3

2

D1578362

JOHN CREASEY'S
CRIME COLLECTION 1984

JOHN CREASEY'S CRIME COLLECTION 1984

An Anthology by members of the Crime Writers' Association

edited by

HERBERT HARRIS

LONDON
VICTOR GOLLANCZ LTD
1984

First published in Great Britain 1984
by Victor Gollancz Ltd,
14 Henrietta Street, London WC2E 8QJ

British Library Cataloguing in Publication Data
John Creasey's crime collection.—1984
1. Detective and mystery stories, English
I. Harris, Herbert, *1911-*
II. Creasey, John, *1908-1973*
823'.0872 [FS]   PR1309.D4

ISBN 0–575–03500–5

Printed in Great Britain by
St Edmundsbury Press, Bury St Edmunds, Suffolk

CONTENTS

Anthony Price: The Chinaman's Garden 9

Eric Ambler: Case of the Gentleman Poet 18

Michael Gilbert: Emergency Exit 27

Julian Symons: The Boiler 44

Celia Fremlin: Accommodation Vacant 55

Dorothy Simpson: Two's Company 71

H. R. F. Keating: A Hell of a Story 89

Joan Aiken: The Jealous Apprentice 93

Celia Dale: Good Investments 103

Herbert Harris: Give Him an Inch . . . 110

Palma Harcourt: A Box of Books 116

Peter Godfrey: The Shadow Behind the Face 132

Clare Dawson: Supergrass 141

Jean McConnell: Germination Period 153

Ella Griffiths: Autumn Crocus 158

Cyril Donson: Heat Wave 170

Tony Wilmot: Open and Shut Case 181

ACKNOWLEDGEMENTS

Eight original stories are included in this edition, those by Joan Aiken, Clare Dawson, Cyril Donson, Ella Griffiths, Palma Harcourt, Herbert Harris, Anthony Price, and Dorothy Simpson.

Acknowledgements are due to the author and Linder AG (Zurich) for "The Case of the Gentleman Poet" by Eric Ambler; to *Mr Calder and Mr Behrens* (Harper & Row) for "Emergency Exit" by Michael Gilbert; to *Ellery Queen's Mystery Magazine* for "The Boiler" by Julian Symons, "Accommodation Vacant" by Celia Fremlin, "A Hell of a Story" by H. R. F. Keating, "Good Investments" by Celia Dale, and "The Shadow Behind the Face" by Peter Godfrey; to *Saint* for "Germination Period" by Jean McConnell; to *Weekend* for "Open and Shut Case" by Tony Wilmot.

INTRODUCTION

During the period that I was selling short stories (some two hundred altogether) to the three evening newspapers which Londoners used to enjoy, one of the latter ran a short story contest for readers, and an avalanche of five thousand stories descended upon the editor's desk.

Since then other short story competitions have drawn an extraordinary number of submissions from readers, which seems to me proof enough, if proof be needed, that the public interest in short stories is still very much alive.

But whereas this interest was once catered for by numerous magazines, short story readers have for some years been shamefully ignored, except for those women's magazines, bless them, which at least provide generous portions of romantic short fiction.

Thus the anthologies being brought out by some of our leading book publishers shine like beacons in an otherwise darkened landscape, and I find it extremely gratifying, as a practising short story writer, to have been associated as editor with so many entertaining collections over the years.

John Creasey's Crime Collection (celebrating its eighth birthday with this edition, and perpetuating an annual literary event which John Creasey, founder of the Crime Writers' Association, himself set in motion) is one such collection. It was recently described as "a substantial anthology recommended to major libraries," and I believe that the generally neglected legion of short story readers will spend happy hours savouring this rare and enjoyable feast.

HERBERT HARRIS

THE CHINAMAN'S GARDEN

Anthony Price

OLD MR MACDONALD sat in the midst of his garden, as he often did when the weather was fine and his work was done, with the book of Chinese poems unopened on his lap.

By the time he sat it was usually too dark to read, and his eyesight wasn't too good now, anyway. But he knew most of the poems by heart, and he liked the feel of the book in his hands. And this was the best time of the day, when the garden gave back to him everything he had put into it, with tenfold interest, in the form of innumerable sweet scents. Indeed, his sense of smell seemed to have sharpened as his sight had weakened, and he could always see the garden in the memory of his mind's eye with perfect clarity —

> *The red flowers hang like a heavy mist;*
> *The white flowers gleam like a fall of snow.*

And finally, when the darkness was complete and the scents at their sweetest, the ghosts of the garden came out of their hiding places and joined him.

Yet, for all that they were the ghosts of a murdered man and his murderers, and he himself was their last fragile link with the world of the living, they never frightened him. They were not vengeful ghosts, and he was not an imaginative man. He could never really think of them as ghosts, only as memories which came to him here without disturbing him, let alone frightening him. The long years, and the scents and the tranquillity of the garden, perfectly erased all the fear and horror of the past: it came back to him like a film he had seen so many times that it had lost its power either to shock or to sadden him, in which the actors no longer had any responsibility for their lines and their actions. And, in any case, the weedy youth who played his part in no way resembled an old man sitting in his garden.

It was odd, though, that his recollections of Reg and Charlie so naturally pictured them on the night when they had killed the old Chinaman, rather than when he had last seen them, in the Jap camp. On that night they had been strapping youths, beside whom he had been smaller and weaker. Three years in the army had filled them out into big men, though they had not been big men when the Japs and the dysentery had finished with them: it was funny how the big strong ones had gone first, while the weedy ones held on. Except that weeds, by their very nature and the world's enmity towards them, were inured to hardship from the start.

It required an effort to see Reg and Charlie dying, and he couldn't hold them like that in his mind for long. So always, as now, they quickly changed back to how they had been when they had been killing, just a few yards away, in the Chinaman's shed where his own little house now stood.

The Chinaman had planned to build his house on the same spot, but the garden had come first in his priorities. Of course, the garden had been the greater work: the wall around it first, then the terracing of an unpromisingly steep hillside, with retaining walls of stone and flagstoned paths; then the raising of trellises and wooden frameworks for the trees and shrubs and vines; and then the planting —

> *I simply bought whatever had most blooms.*
> *Not caring whether peach, apricot or plum.*
> *A hundred fruits, all mixed . . .*

It had been the planting which had fascinated him, even more than the laborious terracing. He had, after all, been a gardener's lad at the time, working for the Municipal Parks and Gardens Department even then. Coming straight from school, barely literate, he hadn't earned much. But he had learnt quickly how to steal flowers and plants and shrubs from his employers, which he had sold to the new people on the Hilltop Road estate, and down Sefton Avenue, on Sunday afternoons.

That had been where he'd met Charlie, who was likewise selling stuff he'd nicked from the building firm he worked for. And it had been through Charlie that he'd met Reg, the clever one, who was a messenger in the bank at Chorleywood, where all the money was. It had been the thought of money which had united their ambitions. If you had money, you had everything else, they had concluded.

But it had been the plants which had led him to the Chinaman, who was making an amazing garden, and who was consequently a good prospect for Sunday afternoon trade.

In the event, the Chinaman hadn't bought anything. The little monkey of a man, gnarled and (so it seemed to him) scarcely human, had stared at him, and the linguistic gap between them had been insuperable. But although the man himself had aroused his profound contempt, the garden had aroused an equally profound curiosity. For it was not simply a great work, but also plainly an expensive one. Had not the Head Gardener in the municipal park sounded off about the high cost of the shrubs which had lately been disappearing? And was not the little Chinaman's garden full of such shrubs — and fruit and flowering trees, too — and obviously exotic plants mixed with them along the terraces, where little fountains played and small waterfalls pattered?

He had said as much to Charlie, and Charlie had said as much to Reg. And Reg had been able to add the crucial piece of intelligence, to complete the blueprint for the Chinaman's murder.

All the same, it had taken months for the blueprint to become legible to them. Summer passed, and autumn, and it had been in winter — cold mid-winter — that need and greed and opportunity had spelt it out for them. Reg had watched all the money coming into the bank for Christmas, and then going out of it. But very little had come their way, except from the sale of Christmas trees stolen with great difficulty from a plantation up Denham way. But most of that had gone by Boxing Day, and the last few shillings in the pub that very evening, as the year 1938 drew to its close.

So there they were, cold and broke and miserable, with the effect of the beer wearing off and nothing in prospect, while all the world around them celebrated the coming of 1939 at parties to which they had not been invited.

And then —

"That bloody little Chink's got money," said Reg.

They each knew what he meant: it had been a secret poisoning them for months, ever since Reg had observed how the Chinaman came to the bank every few weeks to change golden sovereigns into pounds and shillings.

"Yeah. An' under 'is bleedin' bed, like as not," supplemented Charlie, looking at the young MacDonald, who had an avaricious uncle similarly mistrustful of banks. "In that shed of 'is — an' all wasted on bleedin' plants! Right, Mac?"

Mac shook his head. "'E's got 'is garden all planted — 'e's just startin' on 'is 'ouse. Gotta load of bricks an' breeze-blocks there now." Curiosity had kept his eye on the Chinaman's estate.

"Bleedin' Chink!" As a bricklayer, Charlie was hostile to the Chinaman's habit of doing everything for himself.

But Reg was staring at Mac with sudden interest. "He's still livin' in his hut though — ?"

"Yeah." It had long been a source of bewilderment to them that the Chinaman lavished money and back-breaking labour on his garden while living in a ramshackle tar-paper shack among his tools and flower-pots. "Silly old bugger!"

"Yes." There was a different and meaningful note in Reg's voice which made them both look at him. "Silly — eh?"

"What?" Charlie was half a second quicker than Mac.

"So that's where it'll be — right?" said Reg.

"What?" said Mac.

"His money." Reg paused. "The gold." He paused again. "For the bloody taking."

They both looked at him, momentarily transfixed by his vision of El Dorado in a tar-paper shack. Then reality hit them.

"But 'e'll be there," said Charlie. "'E don't go out much — does 'e, Mac?" Mac was the recognized authority on the Chinaman.

But a more cogent objection had struck Mac. "'E knows me. I bin there to see 'im — so 'e's seen me, 'asn't 'e?"

Reg reached forward suddenly and jerked Mac's cap down over his eyes. Then he pulled Mac's muffler up over his mouth. "Now he can't see yer ugly mug, can he?"

"Yeah!" The thought of gold galvanized Charlie's brains into rare action. "An' it'll be dark, like, any road!"

"Yes. And I'll shine my torch into his eyes, won't I!" Reg was proud of his new electric torch, and knew its properties. "Then he won't see nothing at all." He pulled the torch out of his pocket and shone it into Mac's eyes, blinding him.

"But . . . but people'll see us —" Mac was scared and excited at the same time.

"Why should they?" Reg gestured around. "Lots of people out tonight — New Year's Eve. . . . When his house is built, it won't be so easy — an' maybe he'll have spent all his money. We'll never get another chance like this — not like tonight."

Suddenly they were sweating, and their breath smoked in the light of the street lamp above them. Away in the Town Hall across the road the orchestra was playing *One Night of Love*, and all around them were people going home, or going from one party to another, anonymously muffled against the cold of the dying year.

So that was the night they killed the Chinaman.

Of course, they didn't mean to kill him — they didn't even plan to lay a finger on him. But when they'd failed to find the golden sovereigns among his pathetic possessions, and when he'd failed to say a word in answer to Reg's questions, anger had brutalized their greed. And it was then that Charlie had started slapping him. And the slaps had turned into blows — and Charlie's bricklaying muscles were fatally well-developed.

But even then they hadn't meant to kill him — and hadn't killed him, or didn't know that they had; for he was still breathing, unconscious and bloody but still alive, when they'd fled into the night from the wreck of the tar-paper shack. But he was old, and the night was bitter, and it became even colder towards dawn. So, sometime in the dying hours of darkness, the old Chinaman's pulse had fluttered and failed.

All the same, Reg was a good commander, a shrewd judge of situations and opportunities, who held them together then and didn't let them down — who never let them down, in fact, until greater commanders above them all miscalculated in Malaya three years later, up against a more aggressive oriental enemy.

For the police never did find the old Chinaman's killers.

They didn't even find him for a week, and then only by chance. And they never connected his gold-changing at the Chorleywood bank with his death. And, in any case, they concluded that that death was substantially accidental, only indirectly caused by Persons Unknown for an unknowable reason, therefore perhaps manslaughter, but never murder. And he was only an old Chinaman, of unknown origins and eccentric habits, quite without acquaintances, never mind friends, and therefore unimportant in the wider scheme of things.

And, finally, they had much bigger fish to fry before long. So that the Inspector on the case, even before he was promoted to take charge of Air Raid Precautions, overlooked it in preference for the hunt for the Rickmansworth rapist-killer, who was hanged on the day the Germans invaded the Low Countries.

By then, in any case, the Chinaman's killers had been removed from the scene of the crime, and conscripted to kill the enemies of their King and Country, regardless of age and sex and colour, their fear of discovery dulled by more pressing fears.

And so, as Corporal Reg, and Lance-Corporal Charlie, and Private Mac (carefully protected by his friends, as ever), they came to Singapore and the mysterious East, and finally to the Japanese camp. And it was there that the East revenged itself on all three of them with something of their own original brutality, in that it was casual and unplanned in a greater cause. But, while Reg and Charlie died of that revenge, Mac survived to remember the tale of it.

And it was a narrow margin of survival, with a little old Chinaman edging him to life's side of the margin.

He was used to Chinamen by then. They had worried him at first, when he'd been fresh off the troopship, because he'd somehow expected to see the Chinaman's monkey-face among them. But he never did: the funny thing was, while Reg and Charlie and all his mates maintained that Chinks were all alike, they all seemed different to him. And yet there wasn't one of them who looked like his Chink, not even among all the old Chinks whose faces he studied.

It was towards the end of it, long after Reg and Charlie were dead and buried, and things were very bad, that he was put on this working party, doing something the Japs wanted them to do. And that meant an exhausting march, when they were exhausted before they started, so that they had these regular halts by the roadside, each day at the same spot. And one of the halts was beside the Chinaman's garden.

It wasn't much of a garden. It had no terraces, no espalier fruit trees, no showers of blossom — certainly no flowers and water-falls. It was just a vegetable patch, really – with the owner squatting on the edge of it in the hot sun, his face hidden under his coolie hat, near where Mac stretched out to get his breath.

The first time he only just got up, for even weeds aren't immortal. But the second time there was this big leaf near him. And, very slowly, the Chinaman moved the leaf, so that he could see the food underneath it, within reach when the guard wasn't looking.

They did a month on that job, but that was the month during which Mac didn't die. And then they dropped a bomb on a Japanese city, the Yanks did, and that was the end of it: big men, who filled their khaki uniforms the way Reg and Charlie had once done, came striding down the road as though they owned the place, brushing the Japs aside. Only it was not a time he could recall clearly, because he'd been sick then — it was like now, when he'd mislaid his spectacles, the memory was. So he never did get to see that other Chinaman again, and that other garden.

But when he got home things were all right. There was his accumulated pay and his gratuity, and his parents' insurance money, from the bombing in 1941; also the avaricious uncle had died, leaving him what was under the bed; and, as a survivor of the Jap camp, he got his old job back straight off, with promotion in prospect now that he'd educated himself to read books. So he'd been well-placed to buy the derelict wilderness which had once been the first Chinaman's garden.

Indeed, it went dirt cheap, once the lawyers had sorted out its ownership. And that was not only because it was an overgrown jungle, with brambles covering the piles of bricks and stinging-nettles tall on the terraces, but also because it was a place of ill-omen. For it was the place where the Old Chinaman had been murdered (so the story went), and nobody wanted it.

It had taken a terrible lot of work to restore, certainly. Most of the plants had been choked, and many of the shrubs had died, and others had run riot. And the unpruned trees had been a great problem; and his battle with the brambles and the squitch-grass and the nettles had seemed endless, fought year after year in elongated campaigns which delayed the construction of his little bungalow time and again. But the garden always had to come first, and the shed in which he lived was snug enough in winter. And in the summer he often slept outside, under the stars in the midst of the garden, whenever it didn't rain. Compared with the camp, it was heaven. In fact, compared with anywhere, it was heaven.

All the same, it had taken him almost a lifetime to get the garden anywhere near how he wanted it, and even now it wasn't quite right. For there was a vast literature on gardens — and a lot of poetry, too — and it was always giving him new ideas about new things to plant, and old things to change. And after he'd been made Superintendent of Municipal Parks and Gardens there was never enough time — it was amazing how time passed in the garden, there were days when he despaired of ever getting it perfect.

And his other fear had been the thought of the garden without him, for he could remember how it had been when he came back to it and he knew how enviously the nettles eyed it, from the patch of them he had left down by the stream at the bottom, as a sanctuary for butterflies.

But that was no problem now, on this particular night of all others, after he had found the old Chinaman's gold: with the price of golden sovereigns today, he could endow the garden three times over.

It was strange to think that he'd walked over it — how many ten-thousand times? — and never felt that particular flagstone rock unevenly under his foot. It had never moved before, until this very afternoon; and although it had fitted so snugly that nothing had rooted in the cracks around it . . . it had lifted so easily, almost willingly.

But it had rocked, and he had lifted it, meaning to re-bed it firmly. And there underneath it had been the tin box, wrapped in thick tar-paper, the same as had roofed the old Chinaman's shack all those years ago. And in the box were the long cylinders of little gold coins, with only one rank substantially depleted: a king's ransom — once it would have been a Chinaman's ransom — there was there, no doubt about that.

Only for one very brief moment had he wondered about where the old Chinaman had got all that gold. But then, he thought, they hadn't wondered about that on the night, and it was even more useless to wonder about it now. It had belonged to the Chinaman, but if he hadn't died on that night he would certainly have been dead by now. And the dead owned nothing: the dead — Reg and Charlie, as well as the Chinaman — had no claim on it now.

Once upon a time, it would have been different. If they had

found it . . . they might have quarrelled over it, but they would undoubtedly have been caught trying to spend it — three foolish youths — it would have burnt clean through their pockets! And then, although it hardly mattered what would have happened to them — long years in prison, if not the hangman's rope . . . then, while he too might have been dead by now, this garden would have been a wilderness on a dark hillside, with no fruits and flowers and scents.

So now it was his, and he could take it, and do with it what the Governor of Chung-Chou had done eleven centuries ago —

I took money and bought flowering trees,
And planted them out on the bank to the east of the Keep.

But he didn't really need it. And the garden would look after itself in the future. It needed someone to love it, and mere gold wouldn't buy such love.

He could give it away, very easily. There were other gardens, and other gardeners: he had read in the local paper about gardens which opened to the public in aid of gardeners' charities. He had once received a gardener's charity, so it would be appropriate to return the blessing.

The idea pleased him, and he nodded to the ghosts of the garden. He would sleep in the garden with them tonight, and if they invited him to join them . . . well, the flagstone was well-bedded, and some other gardener would find it when it wanted to be found. Tonight he would let the majority vote on his decision.

Meanwhile . . .

The flower-buds fall into my lap.
Alone drinking, alone singing my songs,
I do not notice that the moon is level with the steps . . .

CASE OF THE GENTLEMAN POET

Eric Ambler

IT WAS AFTER the murderer of Felton Spenser had been tried and convicted that Assistant Commissioner Mercer finally became resigned to the occasional intrusions of Dr Jan Czissar into the affairs of New Scotland Yard.

For that reason alone, the case would be worth reporting. The conversion of an assistant commissioner of New Scotland Yard into an ordinary human being must be reckoned a major triumph of the power of reason over the force of habit. But the case has another claim to the interest of students of criminology in general and, in particular, of those who contemplate committing murders of their own. It demonstrated clearly that the first requisite for the committal of a perfect murder is the omniscience of a god.

The world first heard of the death of Felton Spenser late one January evening in the 1930s.

A B.B.C. announcer said: "We regret to announce the death in London tonight of Mr Felton Spenser, the poet. He was fifty-three. Although Mr Spenser was born in Manchester, the early years of his life were spent in the county of Flint, and it was in praise of the Flint countryside and scenery that much of his poetry was written. His first collection of poems, *The Merciful Light*, was published in 1909. Mr Marshall Grieve, the critic and a friend of Spenser's, said of him tonight: 'He was a man without enemies. His verse had a placid limpidity rarely met with nowadays and it flowed with the lyrical ease of his beloved Dee. Although of recent years his work has not received the attention which it has deserved, it remains an enduring monument to a man with many friends and an abiding love of nature.' "

It was left to the newspapers to disclose the fact that Felton Spenser had been found shot in his Bloomsbury apartment. His friend, Mr Marshall Grieve, the author-critic, had reported finding him. There had been a revolver by his side, and it was said that Spenser had recently been suffering from fits of depression.

To Assistant Commissioner Mercer, Detective Inspector Denton ultimately brought further details.

Felton Spenser had lived in the top apartment of a converted house near Torrington Square. There were three other apartments below this. The ground floor was occupied by a dressmaker and her husband named Lobb. On the second floor lived Mr Marshall Grieve. The third floor was unoccupied. The dead man's apartment consisted of two large rooms, used as bedroom and sitting-room, a smaller room used as a study, a kitchen and a bathroom. It had been in the sitting-room that his body had been found.

At about 6.30 that evening the sound of a shot had come from the top of the house. The dressmaker's husband, Mr Lobb, who had just returned home, ran to the door of his apartment. At the same moment, Mr Grieve, who had also heard the shot, had appeared at his door at the head of the first flight of stairs. They had gone up together to investigate.

After breaking down the door of Felton Spenser's apartment, they had found Spenser half sitting, half lying on the sofa, his arms extended and his hands turned back as though he had in the throes of death gripped the edge of the sofa. The body had been rendered rigid by the cadaveric spasm. The appearance of the wound, which was such as to have caused instantaneous death, suggested that when the shot had been fired the revolver had been within an inch or two of the head.

Grieve stated that Spenser had been suffering for some time from fits of intense depression. He knew of several possible causes. Spenser had been profoundly disappointed by the reception accorded to a book of his poems published a year before and had spoken bitterly of being neglected. He had also been in financial difficulties. He had never earned a living from his work and had lived on a small income left to him by his wife, who had died five years previously.

He had, however, Grieve believed, been speculating with his capital. He had also been a very generous man and had lent large sums of money to his friends. Grieve had seen him earlier in the day of his death. Spenser had then told him that his affairs were in a bad way, that he was very worried, and that he was seeing his solicitor the following day in an effort to salvage some of his losses.

This statement was confirmed by the solicitor in question.

Shortly before five o'clock in the afternoon of the day on which
Spenser had died, he had received a telephone call from Spenser
who asked for an appointment for the following day. Spenser
had seemed agitated in his manner on the telephone, but that fact
had not at the time impressed the solicitor, as his client had
always seemed to him to be a trifle neurotic.

The revolver, reported Denton, was an old pin-fire weapon of
French manufacture, and unregistered. Spenser could have
obtained it in a variety of ways. The same applied to the ammunition. Only one shot had been fired from the revolver. The mark-
ings on the bullet extracted from the dead man's head showed
that it had come from that particular revolver. The only distin-
guishing feature about the weapon was a series of marks near the
muzzle which suggested that at some time a silencer had been
fitted to it. No silencer had been found in the apartment.
According to the medical report, the wound showed every sign of
having been self-inflicted.

There was, in Denton's opinion, only one curious thing about
the case. That thing was the draft of an unfinished letter lying on
the desk in the study. It was written in pencil and much corrected,
as if the writer had been choosing his words very carefully. It
began:

"As I told you yesterday, I was serious when I said that unless
the money was repaid to me by today I would place the matter in
the hands of my legal advisers. You have seen fit to ignore my
offer. Accordingly I have consulted my solicitor. Need I say that
I regret the necessity which forces me to take this step? I think
not. Need I say that, if I could afford to overlook the whole
unpleasant matter, I would do so eagerly? Again, I do not think
so. In asking for the return of the money, I . . ."

There the letter stopped.

Mercer considered it. "Looks pretty straightforward to me,"
he said at last. "According to Grieve, he'd been in the habit of
lending people money. It looks as though having found himself
hard pressed he was trying to get a little of it back. What does his
bank account show?"

"Well, sir, he'd certainly got rid of some money. He'd bought
some doubtful stock and lost a bit that way. Six months ago he
drew out £500. Maybe that was this loan he was trying to get back.
Funny idea, though, handing it out in cash. I couldn't find any

note of who had it, either. By the look of his place, I should say he
was the sort who lights his pipe with important papers. I suppose
it's being a poet that does that for you. My wife's got a book
called *Pearls From the Lips of Poets* with one of his pieces in it.
It's about a sunset and it's the kind that doesn't rhyme. I can't say
I cared for it myself. A bit weird." He caught Mercer's eye. "But
I thought that letter was a bit curious, sir. Why should he get up in
the middle of writing a letter and shoot himself?"

Mercer pursed his lips. "Ever heard of impulse, Denton?
That's how half the suicides happen. One minute a man's looking
cheerful. The next minute he's killed himself. 'Suicide while
the balance of his mind was disturbed' is the formula. Any life
insurance?"

"Not that we can trace, sir. There's a cousin in Flint who
inherits. Executors are Grieve and the solicitor."

"Grieve's important. What sort of witness will he make?"

"Good, sir. He looks impressive."

"All right, Denton. I'll leave it to you."

And to Denton it was left — for the moment. It was not until
the day before the inquest was due to be held that Dr Czissar sent
his card in to Mercer's office.

For once, Mercer's excuse that he was too busy to see Dr
Czissar was genuine. He was due at a conference with the commissioner and it was to Denton that he handed over the job of
dealing with the refugee Czech detective.

Again and again during the subsequent conference Mercer
wished that he had asked the doctor to wait and interviewed him
himself. Since the first occasion on which Dr Czissar had entered
New Scotland Yard armed with a letter of introduction from an
influential home office official, he had visited Mercer several
times. And on every occasion he brought disaster with him —
disaster in the shape of irrefutable proof that he, Dr Czissar,
could be right about a case when Mercer was wrong.

He tried to put Dr Czissar out of his mind and concentrate on
the business in hand; but he found his mind wandering from the
larger questions of police administration to the smaller but more
consuming questions raised by Dr Czissar's visit. What did Dr
Czissar want to see him about this time? Could it be the
Birmingham trouble? Surely not. The Soho stabbing? Scarcely.
The Ferring business? Impossible. The questions continued.

There was only one such question that Mercer did not ask himself: "Is it the Spenser suicide?" The idea did not enter into his head.

When at last he returned to his office, Denton was waiting for him, and the expression of exasperated resignation on Denton's face told him all he wanted to know about Dr Czissar's visit. The worst had happened again. The only thing he could do now was to put as stony a face as possible on the impending humiliation. He set his teeth.

"Ah, Denton!" He bustled over to his desk. "Have you got rid of Dr Czissar?"

Denton squared his shoulders. "No, sir," he said woodenly; "he's waiting downstairs to see you."

"But I told you to see him."

"I have seen him, sir. But when I heard what he had to say, I thought I'd better keep him here until you were free. It's about this Spenser business, sir. I'm afraid I've tripped up badly. It's murder.

"No question of opinion, I'm afraid. A clear case. He got hold of some of the evidence from that newspaper friend of his who lends him his pass. I've given him the rest. He saw through the whole thing at once. If I'd have had any gumption I'd have seen through it too. He's darn clever, that Czech."

Mercer choked down the words that rose to his lips. "All right," he said as calmly as he could, "you'd better bring Dr Czissar up."

Dr Czissar entered the room exactly as he had entered it so many times before — thousands of times, it seemed to Mercer. Inside the door, he clicked his heels, clapped his umbrella to his side as if it were a rifle, bowed, and announced loudly: "Dr Jan Czissar. Late Prague police. At your service!"

Mercer said formally: "How do you do, doctor. Sit down. I hear that you have something to tell us about the Spenser case."

Dr Czissar's pale face relaxed. His tall, plump body drooped into its accustomed position beneath the long drab raincoat. The brown, cowlike eyes beamed through the thick spectacles.

"You are busy. I do not wish to interrupt. It is a small matter."

"I understand that you think Felton Spenser was murdered."

The mild eyes enlarged. "Oh, yes. That is what I think, Assistant Commissioner Mercer."

"And may I ask why, doctor?"

Dr Czissar cleared his throat and swallowed hard. "Cadaveric spasm," he declaimed as if he were addressing a group of students, "is a sudden tightening of the muscles of the body at the moment of death, which produces a rigidity which remains until it is succeeded by the lesser rigidity of rigor mortis. The limbs of the dead person will thus remain in the positions in which they were immediately before death for some time. Cadaveric spasm occurs most frequently when the cause of death is accompanied by some violent disturbance of the nervous system such as would be produced by apoplexy or a shot through the head. In many cases of suicide by shooting through the head, the weapon is held so tightly by the cadaveric spasm in the dead hand that great force is required to remove it."

Mercer gave a twisted smile. "And although there was a cadaveric spasm, the revolver was found on the floor. Is that your point? I'm afraid, doctor, that we can't accept that as proof of murder. A cavaderic spasm may relax after quite a short time. The fact that the hand had not actually retained the weapon is not proof that it did not fire it. So . . ."

"Precisely," interrupted Dr Czissar. "But that was not my point, assistant commissioner. According to the medical report, which the inspector has been good enough to tell me, the body was in a state of unrelaxed cadaveric spasm when it was examined an hour after it was discovered. The fingers of both hands were slightly crooked, and both hands were drawn backwards almost at right angles to the forearms. But let us think."

He drove one lank finger into his right temple. "Let us think about the effect of a cadaveric spasm. It locks the muscles in the position assumed immediately before death. Very well, then. Mr Spenser's right hand immediately before his death was drawn backwards almost at right angles to the forearms. Also, the fingers of that hand were slightly crooked. It is not possible, Assistant Commissioner Mercer, to hold a revolver to the head and pull the trigger with the hand in that position. I contend, therefore, that Mr Spenser did not inflict the wound himself."

Mercer looked sharply at Denton. "You saw the body before it was moved. Do you agree with this?"

"I am afraid I do, sir," said Denton.

Mercer contained himself with an effort. "And what did happen, doctor?"

"In the first place," said Dr Czissar, "we have to consider the fact that on the evidence of the dressmaker no one left the house after Mr Spenser was killed. Therefore, when the police arrived, the murderer was still there. Inspector Denton tells me also that the entire house, including the empty apartment on the second floor, was searched by the police. Therefore, the murderer was one of the three persons in the house at the time — the dressmaker, Mrs Lobb, her husband, who returned home shortly before the shot was heard, and Mr Grieve. But which?

"Mr Lobb states that on hearing the shot, he ran to the door of his apartment and looked up the stairs where he saw Mr Grieve appear at the door of his flat. They then went up together to the scene of the crime. If both these men are innocent and telling the truth, then there is an absurdity — for if neither of them shot Mr Spenser, then Mrs Lobb shot him, although she was downstairs at the time of the shot. It is not possible. Nor is it possible for either of the men to have shot him unless they are both lying. Another absurdity. We are faced with the conclusion that someone has been ingenious.

"How was the murder committed?" Dr Czissar's eyes sought piteously for understanding. "How? There is only one clue in our possession. It is that a microscope examination of the revolver barrel showed Inspector Denton that at some time a silencer had been fitted to it. Yet no silencer is found in Mr Spenser's apartment. We should not expect to find it, for the revolver probably belongs to the murderer. Perhaps the murderer has the silencer? I think so. For only then can we explain the fact that when a shot is heard, *none of the three possible suspects is in Mr Spenser's room.*"

"But," snapped Mercer, "if a silencer had been fitted, the shot would not have been heard. It was heard."

Dr Czissar smiled sadly. "Precisely. Therefore, we must conclude that two shots were fired — one to kill Mr Spenser, the other to be heard by the dressmaker's husband, Mr Lobb."

"But only one shot had been fired from the revolver that killed Spenser."

"Oh, yes, assistant commissioner, that is true. But the murder was, I believe, committed with two revolvers. I believe that Mr Grieve went to Mr Spenser's apartment, armed with the revolver you found, at about six o'clock or perhaps earlier. There was a silencer fitted to the revolver, and when the opportunity came he shot Mr Spenser through the head. He then removed the silencer, smudged the fingerprints on the revolver and left it by Mr Spenser on the floor. He then returned to his own flat and hid the silencer. The next thing he did was to wait until Mr Lobb returned home, take a second revolver, which may, I think, have been of the useless kind which is sold for frightening burglars, go up into the empty flat, and fire a second but blank shot.

"Mr Lobb — he will be the most valuable witness for the prosecution — says in his evidence that, on hearing the shot, he ran to his door and saw Mr Grieve coming out of his apartment. It sounds very quick of him, but I think it must have taken Mr Lobb longer than he thinks. He would perhaps look at his wife, ask her what the noise was, and then go to his door. Yet even a few seconds would be plenty of time for Mr Grieve to fire the shot in the empty flat, descend one short flight of stairs, and pretend to be coming out of his door to see what had caused the noise."

"I gathered that you had Grieve in mind," said Mercer grimly; "but may I remind you, doctor, that this is all the purest supposition. Where is the proof? What was Grieve's motive?"

"The proof," said Dr Czissar comfortably, "you will find in Mr Grieve's flat — the silencer, the second revolver, the perhaps pin-fire ammunition. He will not have got rid of these things for fear of being seen doing so. Also I suggest that Mr Lobb, the dressmaker's husband, be asked to sit in his room and listen to two shots — one fired in Mr Spenser's room from the revolver that killed Mr Spenser, the other, a blank shot, fired in the empty flat. You will find, I think, that he will swear that it was the second shot he heard. The two noises will be quite different.

"For the motive, I suggest that you consider Mr Grieve's financial arrangements. Some months ago Mr Spenser drew £500 in cash from his bank. There is no doubt, I think, that Mr Grieve had it. While we were waiting for you, assistant Commissioner, I suggested to the inspector that some information about Mr Grieve's income would be helpful. Mr Grieve, we find, earns a little money writing. He is also an undischarged bankrupt. He would, therefore, prefer to receive so large a sum in notes instead of by cheque. Also, we have only his word that Mr Spenser lent money freely. I have no doubt that Mr Grieve obtained the money to invest on Mr Spenser's behalf, and that he took it for himself. Perhaps you will find some of it in his flat. Mr Spenser had discovered the theft and threatened to expose him. The letter he was writing was to Mr Grieve. But Mr Grieve did not want to receive it. He decided to kill Mr Spenser. The fact that he had this old revolver and silencer no doubt suggested the method."

Dr Czissar sighed and stood up. "So kind of you to receive me, Assistant Commissioner Mercer. So kind, inspector." He gave them a pale smile. "Good afternoon."

"One moment, doctor."

Mercer had risen to his feet. There was nothing left for him to say that would change the fact of his defeat and he knew it. The hope that Dr Czissar would one day prove that he was no more infallible than other men had been deferred too often for him to derive any comfort from it. He did the only thing he could do under the circumstances.

"We're very much obliged to you, doctor," he said. "We'll always be glad of any help you can give us."

Dr Czissar's pale face reddened. "You are too kind," he stammered. And then for once, his English deserted him. "It is to me a great . . ." he began, and then stopped. "It is for me . . ." he said again. He could get no further, and abandoned the attempt to do so. Crimson in the face, he clicked his heels at each of them in turn. "An honour," he said in a strangled voice.

Then he was gone. They heard the long, drab raincoat flapping hastily down the corridor.

EMERGENCY EXIT

Michael Gilbert

IT WAS SIX o'clock, on as foul a morning as could be imagined.

In Warsaw it was raining, in the way it rained just before the rain turned to sleet and the sleet to the first snow of winter. The wind from the east lifted the rain and blew it, in a fine spray, down the Grodsky Boulevard and into Katerina Square. In the far corner of the square the electric sign of the Hotel Polanska was fighting a losing battle with the early-morning light.

A man, dressed in an overcoat which hung nearly to his heels and armed with a long broom, was sweeping down the pavement which fronted the three cafés on the south side of the square; he looked up from his task. Something was happening at the Hotel Polanska across the way.

The front door jerked open and two uniformed policemen came out. They were half carrying, half dragging a man who looked as if he had been pulled out of bed and had not been allowed to put on all his clothes. A police officer raised a gloved hand. A car slid up. The four of them bundled in. The car drove off.

A fresh gust of misty rain blew across the square. It was as though a motion-picture director had said "Dissolve" and the scene had been wiped out. The square was once more quiet and empty.

The sweeper rubbed a frayed cuff over his eyes, and bent to his work. He was paid by all three cafés, and if he swept for one better than the others there would be complaints.

When he had finished, he shouldered his broom and shambled off. His course took him past one of the kiosks which sold newspapers and cigarettes. He stopped to have a word with the bearded stall keeper who was taking down the shutters. The man listened, nodding occasionally. Later that morning he himself did some talking, into a telephone.

The news reached an office in Whitehall with the afternoon tea trays and was passed on to Mr Fortescue, the Manager of the Westminster Branch of the London and Home Counties Bank, as he was getting ready to catch his train home that evening. The message said, "They've taken Rufus Oldroyd."

Mr Fortescue considered the matter, standing in front of the fireplace, with its hideous chocolate-coloured porcelain mantel. From the expression on his face you might have judged that the account of one of his most trusted customers had gone suddenly into the red.

Nine o'clock, on an autumn morning straight from paradise. The sun, clear of the mist, was full and golden, but not yet giving out much heat. In the drawing room of Craysfoot House a log fire was crackling in the grate, and the smell of percolating coffee was scenting the air.

"Damn the girl," said Admiral Lefroy, "how many times have I told her that I like my eggs boiled for four minutes!"

"I've told her a dozen times," said his wife.

"By the feel of this one it's been boiled for fourteen minutes."

"Give it to Sultan."

"I'll do nothing of the sort. The quickest way to ruin a dog's manners is to feed him at table. You'll have him begging next. Balancing lumps of sugar on his nose."

"When you were in command of a ship, I'm sure you were horrid to all the little midshipmen."

"It isn't a captain's job to be horrid to midshipmen." The Admiral glared at the official letter he had just opened. "Damn!"

"What's up now?"

"Got to go to town. The First Sea Lord's called a conference. It's wonderful how busy they manage to keep us, considering we haven't got a Navy."

"I'll go with you. We can come back together on Friday afternoon."

"Who have we got this weekend?"

"Your friend, Captain Rowlandson."

"Good."

"And Mrs Orbiston."

"Oh, God!"

"You'll have to be nice to her. She's on the committee of the Kennel Club. We can't have her blackballing Sultan when he comes up."

Hearing his name, the dog got up from the rug in front of the fire and walked across to Lady Lefroy. He was nine months old, a puppy no longer, but a young dog with plenty of growth to come in his long springy body and barrel chest. A Persian deerhound of royal parentage, he wore the tuft of hair on the top of his head like a coronet. His eyes, which had been light yellow at birth, were deepening now into amber. His nose was blue-black, his skin the colour of honey.

Lady Lefroy tickled the top of his head and said, "Sorry, no scraps for you." And to her husband, "I forgot. There's one more. Mr Behrens."

"Who's he?"

"You ought to know. You invited him."

"Oh, the bee chap. Yes. I met him at my club. He's written a book about them. Knows a lot about mediaeval armour, too."

"He can go for nice long walks with Mrs Orbiston and talk to her about hives and helmets."

Admiral Lefroy abandoned the egg in disgust, and started on the toast and marmalade. He said, "What are you planning to do up in town?"

"Shopping, and having my hair done."

"By — what's the fellow's name — Michael?"

"Who else? And what are you snorting about?"

"You know damned well what I'm snorting about."

"Now, Alaric . . . Michael is adorable. The things he says! Do you know what he told Lady Skeffington last week?"

"I'm not the least interested in what he told Lady Skeffington."

The beauty salon was in two sections. The front had plush settees, low tables covered with glossy magazines, a thick carpet, and indirect lighting. At the back was a row of cubicles, with plain white wooden doors. On each door was the word *Michael's* in letters of brass script, and under each word the stylized painting of a different flower.

From behind the cubicles the snipping of scissors, the sudden gushing of water as a spray was turned on, the humming of a hair dryer. From in front, the hum of conversation. Mrs Hetherington, county to the oblong ends of her brown shoes, was saying to Lady Lefroy, "So *she* said, when they have the next Cabinet reshuffle, Tom's been promised the Navy. Michael said — with a perfectly straight face — 'What'll he do with it when he gets it? Play with it in his bath?' "

A Mrs Toop, who was nobody in particular, and knew it, giggled sycophantically. Lady Lefroy, who had heard the story before, said, "Oh. What did she say?"

"Of course she pretended to be furious. I mean, Michael doesn't bother to be rude to you unless your husband's someone."

How Mrs Toop wished that Michael would be rude to *her*!

"He goes too far sometimes," said Lady Lefroy. "Did you hear what he said to Lady Skeffington?"

"No. Tell, tell."

"Well, you know how she's always carrying on about her husband's polo. What the Duke said to him and what he said to the Duke —"

"Hold it," said Mrs Hetherington regretfully.

The door with a chrysanthemum on it opened and Michael came out. He held the door open for Lady Skeffington, gave her a gentle pat on the back as she went past, and said, "There now, Lady S. You look a proper little tart. I 'ope your 'usband likes it."

"He'll hate it," said Lady Skeffington complacently.

"It'll keep his mind off things. You ought to see the cartoon in the *Mirror*."

"I never read the *Mirror*."

"You don't know what you're missing. They've got him to the life. Quintin as the lion, and 'im as the unicorn."

It was noticeable that Michael dealt with his aitches quite arbitrarily, sometimes dropping them, sometimes not. He helped Lady Skeffington into her coat, showed her out, and came back, casting an eye over the waiting victims.

"Come on Lady L," he said, "I'll wash your hair for you."

Mrs Hetherington said, "What about me? I was next."

"Bert can take care of you," said Michael. "He'll be through in Delphinium in 'alf a mo'."

"It's sheer favouritism."

"You know what Mr Asquith said. 'Favouritism's the secret of efficiency.' "

"It wasn't Asquith," said Mrs Hetherington coldly. "It was Lord Fisher."

"Marcia Lefroy," said Mr Fortescue, "is not English at all, although to hear her speak you would never guess it. She's a French Lebanese girl, of good family." Mr Fortescue paused, as though the next words he had to speak were precious, and needed to be weighed out very carefully. "She has been a trained Communist agent since she was sixteen."

The Under-Secretary of State stared at him in blank disbelief. He said, "Really, Fortescue. This sounds like something Security Executive has dreamed up. I've met Lady Lefroy a dozen times. She's an absolutely charming woman."

"She was trained to be charming. In fact, her earliest assignment was to charm Lefroy. He was only a captain then, in command of our Eastern Mediterranean cruiser detachment. Her instructions were to seduce him. However, it served the purpose of her employers equally well when he carried her off and married her."

"This is quite fantastic. Who started this — this canard?"

"It was started by a disgruntled housemaid. She told us that once, when clearing away the coffee cups, she distinctly heard Admiral Lefroy telling his wife something — she was vague what it was but she was sure it was secret."

The Under-Secretary laughed. "And you believed that sort of evidence?"

"On the contrary, we put her down as a bad and spiteful witness. The information was pigeon-holed. However, three months ago, when Heinrich Woolf defected to us — you remember —"

"Of course."

"One of the things he told us was that details of our agents in Eastern bloc countries were regularly reaching Moscow via Warsaw. They were known to be coming from the foreign-born wife of a senior naval officer with a post in Intelligence. The Lefroys filled the bill exactly. He's the naval representative on the Joint Staffs Intelligence Committee.

"We still didn't believe it, but we had Lady Lefroy watched. And noticed that she had her hair — washed and set, I believe, is the right expression — by a fashionable hairdresser who calls himself Michael, speaks with a strong Cockney accent, was born in Lithuania, and has an occasional and inconspicuous rendezvous on Parliament Hill Fields with a Major Shollitov, who drives the Polish ambassador's spare car.''

The Under-Secretary said, ''Good God!'' and then, ''I hope you realize that this is a case where we can't afford — can't possibly afford — to make any mistake.''

''I can see that it would arouse considerable comment.''

''Comment! God in heaven, man, it's dynamite. And if it went off the wrong way it could — well it could blow quite a lot of people out of the office.''

Mr Fortescue said in his gentlest voice, ''I had not really considered the political angles. My objective is to stop it. You heard they picked up Rufus Oldroyd —''

''Was that —?''

''I imagine so. Admiral Lefroy knew all about Oldroyd. A single incautious word to his wife. The mention of a name even —''

''Yes. I can see that.''

''It must be stopped.'' Mr Fortescue's eyes were as bleak and grey as the seas which washed his native Hebrides.

The Under-Secretary shifted uncomfortably in his padded chair. He was a Wykehamist with a first class degree. The fact that he was a chess player had apparently suggested to his masters that he might have an aptitude for Intelligence matters. It had not proved a happy choice. He disliked Intelligence work, its operations, its operators, and all its implications. It was only the accident of the particular seat he occupied at the Foreign Office which had forced him to have anything to do with it.

He said, ''Alaric Lefroy's a public hero. Has been ever since he got his VC on the Russian convoy. He's a friend of royalty. He could hardly be removed from the committee without public explanation. And suppose we were forced — by questions in the House — to *give* an explanation. Could we prove it?''

''At the moment, almost certainly not.''

''Then couldn't we pull this fellow Michael in?''

''It would be ineffective. Marcia Lefroy is a professional. She'd lie low for a bit. Then she'd open up a new channel of communication — possibly one we didn't know about. Then we should be worse off.''

"I suppose you're right," said the Under-Secretary unhappily. "What are we going to do about it?"

"I had worked out a tentative plan — I could explain the details if you wished — "

The Under-Secretary said hastily that he had no desire to hear the details. He felt confident that the matter could be left entirely in Mr Fortescue's hands.

Michael was uneasy. The causes of his uneasiness were trivial, but they were cumulative. There had been the trouble with the lock on the front door of his flat. The locksmith who had removed and replaced it had found the tip of a key broken off in the mechanism.

Michael had mentioned the matter to the hall porter, and in doing so had discovered that the regular porter, with whom he was on very good terms, had been replaced by a large and surly-looking individual who had treated him in a very off-hand way. And the final straw — there had been trouble with his car.

It had been his custom to make his trips to North London in an inconspicuous little Austin runabout. This had gone in for repairs a week ago, and had been promised to him for today. When he went to get the car it was not ready. Mysterious additional faults had developed. There was nothing he could do but use his second car, the extremely conspicuous, primrose-yellow Daimler with the personal licence plate.

This he parked, as usual, in the backyard of the Spaniards, and made his way on foot down the complex of paths which led to the open spaces of Parliament Hill Fields. It was an ideal place for a rendezvous, with an almost panoramic view of London. Major Shollitov would come from the opposite direction, leaving his car in Swains Lane, and walking up to the meeting place.

And now, to add to, and cap, all the other doubts which had been nagging him, Major Shollitov was late. Michael, although a very minor player in the game, was sufficiently instructed to realize the significance of this. A rendezvous was always kept with scrupulous punctuality. If one party was late, it was a warning — a warning not to be disregarded. The other party took himself off, quickly and quietly.

Michael glanced at his watch. 2:59. From the seat on which he was sitting he could command all the paths leading up from the

Vale. It was one of its advantages. Thirty seconds to go. Major Shollitov was not coming.

When a hand touched him on the shoulder Michael jumped.

The man must have come up across the grass behind him. He was thick-set, middle-aged, and nondescript. He said, "Got a match?"

Michael's heart resumed a more normal rhythm. He said, "Sure."

"Mind if I sit down? Lovely view, isn't it?"

Michael said, "Yes." He wondered how soon he could move. To get straight up and walk off would look rude, and to be rude would attract attention.

The stranger said, "I wonder if you know why they call this spot Parliament Hill Fields?"

"No, I don't."

"You remember that crowd who were planning to blow up Parliament? Fifth of November, sixteen hundred and five. They'd got it all laid out, and were intending to scuttle off up north to start the revolt. And just about here was where they pulled up their horses, to have a view of the fireworks display. Dramatic, wasn't it?"

"Oh, very," said Michael. Give it one more minute.

"Only, as *we* know, the fireworks didn't go off. And they left poor old Guy Fawkes behind to carry the can. Interesting, don't you think?"

"Oh, very."

"I thought you'd be interested."

There was something about this last statement that Michael didn't like. He said sharply, "Why should it interest me, particularly?"

"Well," said the stranger, "after all, it's much the sort of position you're in now, isn't it?"

The long silence that followed was broken by the distant voices of children playing, out of sight down the slope. At last Michael said, "What are you talking about?"

"Your old pal, Major Shollitov — the one you usually meet here. He's gone scuttling back to Warsaw, leaving you sitting here, like Guy Fawkes, waiting for the rack and thumbscrew.

"Who are you?"

"Never mind about me," said the stranger, with a sudden

brutal authority. "Let's talk about you. You're the one who's on the spot. You're a messenger boy for the Commies, aren't you? How did they rope you in? Through your old mum and dad in Lithuania? Not that it matters. They've finished with you now. You're blown."

"You're mad."

"If you think I'm mad I'd advise you to shout for help. Go on. There's a park attendant. Give him a yell. Tell him you're being annoyed by a lunatic."

Michael watched the park attendant approach them. He watched him walk away.

The stranger inhaled the last drop of smoke from his cigarette, dropped it, and stamped on it. He said, "You've had an easy run, so far. Listening to high-class tittle-tattle from Lady This, whose husband's in the Cabinet, and Mrs That, whose brother's on the Staff, and passing it on for a few pounds a time. They don't pay much for third-class work like that. Well, that's all over now. It's you who's going to do the paying and —" The stranger leaned forward until his face was a few inches from Michael's "— it's not going to be nice. They get rough, those Intelligence boys. They know what happens to *their* friends when they get caught, and they like a chance to pay a little of it back. The last one they brought in had both his legs broken. Jumping out of a car, *they* said —"

"He's yellow," said Mr Calder to Mr Fortescue. "Yellow as a daffodil. By the time I'd finished he was almost crying."

"I'm not surprised," said Mr Fortescue. "Verbal bullies are often lacking in moral stamina. You were careful not to suggest any connection between him and Lady Lefroy?"

"Very careful. I kept it quite general. Listening to indiscreet gossip was how I put it."

"Excellent. We must hope that he'll act predictably."

It had not been an easy weekend, even for an experienced hostess like Marcia Lefroy. Captain Rowlandson and Mrs Orbiston had not mixed well. The only real success had been Mr Behrens, who had filled in awkward gaps in the conversation with stories about his bees.

The final straw for Lady Lefroy was when her husband

telephoned that he had to stay in London. The First Lord had called a conference for early the next day.

Lady Lefroy pondered these things as she lay in bed. Usually she fell asleep immediately after turning off the bedside lamp. Tonight she had not done so. Like all trained and experienced agents, she possessed delicate antennae on the alert for the unusual. It was most unusual for a conference to be called on a Saturday morning. If there had been a crisis of some sort, it would have been understandable. But the international scene was flat as a pancake. Why then —"

The first handful of gravel against the window jerked her back to full wakefulness. As she got out of bed, Sultan growled softly. "It's all right," she said. She struggled into her dressing gown without turning on the light.

She made her way downstairs into the drawing-room and opened the long window giving on to the terrace. As a man slipped through, she adjusted the curtains carefully and switched on a single wall light. When she saw who it was her anger exploded. "How *dare* you come here!"

"I wouldn't have come unless I had to," said Michael sulkily.

"Your instructions were clear. You were absolutely forbidden to write, telephone, or even to speak to me, except in your shop."

"But I've got to get out. They're on to me."

"How do you know that?"

"They told me."

"An unusual proceeding," said Lady Lefroy coldly.

"This man, he met me, at the rendezvous. Shollitov's been sent home. He knew all about us."

"*Us?*"

"Well, about me."

"Did he mention my name?"

"Not your name particularly. He accused me of picking up gossip at the salon and passing it on. He made threats. They were going to — do things to me."

"Have they done anything?"

"Not yet. But they will. I tried to get through — to the emergency number."

"Fool. Your line will be tapped."

"I couldn't, anyway. They said it had been disconnected."

"I see," said Lady Lefroy. It was a few moments before she spoke again.

"How did you come down?"

"By car. I'm sure I wasn't followed — I should have known at once. The roads were empty. I hid the car nearly a mile away and walked the rest of the way."

"You showed that much sense." There was no point in panicking him. He was frightened enough already. "What do you want?"

"Help. To get out."

"What makes you think I can help you?"

"You know the ropes. They told me that if I ever had to clear out I was to come to you."

"Then," said Lady Lefroy, "I must see what I can do." She walked across to her desk. As she did so, the door was pushed open. Her heart missed a beat, then steadied. It was Sultan.

"That's very naughty of you," she said. "I told you to stay put."

Sultan yawned. He wanted the man to go so that they could get back to bed.

Lady Lefroy unlocked the desk, and then a steel-lined drawer inside. From it she took a bulky packet which she weighed thoughtfully in her hand. She said, "You see this. It was left with me against such a contingency. But before I give it to you I must have your promise to use it exactly in the way I tell you."

"Of course. What is it?"

"It's called 'Emergency Exit'. Inside you'll find a passport. The photograph resembles you sufficiently. You'll have to make a few small changes. Arrange your hair differently. That should be easy enough for a man of your talents." A smile twitched the corner of Lady Lefroy's mouth. "And wear glasses. You'll find them in the packet too. There's a wad of French and German money, and instructions as to what you're to do when you get to Cologne. From there you'll be flying to Berlin. There's a second passport to use in Berlin, and a second set of instructions. After you open the packet — which you're not to do until you're back in London — all instructions are to be learned by heart and then destroyed. And the first passport is to be destroyed when you reach Cologne. Is that all clear?"

Michael let his breath out with a soft sigh. "All clear," he said. "And thank you."

"A final word. *These things aren't issued in duplicate.* So look after it carefully."

Michael made an unsuccessful attempt to stow the bulky oilskin-covered packet in his coat pocket. Lady Lefroy took it from him. She said, "Open the front of your shirt. That's right. Stow it down there. Now button it up again. Right. Don't open the curtains until I've turned the light off."

She stood for a few moments after Michael had gone. She was taut as a violin string. The young dog, crouched at her feet, sensed it and growled, low in his throat. The sound broke the tension.

"All right," said Lady Lefroy. "Back to bed. Nothing more to worry about."

Among other irritating habits, Mrs Orbiston was accustomed to turning on her portable radio for the seven o'clock news, and retailing the choicer items to the company at breakfast. Lady Lefroy had not appeared, so her audience consisted of Captain Rowlandson, who was never fully awake until he had finished his after-breakfast pipe, and Mr Behrens, whose mind appeared to be elsewhere.

"Burglars," she announced. "Stole jewellery worth fifteen thousand pounds. At Greystone House. That's not far from here, is it?"

"I've no idea," said Captain Rowlandson.

"Well, I'm sure it is nearby. Because the people were called Baynes, and I've heard Marcia talk about them."

"Serve them right. When you go away you ought to put your jewellery in the bank."

"That's just it. That's what made it so terrible. The men went *into* their bedroom, *while* they were there, and helped themselves to the jewel box *off* the dressing table. It makes your flesh creep. I was just saying, Marcia —"

"If it's the Bayneses you're talking about," said Lady Lefroy, who had come into the room at that moment, "I've just heard. Mary Baynes was on the telephone."

"One good thing," said Captain Rowlandson, "they wouldn't get away with it here. Sultan would see them off."

"He's a very light sleeper," agreed Lady Lefroy. "All the same, I can't help thinking that it might be better if he *didn't* give the alarm."

"Oh — why?"

"I gather these burglars are pretty desperate characters. And all my stuff is well insured."

"That's pure defeatism, Marcia. Don't you agree, Behrens?"

Mr Behrens said, "Defeatism might be preferable to being shot."

Mrs Orbiston, seeing the conversation drifting away from her, pulled it back sharply. She said, "And that wasn't the *only* exciting thing that happened in this part of the country. Roysters Cross is quite close to here, too, isn't it?"

"About four miles away," said Lady Lefroy. "Why?"

"There was a terrible accident there last night. A man blew himself up."

"Blew himself up?"

"That's what the news commentator said."

"Curious way of committing suicide," said Captain Rowlandson.

"The possibility of accident has not been ruled out."

"You can't very well blow yourself up by accident," said Mr Behrens. "That is, unless you're carrying some sort of bomb."

"Perhaps it was a tyre blow-out," said Lady Lefroy. "Would you mind passing the marmalade?"

"It didn't sound like a tyre blow-out. They said the man *and* the car were blown to bits."

"Amatol or dextrol," said Mr Calder. "Or just possibly good old-fashioned nitroglycerine. Although that's got rather a detectable smell."

"What sort of fuse?" asked Mr Fortescue.

"Something silent. Wire and acid?"

"Very likely," agreed Mr Fortescue. "It's notoriously inaccurate. I've no doubt the thing was intended to go off a lot further away from Lady Lefroy's house. Or maybe he took longer to walk back to his car than she anticipated. How do you think she arranged it?"

"I imagine it was something she gave him to take back to London. A parcel of some sort."

"The whole thing," said Mr Fortescue, "is most unfortunate. Michael was responding nicely to treatment. He would soon have been ready to co-operate."

"Evidently Marcia thought so, too."

"It demonstrates what we have always suspected — that she's a ruthless and unscrupulous woman."

"It demonstrates something else, too," said Mr Calder. "If she tumbled to what we were doing — twisting Michael's tail so hard that he'd incriminate her — she must have suspected that we were on to her as well."

Mr Fortescue said, "Hmm. Maybe."

"Not certain, I agree. But a workable assumption. And if it's true, it must mean that she's decided to stay put and brazen it out. Because if she had decided to quit she'd have kept Michael on ice for a day or two, while she made all *her* preparations."

"It's not a happy conclusion, Calder."

"It's a very unhappy conclusion. Now that she's been warned she'll sever all her contacts and lie low for a very long time. Possibly forever."

"It would, I suppose, be a halfway solution," said Mr Fortescue. He didn't sound very happy about it. "All the same, I don't think it's a chance we can take. Do you?"

"No," said Mr Calder. "I don't." He added, "I read in the papers that there'd been another burglary down in the Petersfield area. It's some sort of gang. The police say that they're armed, and dangerous. They've put out a warning to all householders in the neighbourhood."

Mr Fortescue thought about this for a long time. Then he said, "Yes. I think that would be best. It'll mean keeping the Admiral up in London for another night. I'll get the Minister to reconvene the conference."

"How's he going to get away with that one? He can't keep senior admirals and generals in London on a Sunday. Not in peacetime."

"Then we'll have to declare war on someone," said Mr Fortescue.

Marcia sat up in bed and said, "Stop it, Sultan. What's the matter with you?"

It had been a savage growl — not a gentle rumbling warning, but a note of imminent danger.

The moon, cloud-wracked, was throwing a grey light into the room. As her sight adjusted itself, Marcia could dimly see the figure at which Sultan was snarling.

She twisted one hand into his collar, and with the other she switched on the bed-table lamp. A man was standing beside the dressing table, examining an opened jewel case. He put the case down and said, "If you don't keep that dog under control I shall have to shoot him. It won't make a lot of noise, because this gun's silenced, but I'd hate to have to mess up a nice animal like that."

"If that jewel case interests you, you're welcome to it. It's got nothing but costume jewellery in it — stop it, Sultan — worth twenty-five pounds if you're lucky."

"And insured for five hundred, I don't doubt," said the intruder. "I'm not really interested in jewellery. That's just an excuse for meeting you. I wanted to get your version of what happened to Michael last night."

"Michael? Michael who?"

"The Michael who's been doing your hair for the last eighteen months. You can't have forgotten about him already. They've only just finished scraping bits of him off the signpost at Roysters Cross. That must have been a powerful bit of stuff you put in the packet you gave him."

"I've no idea what you're talking about," said Lady Lefroy. Her voice gave nothing away. Only her eyes were thoughtful, and the knuckles of the hand which held Sultan's collar showed white.

The door opened quietly. Calder's colleague, Mr Behrens, looked in.

"You've come just at the right moment," said the first intruder. "Have you got the tape?"

"I have it," said Mr Behrens, "and a recorder. I had to wire three rooms to be sure of getting it."

Lady Lefroy's look had hardened. She moved her head slowly, trying to sum up both men, to weigh this new development. It was the reaction of a professional, faced by a threat from a new quarter.

"You know each other, I see."

"Indeed, yes," said Mr Behrens. "Calder and I have known each other for twenty years. Or is it twenty-five? Time goes so quickly when you're interested in your work."

"So you're in this together."

"We often work as a team."

"You do the snooping and sneaking, and he does the rough stuff."

"Exactly," said Mr Behrens. "We find it an excellent arrangement." He was busy with the tape recorder. "Now perhaps we can convince you we're not bluffing. Where shall we start?"

There was a click, and they heard Lady Lefroy's voice say, "It's called 'Emergency Exit'. Inside you'll find a passport — " They listened in silence for a full minute. "Open the front of your shirt. That's right. Stow it down there —"

Mr Behrens turned the machine off.

"A nice touch," he said. "It must have been resting on his stomach when it went off. No wonder there wasn't much of him left."

Lady Lefroy said, "That tape recording proves nothing. You say it's my voice. I say it's a clumsy fake. It doesn't even sound much like me."

"You mustn't forget that I saw Michael, both coming and going."

"Lies! Why do you bother me with such lies?" Again her eyes turned from one man to the other. She was trying to estimate which of them was the stronger character, which one she should attack, what weapons in her well-stocked armoury she should use. It was confusing to have to deal with two at once.

In the end she said, with a well-contrived yawn, "Do I understand that this is all leading up to something? That you have some proposal to put to me? If so, please put it, so that I can get back to sleep."

"Our proposal," said Mr Calder, "is this. If you will make a written statement, naming your employers, and your contacts, giving full details which can be verified in forty-eight hours, we'll give you the same length of time to get out of the country."

"We feel certain," said Mr Behrens, "that you have all *your* arrangements made."

"More efficient, if less drastic, than the ones you made for Michael."

All expression had gone out of Lady Lefroy's face. It was a mask — a meticulously constructed mask behind which a quick brain weighed the advantages and disadvantages of the proposal. When she smiled, Mr Behrens knew that they had lost.

"You're bluffing," she said. "I call your bluff. Go away."

"A pity," said Mr Behrens.

"Very disappointing," said Mr Calder. "We shall have to use plan Number Two."

"You do understand," said Mr Behrens earnestly, "that you've brought this on yourself. We have no alternative."

Lady Lefroy said nothing. There was something here she found disturbing.

Mr Calder said, "It's this gang of burglars, you see. Armed burglars. They've been breaking into houses round here. Tonight they turned their attention to this house. You woke up and caught one of them rifling your jewel case."

"And what happened then?"

"Then," said Mr Calder, "he shot you."

Three things happened together: a scream from Marcia Lefroy, cut short; the resonant twang of the silenced automatic pistol; and a snarl of fury as the dog went for Mr Calder's throat.

Mr Behrens moved almost as quickly as the dog. He caught up the two corners of the blanket on which the dog had been lying and enveloped him in it, a growling, writhing, murderous bundle. Mr Calder dropped his gun, grabbed the other two corners of the blanket, knotted them together.

"It was unpardonable," said Mr Fortescue.

"I know," said Mr Calder. "But —"

"There are no 'buts' about it. It was an unnecessary complication, and a quite unjustifiable risk. Suppose he is recognized."

"All persian deerhounds have a strong family resemblance. Once he's fully grown there'll be no risk at all. I'll rename him of course. I thought that Rasselas might be the appropriate name for an Eastern prince —"

"I can't approve."

"He's beautifully bred. And he's got all the courage in the world. You should have seen the way he came for me. Straight as an arrow. If Behrens hadn't got the blanket over him, he'd have had my throat for sure. What were we to do?"

"You should have immobilized him."

"You can't immobilize a partly grown deerhound."

"Then you should have shot him."

"Shoot a dog like that!" said Mr Calder. "You must be joking."

THE BOILER

Julian Symons

HAROLD BOYLE WAS on his way out to lunch when the encounter took place that changed his life. He was bound for a vegetarian restaurant, deliberately chosen because to reach it he had to walk across the park. A walk during the day did you good, just as eating a nut, raisin and cheese salad was better for you than consuming chunks of meat that lay like lead in the stomach. He always returned feeling positively healthier, ready and even eager for the columns of figures that awaited him.

On this day he was walking along by the pond, stepping it out to reach the restaurant, when a man coming towards him said "Hallo". Harold gave a half-smile, half-grimace, intended as acknowledgement while suggesting that in fact they didn't know each other. The man stopped. He was a fleshy fellow, with a large aggressive face. When he smiled, as he did now, he revealed a mouthful of beautiful white teeth. His appearance struck some disagreeable chord in Harold's memory. Then the man spoke, and the past came back.

"If it isn't the boiler," he said. "Jack Cutler, remember me?"

Harold's smallish white hand was gripped in a large red one.

From that moment onwards things seemed to happen of their own volition. He was carried along on the tide of Cutler's boundless energy. The feeble suggestion that he already had a lunch engagement was swept aside, they were in a taxi and then at Cutler's club, and he was having a drink at the bar although he never took liquor at lunchtime. Then lunch, and it turned out that Cutler had ordered already, great steaks that must have cost a fortune, and a bottle of wine with them. During the meal Cutler talked about the firm of building contractors he ran and of its success, the way business was waiting for you if you had the nerve to go out and get it. While he talked, the large teeth bit into the steak as though they were shears. Then his plate was empty.

"Talking about myself too much, always do when I eat. Can't tell you how good it is to see you, my old boiler. What are you doing with yourself?"

"I am a contract estimator for a firm of paint manufacturers."

"Work out price details, keep an eye open to make sure nobody's cheating? Everybody cheats nowadays, you know that. I reckon some of my boys are robbing me blind, fiddling estimates, taking a cut themselves. You reckon something can be done about that sort of thing?"

"If the estimates are properly checked in advance, certainly."

Cutler chewed a toothpick. "What do they pay you at the paint shop?"

It was at this point, he knew afterwards, that he should have said no, he was not interested, he would be late back at the office. Perhaps he should even have been bold enough to tell the truth, and say that he did not want to see Cutler again. Instead he meekly gave the figure.

"Skinflints, aren't they? Come and work for me and I'll double it."

Again, he knew that he should have said no, I don't want to work for you. Instead, he murmured something about thinking it over.

"That's my good old careful boiler," Cutler said, and laughed.

"I must get back to the office. Thank you for lunch."

"You'll be in touch?"

Harold said yes, intending to write a note turning down the offer. When he got home, however, he was foolish enough to mention the offer to his wife, in response to a question about what kind of day he had had. He could have bitten out his tongue the moment after. Of course, she immediately said that he must take it.

"But Phyl, I can't. I don't like Cutler."

"He seems to like you, taking you to lunch and making this offer. Where did you know him?"

"We were at school together. He likes power over people, that's all he thinks of. He was an awful bully. When we were at school he called me a boiler."

"A *what?* Oh, I see, a joke on your name. I don't see there's much harm in that."

"It wasn't a joke. It was to show his — his contempt. He made other people be contemptuous too. And he still says it, when we met he said, it's the boiler."

"It sounds a bit childish to me. You're not a child now, Harold."

"You don't understand," he cried in despair. "You just don't understand."

"I'll tell you what I do understand," she said. Her small pretty face was distorted with anger. "We've been married eight years, and you've been in the same firm all the time. Same firm, same job, no promotion. Now you're offered double the money. Do you know what that would mean? I could get some new clothes, we could have a washing machine, we might even be able to move out of this neighbourhood to somewhere really nice. And you just say no to it, like that. If you want me to stay you'd better change your mind."

She went out, slamming the door. When he went upstairs later he found the bedroom door locked. He slept in the spare room.

Or at least he lay in bed there. He thought about Cutler, who had been a senior when he was a junior. Cutler was the leader of a group who called themselves the Razors, and one day Harold found himself surrounded by them while on his way home. They pushed and pulled him along to the house of one boy whose parents were away. In the garden shed there they held a kind of trial in which they accused him of having sneaked on a gang member who had asked Harold for the answers to some exam questions. Harold had given the answers, some of them had been wrong, and the master had spotted these identical wrong answers. Under questioning, Harold told the master what had happened.

He tried to explain that this was not sneaking, but the gang remained unimpressed. Suggestions about what should be done to him varied from cutting off all his hair to holding him face down in a lavatory bowl. Somebody said that Boyle should be put in a big saucepan and boiled, which raised a laugh. Then Cutler intervened. He was big even then, a big red-faced boy, very sarcastic.

"We don't want to *do* anything, he'll only go snivelling back to teacher. Let's call him something. Call him the boiler."

Silence. Somebody said, "Don't see he'll mind."

"Oh yes, he will." Cutler came close to Harold, his big face sneering. "Because I'll tell him what it means, and then he'll remember every time he hears it. Now, you just repeat this after me, boiler." Then Cutler recited the ritual of the boiler and Harold, after his hair had been pulled and his arm twisted until he thought it would break, repeated it. He remembered the ritual. It began: *I am a boiler. A boiler is a mean little sneak. A boiler's nose is full of snot. He can't tie his own shoelaces. A boiler fails in everything he tries. A boiler stinks. I am a boiler . . .*

Then they let him go, and he ran home. But that was the beginning of it, not the end. Cutler and his gang never called him anything else. They clamped their fingers to their noses when he drew near, and said, "Watch out, here's the boiler, pooh, what a stink."

Other boys caught on and did the same. He became a joke, an outcast. His work suffered, he got a bad end of term report. His father had died when he was five, so it was his beloved mother who asked him whether something was wrong. He burst into tears. She said that he must try harder next term, and he shook his head.

"It's no good, I can't. I can't do it, I'm a boiler."

"A boiler? What do you mean?"

"A boiler, it means I'm no good, can't do anything right. It's what they call me."

"Who calls you that?"

He told her. She insisted on going up to school and seeing the headmaster, although he implored her not to, and afterwards of course things were worse than ever. The head had said that he would see what could be done, but that boys would be boys and Harold was perhaps over-sensitive. Now the gang pretended to burst into tears whenever they saw him, and said poor little boiler should run home to mummy.

And he often did run home from school to mummy. He was not ashamed to remember that he had loved his mother more than anybody else in the world, and that his love had been returned. She was a highly emotional woman, and so nervous that she kept a tiny pearl-handled revolver beside her bed. Harold had lived with her until she died. She left him all she had, which was a little money in gilt edged stocks, some old-fashioned jewellery, and the revolver. He sold the stocks and the jewellery, and kept the revolver in a bureau which he used as a writing desk.

It was more than twenty years ago that Cutler had christened him boiler, but the memory remained painful. And now Phyllis wanted him to work with the man. Of course she couldn't know what the word meant, how could anybody know? He saw that in a way Phyllis was right. She had been only twenty-two, ten years younger than Harold, when they were married after his mother's death. It was true that he had expected promotion, he should have changed jobs, it would be wonderful to have more money. You mustn't be a boiler all your life, he said to himself. Cutler was being friendly when he offered you the job.

And he couldn't bear to be on bad terms with Phyl, or to think that she might leave him. There had been an awful time, four years ago, when he had discovered that she was carrying on an affair with another man, some salesman who had called at the door to sell a line in household brooms and brushes. He had come home early one day and found them together. Phyl was shamefaced but defiant, saying that if he only took her out a bit more it wouldn't have happened. Was it the fact that the salesman was a man of her own age, he asked. She shook her head, but said that it might help if Harold didn't behave like an old man of sixty.

In the morning he told Phyl that he had thought it over, and changed his mind. She said that he would have been crazy not to take the job. Later that day he telephoned Cutler.

To his surprise he did not find the new job disagreeable. It was more varied than his old work, and more interesting. He checked everything carefully, as he had always done, and soon unearthed evidence showing that one of the foremen was working with a sales manager to inflate the cost of jobs by putting in false invoices billed to a non-existent firm. Both men were sacked immediately.

He saw Cutler on most days. Harold's office overlooked the entrance courtyard, so that if he looked out of the window he could see Cutler's distinctive gold-and-silver-coloured Rolls draw up. A smart young chauffeur opened the door and the great man stepped out, often with a cigar in his mouth, and nodded to the chauffeur who then took the car round to the parking lot. Cutler came in around ten thirty, and often invaded Harold's office after lunch smelling of drink, his face very red. He was delighted by the discovery of the invoice fraud, and clapped Harold on the back.

"Well done, my old boiler. It was a stroke of inspiration asking you to come here. Hasn't worked out too badly for you either, has it?'' Harold agreed. He talked as little as possible to his employer. One day Cutler complained of this.

"Damn it, man, anybody would think we didn't know each other. Just because I use a Rolls and have young Billy Meech drive me in here every morning doesn't mean I'm standoffish. You know why I do it? The Rolls is good publicity, the best you can have, and I get driven in every morning because it saves time. I work in the car dictating letters and so forth. I drive myself most of the time though, Meech has got a cushy job and he knows it. But don't think I forget old friends. I tell you what, you and your wife must come out and have dinner one night. And we'll use the Rolls.''

Harold protested, but a few days later a letter came, signed "Blanche Cutler", saying that Jack was delighted that an old friendship had been renewed, and suggesting a dinner date. Phyllis could hardly contain her pleasure, and was both astonished and furious when Harold said they shouldn't go, they would be like poor relations.

"What are you talking about? He's your old friend, isn't he? And he's been decent to you, offering you a job. If *he's* not snobby, I don't see why you should be.''

"I told you I don't like him. We're not friends.''

She glared at him. "You're jealous, that's all. You're a failure yourself, and you can't bear anybody to be a success.''

In the end, of course, they went.

Cutler and Harold left the office in the Rolls, driven by Meech, who was in his middle twenties, and they collected Phyllis on the way. She had bought a dress for the occasion, and Harold could see that she was taking everything in greedily, the way Meech sprang out to open the door, the luxurious interior of the Rolls, the cocktail cabinet from which Cutler poured drinks, the silent smoothness with which they travelled. Cutler paid what Harold thought were ridiculous compliments on Phyllis's dress and appearance, saying that Harold had kept his beautiful young wife a secret.

"You're a lucky man, my old boiler.''

"Harold said that was what you called him. It seems a silly name.''

"Just a reminder of schooldays,'' Cutler said easily, and Harold hated him.

The Cutlers lived in a big red-brick house in the outer suburbs, with a garden of more than an acre and a swimming pool. Blanche was a fine, imposing woman, with a nose that seemed permanently raised in the air. Another couple came to dinner, the man big and loud-voiced like Cutler, his wife a small woman loaded down with what were presumably real pearls and diamonds. The man was some sort of stockbroker, and there was a good deal of conversation about the state of the market. Dinner was served by a maid in cap and apron, and was full of foods covered with rich sauces which Harold knew would play havoc with his digestion. There was a lot of wine, and he saw with dismay that Phyllis's glass was being refilled frequently.

"You and Jack were great friends at school, he tells me," Blanche Cutler said, nose in the air. What could Harold do but agree? "He says that now you are his right-hand man. I do think it is so nice when old friendships are continued in later life."

He muttered something, and then was horrified to hear the word *boiler* spoken by Phyllis.

"What's that?" the stockbroker asked, cupping hand to ear. Phyllis giggled. She was a little drunk.

"Do you know what they used to call Harold at school? A boiler. What does it mean, Jack, you must tell us what it means."

"It was just a nickname." Cutler seemed embarrassed. "Because his name was Boyle, you see."

"I know you're hiding something from me." Phyllis rapped Cutler flirtatiously on the arm. "Was it because he looks like a tough old boiling fowl, very tasteless? Because he does. I think it's a very good name for him, a boiler."

Blanche elevated her nose a little higher, and said that they would have coffee in the drawing-room.

Meech drove them in the Rolls, and gave Phyllis his arm when they got out. She clung to it, swaying a little as they moved towards the front door. Indoors, she collapsed on the sofa and said, "What a lovely, lovely evening."

"I'm glad you enjoyed it."

"I liked Jack. Your friend Jack. He's such good company."

"He's not my friend, he's my employer."

"Such an attractive man, very sexy."

He remembered the salesman. "I thought you only liked younger men. Cutler's older than I am."

She looked at him with a slightly glazed eye. "Dance with me."

"We haven't got any music."

"Come *on*, doesn't matter." She pulled him to his feet and they stumbled through a few steps.

"You're drunk." He half-pushed her away and she fell to the floor. She lay there staring up at him.

"You bastard, you pushed me over."

"I'm sorry, Phyl. Come to bed."

"You know what you are? You're a boiler. It's a good name for you."

"Phyl. Please."

"I married a boiler," she said, and passed out. He had to carry her up to bed.

In the morning she did not get up as usual to make his break-fast, in the evening she said sullenly that there was no point in talking any more. Harold was just a clerk and would never be anything else, didn't want to be anything else.

On the day after the party Cutler came into Harold's office in the afternoon, and said he hoped they had both enjoyed the evening. For once he was not at ease, and at last came out with what seemed to be on his mind.

"I'm glad we got together again, for old times' sake. But look here, I'm afraid Phyl got hold of the wrong end of the stick. About that nickname."

"Boiler."

"Yes. Of course it was only meant affectionately. Just a play on your name." Did Cutler really believe that, could he possibly believe it? His red shining face looked earnest enough. "But people can get the wrong impression as Phyl did. Better drop it. So, no more boiler. From now on, it's Jack and Harold, agreed?"

He said that he agreed. Cutler clapped him on the shoulder, and said that he was late for an appointment on the golf course. He winked as he said that you could do a lot of business between the first and the eighteenth holes. Five minutes later Harold saw him driving away at the wheel of the Rolls, a cigar in his mouth.

In the next days Cutler was away from the office a good deal, and came into Harold's room rarely. At home Phyllis spoke to him only when she could not avoid it. At night they lay like statues side by side. He reflected that, although they had more money, it had not made them happier.

Ten days after the dinner party it happened.

Harold went that day to the vegetarian restaurant across the park. Something in his nut steak must have disagreed with him, however, because by mid-afternoon he was racked by violent stomach pains. He bore them for half an hour and then decided that he must go home.

The bus took him to the High Road, near his street. He turned the corner into it, walked a few steps and then stopped, unbelieving.

His house was a hundred yards down the street. And there, drawn up outside it, was Cutler's gold and silver Rolls.

He could not have said how long he stood there staring, as though by looking he might make the car disappear. Then he turned away, walked to the Post Office in the High Road, entered a telephone box and dialled his own number.

The telephone rang and rang. On the wooden frame-work of the box somebody had written "Peter loves Vi". He rubbed a finger over the words, trying to erase them.

At last Phyllis answered. She sounded breathless.

"You've been a long time."

"I was in the garden hanging out washing, didn't hear you. You sound funny. What's the matter?"

He said that he felt ill and was coming home, was leaving the office now.

She said sharply, "But you're in a call box, I heard the pips."

He explained that he had suddenly felt faint, and had been near a pay telephone in the entrance hall.

"So you'll be back in half an hour." He detected relief in her voice.

During that half-hour he walked about, he could not afterwards have said in what streets, except that he could not bear to approach his own. He could not have borne to see Cutler driving away, a satisfied leer on his face at having once again shown the boiler who was master. Through his head there rang, over and over, Phyllis's words, *such an attractive man, very sexy*, words that now seemed repeated in the sound of his own footsteps. When he got home Phyllis exclaimed at sight of him, and said that he did look ill. She asked what he had eaten at lunch, and said that he had better lie down.

In the bedroom he caught the lingering aroma of cigar smoke, even though the window was open. He vomited in the lavatory and then said to Phyllis that he would stay in the spare room. She made no objection. During the evening she was unusually solicitous, coming up three times to ask whether there was something he would like, taking his temperature and putting a hand on his forehead. The touch was loathsome to him.

He stayed in the spare room. In the morning he dressed and shaved, but ate no breakfast. She expressed concern.

"You look pale. If you feel ill come home, but don't forget to call first just in case I might be out."

So, he thought, Cutler was coming again that day. The pearl-handled revolver, small as a toy, nestled in his pocket when he left. He had never fired it.

He spent the morning looking out of his window, but Cutler did not appear. He arrived soon after lunch, brought by Meech as usual. He did not come to Harold's office.

Half an hour passed. Harold took out the revolver and balanced it in his hand. Would it fire properly, would he be able to shoot straight? He felt calm but his hand trembled.

He took the lift up to the top floor, and opened the door of Cutler's office without knocking. Cutler was talking to a recording machine, which he switched off.

"Why the hell don't you knock?" Then he said more genially, "Oh, it's you, my old — Harold. What can I do for you?"

Harold took out the little revolver. Cutler looked astonished, but not frightened. He asked what Harold thought he was doing.

Harold did not reply. Across the desk the boiler faced the man who had ruined his life. The revolver went crack crack. Blue smoke curled up from it. Cutler continued to stare at him in astonishment, and Harold thought that he had failed in this as he had failed in so many things, that even from a few feet he had missed. Then he saw the red spot in the middle of Cutler's forehead, and the big man collapsed face down on his desk.

Harold walked out of the room, took the lift and left the building. He did not reply to the doorman, who asked whether he was feeling all right, he looked rather queer. He was going to give himself up to the police, but before doing so he must speak to Phyllis. He did not know just what he wanted to say, but it was necessary to show her that he was not a boiler, that Cutler had not triumphed in the end.

The bus dropped him in the High Road. He reached the corner of his street.

The gold and silver Rolls was there, standing outside his house.

He walked down the street towards it, feeling the terror of a man in a nightmare. Was Cutler immortal, that he should be able to get up from the desk and drive down here? Had he imagined the red spot, had his shots gone astray? He knew only that he must find out the truth.

When he reached the car it was locked and empty. He opened his front door. The house was silent.

The house was silent and he was silent, as he moved up the stairs delicately on tiptoe. He opened the door of the bedroom.

Phyllis was in bed. With her was the young chauffeur, Meech. A cigar, one of his master's cigars, was stubbed out in an ashtray.

Harold stared at them for a long moment of agony. Then, as they started up, he said words incomprehensible to them, words from the ritual of school. "A boiler fails in everything he does. I am a boiler."

He shut the door, went into the bathroom, took out the revolver and placed the tiny muzzle in his mouth. Then he pulled the trigger.

In his final action the boiler succeeded at last.

ACCOMMODATION VACANT

Celia Fremlin

"I'M SORRY . . ." THE woman's eyes slithered expertly down Linda's loose, figure-concealing coat, and her voice hardened. "No, I'm sorry, the room's been taken . . . No, I've nothing left at all, I'm afraid . . . Good afternoon. . . ."

Familiar enough words, by now. Goodness knows, we ought to be used to it, thought Linda bitterly, as she and David trailed together down the grimy steps. She dared not even look up at him for comfort, lest he should see the tears stinging and glittering in her eyes.

But he had seen them anyway. His arm came round her thin shoulders, and for a moment they leaned together, speechless, in the grey, mean street, engulfed by a disappointment so intense, so totally shared, that one day, when they were old, old people, they might remember it as an extraordinary joy. . . .

"Lin — Lin, darling, don't cry! It'll be all right, I swear it will be all right! I promise you it will, Lin . . . !"

The despairing note in his young voice, the pressure of his arms round her, destroyed the last remnants of Linda's self-control. Burying her face against the worn leather of his jacket, she sobbed, helplessly and hopelessly.

"It's my fault, David, it's all my fault!" she gulped, her voice muffled among the luxuriance of his dark, shoulder-length hair. "It was my fault, it was me who talked you into it. You said all along we shouldn't start a baby yet, not until you've got a proper job. . . ."

At this, David jerked her sharply round to face him.

"Lin!" he said, "Never, never say that again! I want this baby as much as you do, and if I ever said different, then forget it! He's *our* baby, yours and mine! I'm his father, and I want him! Get it? I *want* him! And I'm going to provide a home for him! A smashing home, too —" he proclaimed defiantly into the dingy,

uncaring street — "A home fit for my son! Fit for my wife and
son . . . !" His voice trailed off as he glared through the gather-
ing November dusk at the closed doors, the tightly-curtained
windows, rank on rank, as far as they could see. "My God, if I
could only get a decent job!" he muttered; and grabbing Linda's
hand in a harsh, almost savage grip he hurried her away; back to
the main road, back to the lighted buses, back "home".

That's what they still called it, anyway, though they both knew
it wasn't home any more. How could it be, when they had to steal
in through the front door like burglars, closing it in a whisper
behind them, going up the creaking stairs on tiptoe in the vain
hope of avoiding Mrs Moles, the landlady, with her guarded eyes
and her twice-daily inquisitions: "Found anywhere yet? Oh. Oh,
I see. Yes, well, I'm sorry, but I'm afraid I can't give you any
more extension. Six months you've had." (To the day, actually;
Linda remembered in every detail that May morning when she
had come back from the doctor's bubbling over with her glorious
news, spilling it out, in reckless triumph, to everyone in the
house.) "Six months, and I could have got you out in a week if I'd
been minded! A week's notice, that's all I'd have to've given, it's
not like you're on a regular tenancy! Six months I've given you,
it's not everyone'd be that patient, I can tell you! But I've had
enough! I'm giving you till Monday, understand? Not a day
longer! I need that room. . . ."

Sometimes, during these tirades, David would answer back.
Standing in front of Linda on the dark stairs, protecting her with
his broad shoulders and his mass of tangled, cave-man hair, he
would storm at Mrs Moles face to face, giving as good as he got;
and Linda never told him that it only made matters worse for her
afterwards. His male pride needed these shows of strength, she
knew, especially now, when his temporary job at the Rating
Office had come to an end, and the only money he could count on
was from his part-time job at the Cafeteria — three or four afternoons at most.

If only he had finished his course and got his Engineering
degree instead of dropping out halfway! — Linda silenced the
little stir of resentment, because what was the use? No good
needling him *now* about his irresponsible past. Poor Dave,
responsibility had caught up with him now, all right, and he was
doing his best — his unpractised best — to shoulder it. Doing it

for *her*. For her, and for the baby . . . recriminations don't help a man who is already stretched to his limit. Besides, she loved him.

Monday, though! Mrs Moles really meant it this time! *Monday* — only four days away! That night, Linda cried herself to sleep, with David's arms around her, and his voice, still shakily confident, whispering into her ear: "Don't you worry, Lin! It'll be all right. I promise you it'll be all right. . . ."

It wouldn't, though. How could it? They had been searching for months now, in all their free time and at weekends, lowering their standards week by week as the hopelessness of the search was gradually borne in on them. From a three-room flat to a two-room one . . . from one room with use of kitchen to anything, anything at all. . . . If all these weeks of unflagging effort had produced nothing, then what could possibly be hoped from four more days . . . ?

The next morning, for the first time since their search began, David set off for the Estate Agent's alone. After her near-sleepless night, Linda had woken feeling so sick, and looking so white and fragile, that David had insisted on her staying in bed — just as, a couple of weeks earlier, he had insisted on her giving up her job. Before he left, he brought her a cup of tea and kissed her goodbye.

"Don't worry, love, I'll come up with something *this* time, just you see!" And Linda, white and weak against the pillows, smiled, and tried to look as if she didn't know that he was lying.

After he had gone, she must have dozed off; for the next thing she knew, it was past eleven o'clock, pale November sunshine was glittering on the wet windows, and the telephone down in the hall was ringing . . . ringing . . . ringing. . . .

No one seemed to be answering. They must all be out. With a curious sense of foreboding (curious, because what bad news could there possibly be for a couple as near rock-bottom as herself and David?) Linda scrambled into dressing-gown and slippers, and hurried down the three flights of stairs.

"Darling! I thought you were never coming . . ." It was Dave's voice all right, but for a moment she hadn't recognized it, so long was it since it had sounded buoyant and carefree like that — "Darling, listen! Just *listen* — you'll never believe it. . . ."

And she didn't. Not at first, anyway; it was just too fantastic; a stroke of luck beyond their wildest dreams! In those first moments, with the telephone pressed to her unbelieving ear, she couldn't seem even to take it in.

What had happened, she at last gathered, was this. David had been coming gloomily out of the Estate Agent's, with the familiar "Nothing today, I'm afraid," still ringing in his ears — when a young man, red-haired and strikingly tall, had stepped across the pavement and accosted him.

"Looking for somewhere to live, buddy?" he'd asked; and before David had got over his surprise, the stranger was well and thoroughly launched on his amazing, incredible proposition.

A three-room flat, self-contained, with a balcony, and big windows facing south — all for five pounds a week!

"And he'd like us to move in *today*!" David gabbled joyously on, "Just think of it, Lin! *Today*! Not even one more night in that dump! No more grovelling to the old Mole! God, am I looking forward to telling her what she can do with that miserable garret . . ."

"But . . . but, darling . . . !" — Linda could not help breaking in at this point — "Darling, it sounds fantastic, of course it does! But . . . but, Dave, are you sure it's *all right*? I mean, why should this — whoever he is — why should he be letting the flat at such a ridiculously low rent? And . . . ?"

"Just what *I* wanted to know!" David's voice came clear and exultant down the line. "But it's quite simple really — he explained everything! You see, he's just broken up with his girl, she's gone off with another man, and he just can't stand staying on in the place without her. He's not thinking about the money, he just wants OUT — and you can understand it, can't you? I mean, he was nuts about this girl, they'd been together for over a year, and he thought she was just as happy as he was. The shock was just more than he could take . . ."

"Yes . . . Yes, of course . . ." Linda's excitement was laced with unease. "But — David — I still don't quite understand. Why *us*? Why isn't he putting it in the hands of the Agents . . . ?"

"Darling!" — there was just the tiniest edge of impatience in David's voice now — "Darling, don't be like that! Don't spoil it all! Anyway, it's all quite understandable, really. Just think for a minute. A chap in that sort of emotional crisis — the bottom just knocked out of his life — the last thing he needs is a lot of malarky about leases, and tenancy agreements, and date of transfer, and all the rest of it. So he decided to bypass the whole Estate Agent racket and simply —''

"So what was he doing, then, just outside an Estate Agent's?"

The words had snapped out before Linda could check them. She hated her own wariness, her inability to throw herself with total abandon into David's mood of unquestioning exultation.

But this time, David seemed to enjoy her hesitation: it was as if she had played, unwittingly, the very card that enabled him to lay down his ace.

"Aha!" he said — and already she could hear the smile in his voice — the old, cheeky, self-congratulatory smile with which he used to relate the more outrageous exploits of that bunch of tearaways he used to go around with — "*Aha*, that was cleverness! Real cleverness. Just the sort of thing that *I* might have thought of —" — how wonderful it was to hear his cocky, male arrogance coming alive again after all these months of humiliation and defeat! — "He did just the thing that *I* always do in a tricky situation — he asked himself the right questions! Like, what's the quickest way to clinch a deal — any deal? Why, find a chap who's desperate for what you've got to offer. And when the thing on offer is a roof over the head — then where do such desperate chaps come thickest on the ground? Why, outside an Estate Agent's, just after opening time! So that's what he did — just hung about waiting for someone to come out the door looking really sick. . . .''

It made sense. Sense of a sort, anyway. Linda felt her doubts beginning to melt. Joy hovered, like a bright bird, ready to swoop in.

"It — Oh, darling! It seems just too good to be true!" she cried. "Oh, Dave, I'm so happy! And this young man — once we're settled, and you've got another job, we must insist on him taking more than five pounds — we mustn't take advantage of his misery! Not when *we're* so happy . . . so lucky . . . ! Oh, but we don't even know his name . . . !''

"We do! It's Fanshawe!" David countered exultantly. "It's on the name-slip outside the door — 'R. Fanshawe'. But I've changed it, darling, I'm right here, and I've changed it already! It says 'Graves' now! 'David and Linda Graves'! Oh, Lin, darling, how soon can you get here . . . ?''

*   *   *

It was bigger even than she'd imagined, and much more beautiful. It was on the fifth floor of a large modern block, and even now, in winter, the big rooms were filled with light. The sunshine hit you like a breaking wave as you walked in, and through the wide windows, far away above the roofs and spires of the city, you could see a blue line of hills.

Linda and David could hardly speak for excitement. They wandered from room to room as if in a trance, exploring, exclaiming, making rapturous little sounds that were hardly like words at all; more like the twittering of birds in springtime, the joyous nesting time.

Deep, roomy shelves. Built-in cupboards and wardrobes. Bright, modern furniture — and not too much of it; there would be plenty of room for their own few favourite pieces.

"Your desk — it can go just here, Dave, under the window. It'll get all the light," exclaimed Linda: and, "See, Lin, this alcove — I can build his cot to exactly fit it! This will be *his* room . . . !" and so on and so on until at last, exhausted with happiness, one of them — afterwards, Linda could never remember which, and of course, at the time, it did not seem important — one of them suddenly noticed the time.

"Gosh, look, it's nearly two!" exclaimed whichever one it was; and there followed quite a little panic. For by 2.30 David was supposed to be at the Cafeteria, slicing hard-boiled eggs, washing lettuces, sweeping up the mess left by the lunchtime customers . . . it would never do for him to lose this job, too. Hand in hand they raced out of the flat . . . raced for the bus . . . and managed to reach home in time to get David out of his leather jacket and into a freshly-ironed overall just in time to be not much more than ten minutes late for work. Kissing him goodbye, Linda was careful not to muss up his hastily-smoothed hair — the curling, shoulder-length mane was a bone of contention at the Cafeteria — as, indeed, it had been at all his other jobs — but *she* loved it.

At the door he paused to urge her to rest while he was gone; to lie down and take things easy.

"You weren't too good this morning," he reminded her. "So whatever you do, don't start trying to do any packing — we'll do it this evening, together. Oh, darling, just imagine Mrs M's face when she sees us bumping our suitcases down the stairs this very night . . . ! 'Monday', indeed! *I'll* give her 'Monday' . . . !''

Obediently, after he'd gone, Linda pulled off her dress and shoes, and climbed into bed. It was quite true, she *was* tired. For a few minutes she lay, staring up at the ceiling, and trying to realize that she was looking at those familiar cracks and stains for the very last time. She couldn't believe it, really; the change in their fortunes had been so swift, so dreamlike somehow, that she hadn't really taken it in.

"Rest," David had urged her; but it was impossible. Excitement was drumming in her veins, it was impossible to be still, with all this happiness surging about inside her. She must *do* something. Not the packing — she'd promised to wait for David before starting on that; but there'd be no harm in getting things sorted out a bit . . . get rid of some of the rubbish. Those torn-off pages of "Accommodation to Let", for a start: they'd never need *those* again . . . !

Clumsily — for she was nearly eight months gone now — she heaved herself off the bed, and as she did so, David's leather jacket, hastily flung aside when he'd changed for work, cascaded off the bed on to the floor, with a little tinkling, metallic scutter of sound.

The keys, of course. The keys of the new flat: and as she picked them off the floor, Linda was filled with a surge of impatience to see again her beautiful new home — "home" already, as this place had never been. She ached to look once more out of the wide, beautiful windows, to gloat over the space, the light, and the precious feeling that it was *hers*! Hers and David's, and the new baby's as well! She wanted to examine, at leisure and in detail, every drawer and cupboard; to make plans about where the polished wooden salad-bowl was to go, and the Israeli dancing girl: and the books . . . and the records. . . .

Well, and why not? The whole afternoon stretched ahead of her — David wouldn't be home till nine at the earliest. What was she waiting for?

The flat did not seem, this time, quite the palace of light and space that it had seemed this morning; but it was still very wonderful. The rooms were dimmer now, and greyer, because, naturally, the sun had moved round since this morning, and left them in shadow.

But Linda did not mind. It was still marvellous. Humming to herself softly, she wandered, lapped in happiness, from room to room, peering into cupboards, scrutinizing shelves and alcoves, planning happily where everything was to go.

What space! What lovely, lovely space! Opening yet another set of empty, inviting drawers, it occurred to Linda that, for a man with a broken heart, their predecessor had left things quite extraordinarily clean and tidy. In the turmoil of shock and grief, how on earth had he forced himself to clear up so thoroughly — even to Hoover the carpets, and dust out the empty drawers? Or maybe the defecting girlfriend had done it for him? A sort of guilt-offering to assuage her conscience . . .?

Musing thus, Linda came upon a cupboard she had not noticed before — it was half-hidden by a big, well-cushioned armchair pulled in front of it. It looked as if it might be big enough to store all the things for the new baby . . . Linda took hold of the handle and pulled — and straightaway she knew that it was locked. This, then, must be where the ultra-tidy Mr Fanshawe had stored away his things? Spurred by curiosity, Linda tried first one and then another of the keys on the bunch David had been given — and at the third attempt, the door gave under her hand. Gave too readily, somehow. It was as if it was being pushed from inside . . . a great weight seemed to be on the move . . . and just as the fear reached her stomach, making it lurch within her, the door swung fully open, and the body of a girl slumped out on to the floor. A blonde girl; probably pretty, but there was no knowing now, so pinched and sunken were the features, already mottled with death.

Linda stood absolutely still. Horror, yes. In her recollections afterwards, and in her dreams, horror was the emotion she remembered most clearly. And what could be more natural?

But not at the time. At the time, in those very first seconds, before she had had time to think at all, it was not horror that had overwhelmed her at all, it was fury. Sickening, stupefying fury and disappointment.

"Damn you, damn you, damn you!" she sobbed, crazily, at the silent figure on the floor. "I *knew* it was too good to be true! I *knew* there would be a snag . . . !" and it was the sound of her own voice, raised in such blind, self-centred misery, that brought her partially to her senses.

She must *do* something. Phone somebody. Scream "Murder!" out of the window. Get help.

Help with what? How can you help a girl who is already dead . . . ? With the strange, steely calm that comes with shock, Linda dropped to her knees, and peered closely at the slumped, deathly figure. No breath stirred between the bluish lips; no pulse could be felt in the limp, icy wrist. The girl lay there lifeless as a bundle of old clothes, ruining everything.

Because, of course, the flat was lost to them now. Had, in fact, never been theirs to lose. The whole thing had been a trick, right from the beginning. What they had walked into, so foolishly and trustingly, was not a flat at all, but a dreadful crime. Presently, the police would be here, cordoning everything off, hunting down the real owner of the flat, bringing him back for questioning. They would be questioning herself and David, too. . . . That, of course, had been the whole point of the trick! Linda could see it all now. They had been lured here deliberately by the phoney offer of a home, in order that they should leave their fingerprints all over the place and be found here when the police arrived. A pair of trespassers, roaming without permission or explanation around someone else's flat! Because that's how it would look: why should the police — or indeed any other sane person — believe such a cock-and-bull story as she and David would have to tell? A ridiculous, incredible tale about having been offered, by a total stranger, an attractive three-room flat in a pleasant neighbourhood for only five pounds a week. All that this Fanshawe man had to do now was to deny totally the encounter with David outside the Estate Agent, and it would be his word against David's — with, to him, the overwhelming advantage that his denials would sound immeasurably more plausible than David's grotesque assertions!

Neat, really. "*Aha*, that was cleverness!" as David had so light-heartedly remarked, only a few hours ago!

At the thought of all that happiness — of David's pride, his triumph, all to be so short-lived — a cold fury of determination seized upon Linda's still-shocked brain, and she knew, suddenly, exactly what she must do.

The dead cannot suffer. They are beyond human aid, and beyond human injury, too; so it wasn't really so terrible, what she was going to do.

Cautiously, and without even any great distaste, so numbed was she with shock, Linda got hold of the limp figure by the thick polo-neck of its woollen sweater, and began to pull.

Luckily, at this dead hour of the afternoon, the long corridors were empty as a dream. The lift glided obediently, silently downwards with its terrible burden . . . down, down, past the entrance-floor, past even the basement . . . down, down to the lowest depths of all . . . and there, in an icy, windowless cellar, stacked with old mattresses and shadowy lengths of piping, Linda left her terrible charge.

It would be found — of course it would be found — but now there would at least be a sporting chance that the clues — now so thoroughly scrambled — would no longer lead so inexorably to the fifth-floor flat into which the new tenants had just moved. It would be just one more of those unsolved murders. There were dozens of them, every year, weren't there?

It would be all right. It *must* be all right. It must, it must. . . .

All the same, Linda couldn't get out of the beautiful flat fast enough that afternoon. While the grey November day faded — she dared not switch on any lights for fear of advertising her presence here — she pushed the big chair back in front of the cup-board again, and set the room to rights. Then, still trembling, and feeling deathly sick, she set off for home. It was only five o'clock: four whole hours in which to recover her composure before David got back from work.

And recover it she must. At any cost, David must be protected from all knowledge of this new and terrible turn of events. She recalled his triumphant happiness this morning, the resurgence of his masculine pride . . . she pictured how he would come bounding up the stairs this evening, three-at-a-time; carrying a bottle of wine, probably, to celebrate. . . .

And celebrate they would, if it killed her! Not one word would she breathe of her fearful secret — not one flicker of anxiety would she allow to cross her face.

Celebrate! Celebrate! Candles: steak and mushrooms, even if it cost all the week's housekeeping! She would wash and set her hair, too, as soon as she got in, and change into the peacock-blue maternity smock with the Chinese-y neck-line . . . she thought of everything, in fact, hurrying home through the November dusk that evening, except the possibility that David would be in before her. . . .

She stood in the doorway clutching her parcels, speechless with surprise, and staring at him.

"*Where the hell have you been*?"

Never had she heard his voice sound so angry. How long had he been here? Why had he come back so early . . . ?

"I said you were to *rest!*" he was shouting at her. "You promised me you'd stay here and rest! Where have you *been*? I've been out of my mind with worry! And where are the keys? The keys of the flat? They were here . . . in my pocket . . . !"

He was sorry, though, a minute later; when she'd handed over the keys, and had explained to him about her excitement, about the sudden, irresistible impulse to go and look at the beautiful new flat once more. He seemed to understand.

"I'm sorry, darling, I've been a brute!" he apologized. "But you see it was so scary, somehow, coming in and finding the place all dark and empty! I was afraid something had happened. I thought, maybe, the baby . . ."

The reconciliation was sweet: and if he questioned her a little over-minutely about her exact movements that afternoon, and exactly how she had found things in the flat — well, what could be more natural in a man thrilled to bits about his new home, into which he is going to move this very night?

And move that very night they did.

No more Mrs Moles! No more tiptoeing guiltily up and down dark stairs! Everywhere, light, and space, and privacy! And on top of this, a brand-new, modern kitchen, and a little, sunny room exactly right for the baby — only a month away he was, now! For a day or so, Linda had feared that the birth might be coming on prematurely; she had been having odd, occasional pains since dragging that awful weight hither and thither along cement floors, through shadowy doorways. But after a few days it all seemed to settle down again — as also, amazingly, did her mind and spirits.

At first, she had been full of guilt and dread: it was all she could do not to let David notice how she started at every footfall in the corridor . . . every soft moan from the lift doors as they closed and opened. Sometimes, too, she was aware — or imagined she was aware — of David's eyes on her, speculative, unsmiling. . . . At such times she would hastily find occasion to laugh shrilly . . . clatter saucepans . . . talk about the baby . . . anything.

But presently, as the days went by, and nothing happened, her nerves began to quieten. Indeed, there were times when she almost wondered whether she hadn't imagined the whole thing? Because there was nothing in the papers: nothing on the radio — though she'd listened, during those first few days, like a maniac, like a creature obsessed, switching-on every hour on the hour.

Nothing. Nothing at all. Had the body, conceivably, not been found yet? Surely it was *someone's* business — caretaker, night-watchman or someone — to go into that cellar now and again. Or — was it possible that the murderer himself had discovered where it had been moved to — had, perhaps, even watched her moving it, from some hidden vantage point . . . ? The lift, the corridors, had all *seemed* to be totally deserted, but you never knew. . . .

To begin with, weighed down as she was by guilt and dread, Linda had tried as far as possible to avoid contact with the neighbours; but inevitably, as the days went by, she found herself becoming on speaking-terms with first one and then another of them. The woman next door . . . the old man at the end of the corridor . . . the girl who always seemed to be watering the rubber-plant on the second-floor landing. Bits of gossip came to her ears, of tenants past and present, including, of course, snippets of information about her and David's predecessor in the flat . . . and slowly, inexorably, it was borne in on her that practically none of it fitted with David's story in the very least degree. The previous tenant had been neither red-haired nor tall — hadn't, in fact, been a man at all, but a woman. A young, blonde woman, Linda learned, who had rather kept herself to herself . . . Oh, there'd been goings-on, yes, but there, you have to live and let live, don't you? Quite a surprise, actually, when the young woman gave up the flat so suddenly, no one had heard a thing about it, but there you are, the young folk are very unpredictable these days. . . .

And it was now, for the very first time, that it dawned on Linda that she only had David's word for it that the bizarre and improbable encounter with "Mr Fanshawe" had ever taken place at all. Or, indeed, that any "Mr Fanshawe" had ever existed!

This terrible, traitorous thought slipped into her mind one early December evening as she sat sewing for her baby. And having slipped in, it seemed, instantly, to make itself horribly at home . . . as if, deep down in her brain, there had been a niche ready-prepared for it all along.

Because everything, now, slid hideously, inexorably into place: David's disproportionate anger when he found she had visited the flat by herself that first afternoon: his unexplained, mysteriously early return from work on that same occasion. Perhaps, instead of going to the Cafeteria, he had slipped off that working overall the moment he was out of sight, and gone rushing off to devise some means of disposing of the body: his preparations completed, he would have arrived at the flat, scared and breathless — to find that the body had already disappeared! What then? Bewildered and panic-stricken, he would have hurried home — only to find that she, Linda, had been to the flat ahead of him! Had he guessed that she must have found the body? And if so, what had he made of her silence all these days? What did he think she was thinking as she sat there, demure and smiling, evening after evening, sewing for the baby? No wonder he had been giving her dark, wary glances! . . . What sort of a look would it be that he'd be giving her tonight, when he came in and saw the new, terrible fear in her eyes . . . the suspicion flickering in her face and in her voice . . .?

Suspicion? No! No! She *didn't* suspect him — how could she? Not *David*! Not her own husband, the man she loved! How *could* she, even for an instant, have imagined that he might be capable of . . .!

Well, and what *is* a man capable of? A proud, headstrong young man who not so long ago was the daredevil leader of the most venturesome teenage gang in his neighbourhood? To what sort of lengths *could* such a young man go, under the intolerable lash of humiliation? He, who had set out in proud and youthful arrogance to conquer the world, and now finds he cannot even provide any sort of home for his wife and child? Such a young man — *could* he, in such extremities of shattered pride and of self-respect destroyed? — *could* he simply walk into a strange flat, murder the occupant, and coolly take possession . . .?

And even if he couldn't — couldn't, and hadn't, and never would — what then? What about *her*? How could she, having once let the awful suspicion cross her mind, ever face him again? How was she to behave . . . look . . . when he came in from work tonight? What sort of supper should one cook for a suspected murderer . . .?

And as she sat there, crouched in the beautiful flat, while

outside the evening darkened into night, she heard the soft whine of the lift — the opening and closing of its doors.

And next — although it was only a little after five, and David shouldn't be home till nine — next there came, unmistakably, the sound of the key in the door.

Afterwards, Linda could never remember what exactly had been the sequence of her thoughts. "*Why*?" had been one of them, certainly — *Why* is he arriving home so early? — and then, swift upon the heels of this, had come the blind, unreasoning panic . . . What is he *doing* out there? Why doesn't he come right in . . . shut the front door behind him? Why isn't he calling "Lin, darling, I'm back" the way he always does? Why is he being so quiet, so furtive . . . ? Lurking out there . . . standing stock still, to judge by the silence. . . .

But after that, in Linda's jumbled memory, all was confusion. Had she recognized the blonde girl at once — so different as she now looked — or had there been several minutes of stunned incomprehension as they gaped at one another in the little hall, all at cross-purposes in their questions and ejaculations?

Because, of course, this was the rightful tenant of the flat, Rosemary Fanshawe by name; as astounded (on her return from a stay in hospital and a fortnight's convalescence) to find a strange girl in possession of her flat as Linda was at this sudden invasion by a stranger. Linda could never remember, afterwards, who it was who finally made coffee for whom, or in what order each had explained herself to the other; but in the end — and certainly by the time David got back at nine o'clock — all had been made clear, and a sort of bewildered friendship was already in the making.

For this bright, well-groomed girl was indeed the same that Linda had found and taken for dead; and there had indeed been a terrible lovers' quarrel, just as the red-haired young man outside the Estate Agent's had affirmed. What he had told David hadn't been a lie, exactly; rather a sort of mirror-image of the truth, with all the facts in reverse. Thus it had been he, not Rosemary, who had ended the relationship: it had been her heart, not his, that was broken. It was she, not he, who had declared that she couldn't bear to stay in the flat for so much as another day. Hysterically, she had flung her things into cases . . . ordered a car to take them to a friend's house . . . and then, in less than an hour, had returned, half-crazy with grief and fury, to storm at him for not having tried to prevent her going. There had been a final, terrible quarrel, at the climax of which Rosemary had threatened dramatically to take a whole bottle of sleeping pills. Enraged by this bit of melodramatic blackmail (as he judged it), the red-haired boyfriend — Martin by name — had slammed out of the flat; but later, growing scared, he had crept back, and found to his horror that she really *had* taken the pills, and was lying — dead, as he thought — on the floor. (Actually, as they'd explained to Rosemary in the hospital, she'd only been in a deep coma, but a layman could not be expected to realize this, as both breath and pulse would be too faint to be discerned.) Appalled — and terrified at the thought that he might be blamed — Martin had bundled the "body" out of sight in the nearest cupboard, and set himself frantically to cleaning up the flat and removing all traces of their joint lives. All night it had taken him; and while he packed and scrubbed his brain had been afire with desperate schemes for shuffling-off the responsibility — preferably on to some anonymous outsider — while he, Martin, got clean away . . . by the time morning came, and his task was finished, his plans were also ready; he washed, shaved, and off he went to the Estate Agent. . . .

And in fact, it all worked out much as he had hoped — with the fortunate addition that, as it turned out, it was probably Linda's action in dragging the "body" down to the basement that had saved Rosemary's life — the jolting, the knocking-about, and the icy chill of the cellar, had prevented the coma becoming so deep as to be irreversible. That same night, she had recovered consciousness sufficiently to stagger out into the deserted street and wander some way before being picked up and taken to hospital.

And David, when he came home and heard the whole story? He was unsurprised. David was no fool, and he had realized right from the start (despite his show of bravado) that there was something very phoney indeed about that offer outside the Estate Agent's, but had decided (being the kind of young man he was) to gamble on the chance of being able to cope with the tricksters, whatever it was they were up to, when the time came. However, with his mind full of the possible hazards of the venture, he had naturally been thrown into a complete panic by the discovery that

Linda had gone off alone that first afternoon into what might well prove to be a trap of some kind; and even after his immediate fears had been set at rest, he had not failed to notice, in the succeeding days, that Linda was oppressed and ill-at-ease. He knew nothing, of course, about the "body", but he could see very well that there was *something* . . .

Now, he shrugged. He'd gambled and lost before in his short life.

"Oh, well. It's back on the road for us, then, Linda my pet," he said, reaching out his hand towards her . . . but at that same moment Rosemary gave a squeal as if she'd been trodden on.

"Oh *no*! Not *yet*! Oh, *please*!" she cried. "I can't possibly stay on in the flat by myself, I *must* have someone to share, now that . . ."

Of course, it wasn't quite the same as having the place to themselves; but it was much, much better than living at Mrs Moles'. And for Rosemary, likewise, it wasn't quite the same as having Martin there; but it was much, much better than having to pay the whole of the rent herself. She found, too, that she enjoyed the company; and when, soon after his son was born, David resumed his engineering studies and began bringing friends home from college, she found she enjoyed it even more.

"Wasn't it lucky that I took those pills just when I did?" she mused dreamily one evening, after the reluctant departure of one of the handsomer of the embryo engineers; and Linda, settling her baby back in his cot, had to agree that it was.

Indeed, when you thought of all the ways the thing *might* have ended, "lucky" seemed something of an understatement.

TWO'S COMPANY

Dorothy Simpson

FRANCIS LOWERED THE newspaper which he had been pretending to read and glanced over the top of it at his daughter's
head, bent in absorption over her school books. "By the way,"
he said casually — too casually? — "there's someone I'd like
you to meet."

For a moment he felt dizzy with relief, that he had actually
spoken the words aloud at last. But the worst might yet be to
come and he found that he was holding his breath, waiting for her
reaction. He didn't quite know what he was expecting — shock,
perhaps? Recoil? Some kind of resistance, anyway. It was, after
all, three years since they had received a guest into their home.

Becca's response was something of an anticlimax. She raised
her head slowly, smoothing back in an habitual gesture the tawny
hair which framed her small, pointed face with its high cheek-
bones and slanting, amber-coloured eyes.

For a disconcerting moment Francis was reminded of the tiger
in the jungle alerted by the first scent of danger but the impression slipped away almost before the thought was formulated;
Becca was merely looking at him in polite enquiry.

"Someone I met at the Hodgsons'," he went on, the well-
rehearsed words sounding uncomfortably stilted. Mr Hodgson
was Francis's boss, the regular Bridge evening Francis's one taste
of freedom. "A Mrs Jarvis," he said, shaken by Becca's continuing silence. "She's a friend of Mrs Hodgson and hasn't been
living in the area long, doesn't know many people here yet. I . . .
I thought that we could perhaps ask her to tea one Sunday."

"Why not?" Becca carefully capped her fountain pen. "If you
think she'd like to come."

"Oh she would." Francis was aware that relief was infusing his
words with an enthusiasm he would have preferred not to show.
"She's longing to meet you. You'll like her, I'm sure you will."

"She could come this Sunday, if you like."

"I'll be seeing her at Bridge on Thursday. I'll ask her then. What time shall I say?"

A slight shrug. "Whatever time you like."

"Three o'clock, then?"

"Fine." Becca uncapped her pen and returned to her books.

Francis went back to his newspaper, elated yet somehow uneasy. He had been so certain of Becca's opposition that he found her apparent indifference and lack of curiosity vaguely alarming. There was, too, a distinct sense of anticlimax. He felt like a mountaineer who had set out to climb Everest and found himself confronted by a molehill. He chided himself for his sense of dissatisfaction. Had he not, after all, gained his objective? His anticipatory fears had evidently had no foundation in reality. He had blown the whole thing up out of all proportion and should be thankful that the dreaded confrontation had proved so painless. Gradually he persuaded himself into a calmer state of mind and by the time he rang Laura, later that evening when Becca was in bed, he felt positively euphoric.

"No, no problem at all," he said. "You're invited for Sunday."

"She really didn't raise any objections?"

"Not one!" Francis laughed, a joyous sound.

"Wonderful! Let's hope she doesn't take an instant dislike to me."

"Of course she won't. Why should she?"

"I shall be terrified."

"Nonsense. It's going to be all right, darling. I can feel it in my bones."

On Sunday morning Francis was touched to see the trouble Becca took over her preparations for the visit. She rose early, cleaned the sitting-room, washed the best tea service, which since her mother's death had languished unused in the little rosewood china cabinet, and then launched into an orgy of baking, turning out scones, angel cakes and a sumptuous chocolate gâteau with an ease which filled Francis with pride and guilt. How many fourteen-year-olds could run a home, cook like an angel and still stay top of their class, he wondered. At the same time he felt passionately, as he had so often felt before, that it should not be necessary for her to do these things, that her childhood and youth were slipping away from her unnoticed and uncherished. She always denied it, of course. "I *like* to do it, daddy," she invariably said, when he expressed such feelings. And, "I don't want to go out with my friends. I'd much rather stay at home with you."

At first he had been able to accept and sympathize with this attitude, telling himself that the shock of losing her mother would naturally make Becca more dependent upon him, but gradually, as time went by and she showed no signs of wishing to change the status quo, he became restless, more and more resentful of the emotional burden which her attitude imposed upon him. He found the atmosphere of the little flat into which they had moved after Marion's death increasingly claustrophobic and the long, quiet evenings and uneventful weekends drove him to a screaming pitch of restlessness. He had leapt at Hodgson's suggestion of a weekly Bridge evening like a starving man grabbing for a crust of bread.

For a while this innocuous extension to his social life had satisfied him but after a few months he had found that it was not enough; he found himself yearning more and more for the company of a woman, for the release and delight of lovemaking. He and Marion had been fortunate indeed, their sexual relationship a continuing joy to both. To have had to adjust himself to celibacy so suddenly after Marion's death had been hard indeed, a struggle of which he had felt ashamed at the time. There was, he had felt, something almost indecent about missing sex when one's wife was barely cold in her grave. So when, about a year ago, Laura made her first appearance at the Bridge table, he had been more than ready to fall in love. Fortunately she too was free, the attraction had been mutual and their happiness was marred only by their anxiety over Becca's reaction to the prospect of a stepmother. Endlessly, obsessively, they had discussed ways and means of winning her co-operation and they now looked forward to this all-important first meeting with a mixture of eagerness and dread.

By three o'clock Francis and Becca were ready and waiting. Francis had been unable to do more than pick at his lunch and now his stomach was knotted, his palms slippery with apprehension. As the minutes ticked away he was seized by panic. What if, after all Becca's preparations, Laura didn't come? What if she had had an accident, if there had been some emergency, if her bus simply hadn't turned up? Sunday services were notoriously unreliable. He had offered to fetch her by car, but she had been adamant in her refusal.

"Far better for me to arrive alone, darling," she'd said, "just like any ordinary visitor."

Now, he wished that he had insisted. At least, then, he would not have had to sit here in this agony of uncertainty. He glanced surreptitiously at Becca, calmly engrossed in one of the Sunday supplements. What was she thinking, beneath that unruffled exterior?

The doorbell rang. "There she is," he said, jumping to his feet.

Laura looked just right, he thought, as he opened the door to let her in. Her simple summer dress in a cornflower-blue linen which matched her eyes was neither too casual nor too formal, pretty without being inappropriately elegant. They exchanged polite greetings, conscious that Becca could hear what they were saying, only their eyes and a quick squeeze of their hands betraying their mutual need for reassurance.

Francis led the way into the sitting-room. "This is Becca, Laura," he said. "Becca, Laura Jarvis."

It was going to be all right, he thought, watching them shake hands and greet each other. More than once, during the hours that followed, he wondered what on earth he had been worrying about. Laura and Becca were getting on wonderfully well and was it not, after all, logical that they should? Linked by his love for them and theirs for him, did they not already have a head start in their relationship? Laura's manner was perfect, he thought complacently, warm without being over-effusive or condescending. And Becca's behaviour far outstripped his expectations. He could not have faulted it in any way. Perhaps this was what she, too, needed: feminine company and an opening up of the narrowness of their life together.

Promptly at half-past five Laura said that it was time for her to go. Becca and Francis both protested, but she was determined.

"I'll run you home, then," Francis said. This was contrary to what they had aranged, but the afternoon had gone so well that he felt she could not possibly object. Besides, he longed to share his euphoria with her.

"It's not necessary, really," Laura said. "There's a bus in just a few minutes."

"Nonsense," said Francis. "It'll take you three quarters of an hour by bus — you have to change in the town and you know what Sunday connections are like. What's the point, when I could have you home in ten minutes?"

"No, really . . ."

"Let daddy take you, Mrs Jarvis," Becca said, smiling.

Her seal of approval was all they needed. Becca came down to see them off and in a flurry of farewells they were on their way.

"Well?" Francis burst out triumphantly, the moment they were out of sight.

Laura said nothing and he glanced at her, surprised at her silence. She was frowning, her underlip caught beneath her teeth.

"What's the matter? Didn't you think it went well?"

"She didn't like me."

"Nonsense! You got on like a house on fire!"

Laura shook her head, a quick, decisive little shake. "On the surface, perhaps. But underneath . . ."

"Darling, you're imagining things. I *know* Becca. She liked you, she really did."

Laura compressed her lips, said nothing.

"I just don't understand," said Francis in exasperation. "Can you tell me one single thing that Becca said or did that will bear out what you're saying?"

Laura remained silent.

"You see? You can't."

"She didn't like me," Laura repeated stubbornly. "Oh, I admit there's nothing I can put my finger on, but I'm convinced of it all the same."

"A woman's intuition, I suppose."

"If you choose to call it that."

Francis shook his head. "I just don't understand you. If she'd been rude, uncooperative, you'd have reason to complain, but as it is . . ."

"Do you realize," Laura said, so softly that Francis had to strain to decipher the words above the noise of the engine, "that this is the first time we have ever come anywhere close to quarrelling?"

They had arrived, Francis noted thankfully and he pulled in to the kerb. "You're right," he said ruefully.

"And," Laura went on, "that if she had been difficult, the

effect would have been quite different? Then we would have been united, in condemnation of her behaviour. We would, wouldn't we?''

"True, but . . . oh, come on! Surely you're not suggesting she's as devious as that?''

"Not consciously, perhaps. In any case, I think she values your good opinion too much to have behaved badly.''

"Well it's only natural that she should be a little wary,'' Francis said defensively. "After all, she must suspect what we have in mind.''

"You haven't told her yet, I hope?''

"No. You . . . haven't changed your mind?''

"About us?'' Laura shook her head, her slow smile lighting her eyes. "Of course not. I think we'll just have to go very gently with Becca, that's all. Give her plenty of time to get used to the idea of having to share you again.'' Laura hesitated, then went on, "I've never asked you before, but was she very fond of her mother?''

"Not terribly, no, I wouldn't say. They were so very different. Becca's a very neat, organized sort of person and Marion was just the opposite. She painted, you know, and when she was working she just used to forget about the time. Often, when Becca came home from school she'd find the breakfast dishes still on the table, the housework undone and no supper prepared. She used to set to and do it herself, but naturally she got a bit fed up with it. Of course, it was still a terrible shock for her when Marion . . . died. She was there, you see. Becca, I mean. She was only eleven . . .''

"Where?'' said Laura, softly.

Francis had never told Laura the details of Marion's death and even now he hated talking about it.

"Marion was killed in an accident. By a bus. She was wearing high heels and witnesses thought that she must have caught one of them on the edge of the pavement. Luckily she wasn't holding Becca's hand at the time . . .''

Laura shivered. "Poor kid.''

"I know. Not that she ever shows her feelings much, but after that she just dropped all her outside interests . . . I was hoping that in time she'd start to go out with her friends again, but she never did. That's one of the reasons why you'll be so good for her.''

Laura gave a wry grin. "You make me sound like a dose of medicine.''

"A breath of fresh air," said Francis, leaning across to kiss her.

Her lips were soft, warm, infinitely inviting.

"Shall I come up?" he whispered.

She pulled away. "Better not. Becca'll be expecting you back."

"See you on Thursday?" It seemed a lifetime away and for the thousandth time he thought how wonderful it would be not to have his time alone with Laura rationed to such brief intervals.

He drove home dreaming of the future.

Back at the flat Becca stacked the dirty dishes on a tray and carried it into the tiny kitchen. She had refused Laura's offer of help with the washing-up and now she set about the task in her usual methodical manner, a complacent little smile on her lips. Yes, she thought, the afternoon had gone very well indeed. She had a feeling that Laura had seen through the friendly façade, but that didn't matter. The important thing was that her father had been well and truly taken in.

It was obvious, of course, that he and Laura were crazy about each other. Becca had suspected the truth for some time and it was a relief that they had at last come out into the open. She had looked forward to this afternoon. It was always interesting — indeed essential — to study one's enemy. Only thus may one begin the search for his Achilles heel.

Now, as she washed, rinsed and dried the delicate china, Becca thought back over the afternoon with the clinical detachment of a chess player considering the moves of his latest game. Laura was a promising victim, no doubt about that. She was kind, warm, genuine . . . and therefore vulnerable. It really shouldn't be too difficult to dispose of her. It would simply be a matter of waiting and watching and of being prepared to seize the opportunity when it arose, like last time . . . Becca's hands became still and her eyes glazed as she relived once more that moment of supreme satisfaction when, of its own volition, her hand had darted forward to give her mother that vicious and timely shove in the small of the back. The act had been unpremeditated but Becca had never felt a vestige of remorse. On the contrary, it had been bliss to be free of her mother's sluttishness, to revel in the neat orderliness of her home and, above all, to be the sole object of her father's love and attention.

Until now.

Becca had every intention of ensuring that no other woman, ever, would permanently take first place in her father's life.

Meanwhile, of course, it was vital that he should not suspect her true feelings and over the next months Becca gave him no reason whatsoever to do so. She continued to be polite, well-mannered and even welcoming to Laura, pretended delight when they finally plucked up sufficient courage to inform her of their plans for marriage. She entered with exactly the right degree of enthusiasm into their discussions about the future, agreed to be bridesmaid with a carefully calculated degree of shy pleasure.

And all the time she secretly watched Laura with the single-minded intensity of a cat watching a mouse-hole. Laura's death, when it came, must appear to be the inevitable consequence of some facet of her character, some apparently innocuous habit. Patiently, Becca noted them all, confident that sooner or later Laura herself would provide Becca with the perfect solution.

As, eventually, she did.

The first piece of relevant information did not at the time appear to be particularly significant. It was a few days before the wedding and the three of them had spent the evening discussing final details. Becca was to stay with a neighbour until Francis and Laura returned from their brief honeymoon. Afterwards, Laura would move into the flat until a larger one could be found. Accommodation in the area was both scarce and expensive and they had not as yet succeeded in finding anything suitable.

At ten o'clock Laura said that it was time she went home. Becca politely went to fetch Laura's coat and on the way back through the narrow hall was intrigued to find Laura in the bathroom, bending over the bath.

Becca paused in the doorway. "What's the matter?"

"A spider, look." Laura had taken a towel and was trying to scoop the creature up.

"Flush it down the loo."

Laura raised a shocked face. "It would drown." She managed to capture it at last and shook it out of the window. "There," she said triumphantly.

This tiny incident, Becca found, epitomized Laura's attitude to animals. Stories of ill-treated or abandoned pets upset her for days. Becca began to think that here, perhaps, was something she might be able to use.

The second and most crucial piece of information emerged, surprisingly enough, from a visit to the theatre. It was Becca's birthday and Francis had reserved the tickets by telephone. When they arrived at the theatre he was disappointed to find that their seats were not in the dress circle, as he had expected, but in the upper circle. The show was a popular one and an exchange not possible.

"It really doesn't matter, Daddy," Becca said. "I don't mind sitting in the Gods. It's rather fun."

"But it's supposed to be a special treat. The best of everything."

"It *is* a treat. I've been longing to see this show for ages."

Grumbling, Francis allowed himself to be coaxed towards the stairs. Engrossed in their little drama neither of them noticed Laura's silence until they stepped out on to the narrow cat-walk. Below them, steeply tiered seats dropped giddily away. Francis courteously stood back for Laura and Becca to precede him.

"You go first," Laura said to Becca.

Becca, ever sensitive to the nuances of Laura's behaviour, looked at her sharply.

"Are you all right?"

"Fine." But Laura's smile was more a baring of teeth.

Becca cottoned on at once, and her stomach clenched with excitement: Laura was afraid of heights. She studied her stepmother covertly as they made their way down the precipitous steps and found their places, noting with satisfaction that even when they were seated Laura was pressing herself back in her chair, her knuckles white on the armrests.

Becca's instant diagnosis was correct. Laura had suffered from vertigo as far back as she could remember and took extreme care to avoid finding herself in this sort of situation. It was unfortunate for her that her father had been the boisterous, insensitive type who found other people's fears incomprehensible and believed that the only cure was confrontation. Through years of being hauled up lighthouses, forced to look over the sides of multi-storey car parks and dragged near the edge of cliffs, Laura had reached a state in which the terror was a near-paralysis of thought and movement. Escaping at last from her father's sneers and bullying she had sworn that never, ever again would she allow herself to become vulnerable in this particular way; never again would she reveal her fear to anyone, no matter what the circumstances. Tonight as she sat grimly through the performance she was sorely tempted to confide in Francis. Francis, surely, was different, a kind and gentle man. But there was Becca . . . Laura knew with a deep, instinctive certainty that although she could trust the father, she could not trust the daughter. Becca was Francis's blind spot, and if Laura were to tell him of her phobia and ask him not to tell Becca, she would have to explain why. Inevitably there would be arguments, quarrels, even. Laura was not prepared to put her relationship with Francis at risk. Becca was growing up fast, would one day (please God!) remove herself from their orbit. Until then, Laura was determined to hide her mistrust and go along with the sweetness-and-light image which Becca invariably projected.

So this evening Laura elected to suffer in silence and in response to Francis's whispered solicitude merely murmured that she had a slight headache, that was all, and would be fine once they were back in the open air.

But for Becca the evening was one of exquisite, orgasmic pleasure. Here at last was the weapon for which she had so long and patiently waited. Her imagination seized greedily upon it and the music of the show, the wave after wave of enthusiastic applause became simply the background to the far more exciting scenarios for Laura's death which played themselves out in her mind. Laura's silent suffering, beside her in the darkness, was a bonus, an extra dimension of delight, a foretaste of the pleasure to come. Becca was possessed by a fierce exultation. Her eyes glowed, her cheeks burned and when they left the theatre her father smiled indulgently, put her arm around her shoulders and gave her a gratified hug.

"No need to ask if you enjoyed it."

When the euphoria ebbed it left behind a cold, implacable determination not to ruin everything by rushing in too soon. She could afford to wait, now. Systematically she began to consider plans for Laura's murder, discarding, adapting, adjusting, amplifying with a meticulous attention to detail.

At last she was satisfied and it was time for the next stage to begin.

She chose a Saturday morning, when the three of them invariably lingered over breakfast.

"Daddy," she said diffidently.

"Yes?"

Becca shook her head. "Oh, nothing," she mumbled.

"Go on," her father urged. "What were you going to say?"

Reluctantly, Becca allowed herself to be coaxed into speech. "I was wondering how soon we might be able to move, that's all." She was aware that Francis and Laura had exchanged puzzled glances. Good. As she had intended, they were obviously wondering why such an impersonal topic should cause such diffidence.

"Well, we keep on looking, as you know," Francis said. "But it's difficult. There's not much on the market at present, particularly as far as flats are concerned. And we don't want to rush into anything unsuitable. I know this place is a bit cramped, but surely we can manage here until the right thing comes along, can't we?"

Becca bit her lip, avoided his eye.

"What's the matter?" Bewilderment was making him slightly exasperated. "Becca?"

Becca ducked her head, shook it.

"Becca, what is it?" Laura now joined in.

If it hadn't been so important to get this scene just right, Becca felt that she could have burst out laughing at the sight of their concerned faces. But she couldn't afford to make even the slightest mistake at this point.

"It's just that this flat's so small," she murmured.

"Well, we know that," Francis said impatiently. "We're all agreed on that."

"And my bedroom's right next door to yours . . ." Becca said, so softly that she sensed, rather than saw that they both had to lean forward to catch her words.

But they had heard her, all right. There was a profound silence. The shock in the air was almost tangible. Deliberately Becca maintained her façade of embarrassment and it was a moment or two before she risked a darting glance at their faces. She had, she saw, achieved precisely the effect for which she had striven. They were both sitting there like stuffed dummies, their faces stamped with identical expressions of mortification.

She waited.

Francis cleared his throat. "Yes, well," he said, standing up so abruptly that he almost overturned his chair and had to put out a hand to catch it. "I see what you mean. We hadn't . . . it hadn't . . ." He had crossed to the window and now he fell silent, looking out.

"I'd better clear away," Laura said brightly, jumping up and beginning to pile the dishes one on top of the other with movements that were a little too brisk, a shade too noisy.

So far, so good, thought Becca, watching them depart for the Estate Agents, half an hour later. Manipulating people, she decided, was really rather fun. The highest hurdle was of course yet to come, but she was confident now that she could clear it.

It took every last scrap of patience she could muster.

"Houses, bungalows, bungalows, houses!" Francis threw the stack of House Agents' details down in disgust. "Why on earth they bother to send these when they know it's a flat we're looking for, I can't imagine."

It was three months later and they still hadn't found anything even remotely suitable.

"I suppose they hope that one of these will catch our fancy. Perhaps we ought to settle for a house after all," said Laura, retrieving some of the typed sheets. "This one doesn't sound too bad. Listen." She read out the details.

"But you both loathe gardening," Becca put in gently.

It was true. This was the main reason why they were restricting their search to flats.

There was a frustrated silence.

"Oh, it's hopeless," Laura said. "There just aren't enough flats in the area, that's the trouble, and there are always queues of people waiting for them."

"Surely we ought to be well up the list by now," said Francis.

"If they're working through it fairly," said Becca.

"That's a thought." Francis looked at her thoughtfully. "Perhaps I'll try some new tactics. Make a bloody nuisance of myself." He stood up purposefully, went to fetch his coat. "And I'll begin right now."

Almost at once this new approach began to pay off. A thin trickle of details of flats began to plop through the letterbox and then, one Saturday morning some three weeks later, Francis returned in a state of high excitement.

"Come on. Get your coats on, both of you. We're not going to miss this one. I haven't even seen it yet, but I've already made a verbal offer and said I'll be back in an hour with a written one."

Becca's heart sank. If the flat turned out to be unsuitable for her purpose, there could be problems ahead.

But it didn't.

"Random Towers!" she said in excitement as Francis drove into the car park behind the tall tower block. Flats in this and in its twin block across the road were the most coveted in the area and very rarely came on to the market.

"I know. What a stroke of luck, eh? You'll both love it, I know you will." Francis shepherded them eagerly to the main entrance and into the lift. Unlike Becca he did not notice Laura's lack of response, simply took her enthusiasm for granted.

Two pairs of eyes watched in equal suspense as he selected the appropriate button.

The fourth floor.

Laura relaxed a fraction. Any higher and she would have had to speak out. The fourth floor was bad enough, but she might just be able to cope.

Becca expelled her breath in a long, slow sigh of satisfaction. The fourth floor would be fine. Any lower and she would have had to prepare for battle.

And the flat, they all saw at once, was perfect. There was a spacious living room, a beautiful modern kitchen, and two bedrooms separated by a luxurious bathroom. The latter, Becca noted, had only one small window, high up. She went into the smaller of the two bedrooms, threw up the window and glanced down. She could scarcely believe her eyes. The whole place was tailored to her requirements. They had to take it, they just had to.

She returned to the living-room determined to fight with every weapon she could muster.

She could tell at a glance that Laura had been registering some objection to the place. Becca whirled into action. She ran across the room and threw her arms around her father's neck, gave him an enthusiastic hug. "It's wonderful, daddy," she cried. "Really marvellous." She felt some of the tenseness drain out of his body.

He put her gently away from him. "Laura's not sure if it's suitable," he said.

This was the moment. She had to get it right.

"Oh," Becca said, allowing the excitement and enthusiasm slowly to drain from her face. "But why?" She was carefully non-aggressive, an adult prepared to listen to another adult's point of view. Nothing betrayed the agonized suspense in which she waited. She knew only too well that if Laura revealed her phobia, all would be lost. She couldn't understand why Laura had not confided in Francis long before now, was simply grateful that Laura evidently had some powerful reason for holding back. Powerful enough to restrain her even now?

"It's just that it's rather expensive," said Laura.

"But worth it, surely," said Francis. "I know things would be a bit tight, but we could manage." Then, as Laura still hesitated, "What is it that you don't like about it, darling?"

Laura shook her head, a trapped, uncertain movement.

With trepidation Becca played her ace. "It's no good, daddy. If Laura doesn't like the place, there's no point in even considering it, is there?"

Laura looked helplessly from one expectant face to the other. Becca's apparent generosity had put her in an impossible position. If she stood firm there was no doubt which of them would appear in the better light to Francis. She glanced at the windows, which framed a view of the block of flats across the road. At least she would not have to live with the prospect of a dizzying expanse of sky. And it was only two floors higher than their present flat . . .

"Darling?" pleaded Francis. "Are you sure? We'll never get another chance like this."

They looked at each other, thinking of the endless, interminable search for anything remotely suitable, remembering how inhibited their lovemaking had become since Becca's shattering plea that sunny Saturday morning six months ago.

With a dragging sensation in the pit of her stomach, Laura capitulated. "I suppose you're right. Oh, of course you are, darling. It would be madness to turn it down."

The look of delight on Francis's face was her reward.

"That's settled, then." He put one arm around Laura, the other around Becca and hugged them both. "We'll go straight back to the Estate Agent and clinch it. And tonight, we'll celebrate."

They managed to get completion in the record time of six weeks, and Becca used this interim period to prepare the ground for acquiring the other essential ingredient of her plan, a kitten. It was simple to overcome Laura's objection on the grounds that it was unkind to keep an animal cooped up in a flat.

"Better than being drowned in a bucket of water," said Becca.

That shut Laura up, as she had known that it would. Finding a kitten presented no problem. Enquiries at school quickly produced one and Becca arranged to collect it the day after the move.

Now all she had to do was wait for the right moment.

It came sooner than she had dared to hope, just a week after they moved in. It was a Friday, the second day of Becca's half-term holiday. Laura had complained of feeling unwell the previous evening and today her temperature was up, her head ached and she thought that she was probably in for a bout of 'flu.

"Better have the day off," said Francis. "Becca'll look after you, won't you, Becca?"

It was difficult for Becca not to show too much alacrity. Together, she and Francis persuaded Laura back to bed.

As soon as Francis left for work Becca made sure that Laura was dozing and that her window was open, then shut herself into her room to make her preparations.

First, she checked the weather: perfect. A calm, still day, ideal for her purpose.

Then, taking the reel of strong, sand-coloured thread which she had bought in readiness, she measured and cut off two fourteen-foot lengths. She knotted one end of each piece of thread around the legs of her dressing table and then went in search of the little black and white bundle of fur they had named Nemo.

Nemo did not appreciate being hamstrung. Becca had been careful to make sure that her hands were permanently covered in scratches, but by the time she had finished tying the two stray ends of thread securely around Nemo's back legs, she had acquired several more.

Then, carrying the kitten, she went to the window, opened it and looked out. The street below was deserted and she could see no sign of life in the flats opposite. She checked again, just to be certain, and then quickly leaned out and set Nemo down on the broad ledge which ran along the front of the building a few feet below. Then she closed the window, snatched up her coat and bag and left the room, locking the door behind her and pocketing the key. Before leaving the flat she returned to Laura's room and, with an apology for rousing her, said that she was going into the town. Did Laura need anything?

Laura, flushed and drowsy, shook her head.

In the entrance hall downstairs Becca stopped to chat briefly to Mr Brierson, the caretaker, who was washing the floor with a long-handled mop. Then she hurried across the road and glanced up at her window.

She could see Nemo clearly, a black blob against the sand-coloured façade of the building. As she had hoped, he had moved along the ledge towards Laura's open window, hoping for access to the flat. Praying that no one spotted him she hurried along to the telephone box on the corner and dialled.

There was a telephone beside Laura's bed and she answered on the third ring, her voice hoarse and blurred with sleep.

"Laura? Becca here. I'm sorry to disturb you, but I'm down in the town and I'm worried about Nemo. I've got a horrible feeling I left the door of your room open and as the window's open too I'm afraid he might try to get out . . ."

"I'll check," said Laura, sounding more awake and a little annoyed. "But really, Becca . . ."

"I know." Becca was contrite. "I'll be more careful in future, I promise. And I really am sorry to have disturbed you. I do hope he's okay."

Laura made some non-committal noise and rang off.

Now, Becca thought, the palms of her hands growing moist, now we'll see if it's going to work. She took several deep breaths. This was no time for an attack of nerves. Even if her plan didn't come off, she would have to act swiftly to remove those incriminating threads, make a split-second decision to stay in the street or to hurry unobtrusively up to the flat, according to whether Laura pulled Nemo down with her or not.

Becca had already chosen her vantage point, a bus shelter opposite the entrance to Random Towers. From here she had a grandstand view of the drama being played out above her.

Nemo, prevented from attaining his goal by the fetters on his back legs, was standing quite still some four or five feet away from Laura's window. Becca's stomach lurched with excitement as that window opened further and Laura's head appeared. Now Laura had seen the kitten, was calling it, extending her hand towards it. . . .

This, Becca knew, was the crucial moment, when Laura's fear of heights was going to have to battle with her tender heart. Becca was pretty certain which would win, but even so she found that her fists were clenched so tightly that her fingernails were cutting into her palms. A quick glance up and down the road reassured her that she was still the only spectator to the drama — surely a good omen? Even so, she dared not gaze fixedly upwards, forced herself to be content with quick, darting glances.

It was working! Laura was leaning out of the window now, stretching further and further towards the cat. Becca's heartbeat thundered in her ears and she prayed that she had calculated aright, that Laura's body would have to pass the fulcrum before she succeeded in reaching Nemo, and that the thread was as invisible to Laura as its careful selection of colour should make it.

Becca poised herself for action, attention divided between Laura and the kitten. The moment Laura fell . . .

It was now. Laura grabbed for the kitten, missed, and Becca ran across the road and into the entrance to the flats as the cartwheeling body windmilled down on to the pavement with a sickening crunch against which Becca closed her ears. Strangely, Laura had made no sound.

Mr Brierson was putting away his mop and bucket in a cupboard at the rear of the hall.

"Forgot my purse!" she said, with a little laugh.

He ignored her, turned, head cocked. "What was that?"

"What?" Becca pressed the lift button.

"Thought I heard something . . ." And be began to walk towards the glass doors.

Becca entered the lift as he stepped out on to the pavement.

In her room she raised the window and peeped out. There were already several people bending over Laura's body, but no one was looking up. Quickly she rescued Nemo by hauling on the threads, cut them off and flushed the evidence of her guilt down the lavatory. Then she prepared for the part she would have to play — shock, grief, self-reproach. . . .

An hour later, clasping Becca tightly in his arms, Francis was still trying to calm her down.

"I shouldn't have gone out . . . I should have realized she'd be all muzzy, from the 'flu . . . I shouldn't have left her door open, then Nemo couldn't have got out . . ."

"Hush." Francis thrust aside his own grief and stroked Becca's hair. "What's the point of going on like this? Nothing can bring her back. It's over. You really mustn't reproach yourself like this . . ." He blinked back his tears and said hoarsely, "At least we've still got each other."

Becca raised her tear-stained face, inwardly exulting. Mine, she thought, as she looked up at him, rubbed her cheek against the rough tweed of his jacket, inhaled the familiar smell of him, so long denied her. All mine. And nothing, but nothing, is ever going to take him away from me again.

In the fourth-floor flat of the block across the road the woman in the wheelchair watched them embrace and came to a decision. She hated getting involved in other people's affairs but she really couldn't sit by any longer.

She laid down the powerful binoculars which made bearable the limitations imposed upon her life by her paralysed legs and reached for the telephone.

It was time that she rang the police.

A HELL OF A STORY

H. R. F. Keating

THEY SNATCHED THE Oil Sheik's kid, exactly as planned, at 11:06 precisely. There were no difficulties. The girl they'd got for the job distracted the boy's bodyguard for just long enough. The boy himself reacted to the little flying helicopter on a string just as they'd calculated he would. But then a kid of eight, and an Arab from the sticks first time in London, that part couldn't have gone wrong. Worth every penny of all it had cost, that toy.

Everything else had gone like clockwork too. No traffic hold-ups when they were moving away from the Park. No trouble in the change-over of cars. No one about in the mews to see it, and not a bit of fuss out of the lad. Quiet, big-eyed, doing what he was told, scared to death most likely.

So inside half an hour he was safely in the room they'd prepared for him in the old house waiting for demolition up over Kilburn way. No one had spotted them taking him in. He hadn't had time to see enough of the outside of the place to remember it again when they'd got the cash and let him go. And Old Pete was there minding him. Dead right for the job.

Forty years in and out of the nick had soured Old Pete to such a point that anybody who met him accidentally began at once to think how they could get away. No one would come poking their nose into the Kilburn place when there was sixteen stone of Old Pete there, fat but hard, never much of a one for shaving, always a bit of a smell to him. The kid was in as safe hands as could be while they conducted the negotiations.

They put in the first call to the rented Mayfair house at six o'clock that evening when they calculated the Sheik would have had just about enough time to have unpleasant thoughts and be ready quietly to agree to dodge the police and pay up. "The kid's safe," they said. "He'll be having his supper now. He's being well looked after."

It was true. Old Pete was just going into the room with the boy's supper, baked beans and a cup of tea, prepared on the picnic stove they'd put into the place. The boy looked at the extraordinary food — extraordinary to him — without seeming to be much put out by it. Old Pete even grunted a question at him, which he hadn't meant to. Only the kid's calm was a bit unexpected. It threw Old Pete a little. "All right, are you?" he grunted.

The boy looked at him, his large dark eyes clear and unwavering.

"Will you mind being in Hell?" he asked.

Old Pete, lumbering toward the door with its dangling padlock, stopped dead in his tracks and turned round.

"English," he said dazedly. "English. You speak English."

"Of course I do," the boy replied. "I always speak English with the Adviser. Talking with me is all he has to do, now my father has the oil and doesn't need advice any more."

Old Pete, crafty enough in his way but not one for confronting new situations easily, stood blinking, trying to fit this into the framework of his knowledge. And there was something else. Something at the back of his mind that had to be dealt with too. And it was that, surprisingly, that pushed itself forward first.

"'Ere," he said suddenly, "what d'you mean 'Hell'?"

"Will you mind being in Hell forever?" the boy asked.

"What d'you mean, me being in Hell?"

"Well, you will have to go there. Kidnapping is a sin. If you commit sins you go to Hell."

The simple, fundamental philosophy of the desert fell like drops of untarnished water from his lips.

Old Pete, tyre-tummied, dirt-engrimed, looked at the kid for a long while without speaking a word. Then at last the machinery of his mind ground out his answer.

"Look, lad," he said, "that's all gone out. They finished with all that. Word may've not got round to where you come from, but they found out all that's wrong. Just tales. You know, what ain't so."

He stood, bending forward a little, examining the slight form of the boy in his neat, expensive Western shirt and shorts.

"Yes," he said, ramming it home, "you take my word for it, lad. That's all past-times stuff now. Gone and forgotten."

He made his way out, an evil-smelling forty-ton tank, and carefully refitted the padlock to the little secure room.

But the next morning, when the Sheik was still holding out and the rest of them were considering what would be the easiest way of putting the pressure on a bit, the boy proved not to have absorbed the latest developments in Western thought at all. When Old Pete brought him his breakfast, the kid accepted the big bowl of cornflakes eagerly enough, but in his conversation he was making no concessions to modernity.

"You will go to Hell, you know," he said, picking up from where they had left off. "You have to — you've done wrong."

"But I told yer," said Old Pete. "They changed all that."

"You can't," the boy said, with all the calm certainty of someone pointing out an accidental breach in the rules of a game. "If you do something wrong, you have to be punished for it. Isn't that so?"

"Well, I don't know about that," said Pete. "I mean, the cops don't always catch you. Not if you're sharp. They're not going to catch us for this lot, that's for sure. Those boys has it worked out a right treat."

"Yes," said the Sheik's son, "but that's just the reason."

"Just the reason?"

"Yes, if you do not get caught and punished here, you must be punished when you are dead. When you cross the Bridge of Al Sirat, which is only as wide as the breadth of a hair, the weight of your sin makes you fall. Into Hell."

His large brown eyes looked steadily into Pete's battered face.

"It's for ever, of course," the boy added.

Old Pete left the room in too much of a hurry to collect last night's dirty baked-beans plate.

He did not come back at lunchtime as he had meant to do. But at about six that evening — when the Sheik, after talk of making life hard for the boy, had just caved in and promised to deliver the cash — Old Pete once more removed the heavy padlock on the door and entered with another plate of steaming baked beans. The boy said nothing but seized eagerly on the beans. Old Pete turned to the door. But then he stopped, and began to gather up the two previous lots of dirty crockery. The boy ate steadily. Pete picked up the plates and put them down again. At last he broke out.

"For ever?" he said.

"Of course," the boy answered, knowing at once what they were talking about. "If you go to Paradise for ever if you've been good, then you must go to Hell for ever if you've been bad."

"Yeah," said Pete. And after a little he added, "Stands to reason, I suppose."

He put the now emptied second baked-beans plate on top of the others.

"I'm not meant to tell yer," he said, "but you'll be going back 'ome soon. Yer old man's coming up with the dibbins."

"It won't make any difference," the boy said, again answering an unspoken question.

Pete blundered out of the room, snapping the big padlock closed with a ferocious click. And entirely forgetting the dirty crockery.

But he was back within twenty minutes.

"Look," he said. "If I'd forgotten to lock the door when I brought you your nosh just now, you could've sneaked out and nobody the wiser."

"No," said the boy. "You must *take* me home, all the way. Otherwise it wouldn't count."

Sweat broke out under the dirt of Pete's broad, fat-bulged face. "I can't do that. They'd catch me. Catch me for sure."

At the steps leading up to the door of the big corner house in Mayfair the boy turned to his companion.

"All right," he said. "I will ring myself. You can go now."

Pete swung away and lumbered off round the corner, fast as if he was a tanker lorry out of control on an ice-slippery hill. But his legs were too jelly-like to support him for long, and once safely round the corner out of sight, he just had to stop and lean against the tall iron railing and let the waves of trembling flow over him.

For two whole minutes he did nothing but lean there, shaking. Then he began to relieve his feelings in dredging up from a well-stored memory every foul word he had ever heard. He only came to a halt, after some ten minutes, in order to draw breath.

When he did so the cool, clear, horribly familiar voice of the boy spoke from the open window over his head.

"I'm afraid with all that you will have to go to Hell after all," the boy said.

THE JEALOUS APPRENTICE

Joan Aiken

OF COURSE THE academy of which my aunt Gwen is Dean can't be spoken of by its true name. Graduates refer to it affectionately as Crib College. But its full title is the Antient & Singular Academie of Farcing, Charmerie, Prigging Law, and Cracksmanship. There are no written records kept, naturally, but the college has been in existence, one way or another, since the fifteenth century, and very probably much longer. It moves about the country, since a permanent headquarters would be undesirable; under Henry the Eighth was the longest tenure of one spot, an expropriated monastery, but then some up-and-coming nobleman moved in, and the staff and students moved out, hastily, by night.

Courses, naturally, have changed during the centuries; dummering, swadding, and demanding for glimmer are no longer on the syllabus; but the Black Art (lock picking), Lifting Law (parcel stealing) and Motor-prad Law (theft of wheeled vehicles) are still on the regular timetable and form part of the basic groundwork of lore which students are expected to absorb in their first year. They are not, in fact, referred to as students; early usages still obtain in the college and novices for their first seven years are bound by strict agreements of indenture, and are known as apprentices. Then they serve a further two years as journeymen. After this period they are formally invested with the black velvet mask, fine steel chain, and gilt nutcrackers of the Master Cracksman.

However, as the conditions of service are somewhat hazardous, it is doubtful whether more than about thirty per cent of apprentices ever work through to full mastership. Those that do so are principally in the more studious and sedentary branches: cursitor work, forging, Barnard's law, cheating at cards, and, nowadays, computer-scripping and tax-versing. But, since

apprentices are sent out to cribs with the more experienced journeymen (as, of course, they must be, or how will they ever acquire
experience?) if the peelers should rumble the ken and arrive on
the spot, it is college law that the santer, or apprentice, shall if
possible help his journeyman to escape (with the pelfry if he can)
and allow himself to be taken, in order to let his senior get clear.
Apprentices are not so nimble at getting away and at most
periods, therefore, the ranks of the second-, third-, and fourth-
year students are thinned because many of them will be in the
clink, or pokey. (Their fees are remitted during this time.)

It is, of course, unusual for a woman to be Dean of the college,
and indeed my aunt Gwen Thornbush was the first female to be
so honoured as far as the verbal annals record. But the college
was founded by a famous wild rogue, Wat Thornbush, about
whom there are no proved tales but innumerable legends, and
there has always been a member of the Thornbush tribe to continue the tradition ever since. Lambert Thornbush, Gwen's great-
grandfather, was one of the last highwaymen, or high-lawyers,
who achieved a highly correct and exemplary end, being hanged
at Tyburn; her grandfather was caught prigging a gross of gold
snuffboxes from the Pavilion at Brighton, and was transported
to Botany Bay; her great-uncle, branching into more intellectual
pursuits, made a very comfortable fortune by fraudulent company promotion.

The college does not advertise. And its current whereabouts, at
any one time, are not widely known. Would-be students must be
endowed with pertinacity and firm intentions, they must pass
through a lengthy channel of inquiry and referral, question and
answer, all by word of mouth, before they, so to speak, even
reach the porter's lodge. There has been only one instance of a
peeler's spy, or smoke, managing to bluff his way in and enter as
a student. What happened to him has passed into legend and is a
deterrent for any member of the academy who might consider
blabbing on a fellow-practitioner or grassing to the police about
college activities: it began with having his tongue burned out by
hot irons and went on for five days. Apprentices, when they sign
their indentures, take what is known as the *Bitter Oath*, which
binds them for life, as the Aesculapian oath does members of the
medical profession.

There are, of course, as well as the regular syllabus, weekend courses, seminars, refresher courses, and high-pressure intensive classes to keep graduates up to the minute in new techniques such as laser work and computer fraud. My aunt Gwen was herself a computer expert — she had done that beautiful little job on meat supplies for Whiplash Worldwide Hamburger Bars which netted her a cool million; she could easily have retired, and indeed she invested much of the money in new equipment for the college; but my aunt was a natural hard worker and enjoyed practising the art for its own sake; she often voiced her ambition to die in harness like great-grandfather Lambert. She did not, however, very often go out on a crib herself. The case I am going to relate was one of the rare exceptions.

It was an unusual mark altogether. In the first place, my aunt was approached by an outside, a simpler, which is extremely uncommon. After a series of messages a meeting was arranged at a small Indian restaurant in a medium-sized northern town of no interest called Bucklawrie. Confidence was rapidly established between my aunt, a shrewd judge of character, and the simpler, who identified himself as a member of a distinguished north-country family. His errand was an odd one. It seemed that the family mansion was to be sold up. This was partly a matter of necessity. He explained that the house, Normanley Priory, was disastrously situated on a ridge underneath which a whole series of coal shafts had been dug (in fact it was from these mines that the Normanley family had made their very substantial fortunes). Somewhat short-sightedly, they had not, in burrowing for riches underground, realized the hazard to the family home, custom-built for them on the ruins of the ancient abbey by the Adam brothers and custom-furnished by Sheraton; but now the mines had been nationalized, the family had fallen on hard times, and the National Trust refused to take on the mansion, which was about to fall in half, if not vanish entirely into a huge crack which was opening across the hillside. The coal shafts, now worked out, could not be filled in because of the danger from springs of water; the only course was to abandon the house and realize the value of its contents. This value, of course, was immense: furnished at the heyday of the family's prosperity, the priory contained treasures of every possible kind, paintings by Raeburn, Romney, Rembrandt and Goya, tapestries, china, gold, marble, jewellery and antiques of all periods.

What my aunt's customer wanted was nothing much; he introduced himself as Cyril Normanley, a younger brother in a cadet branch of the family. He would not, he said, be personally benefiting in any way by the sale of the contents, and he was angry about it: Lord Normanley, his cousin, was selling all the family treasures to overseas collectors and nothing would be left in this country. He felt it a slur on the family honour and was resolved that one article, at least, should be saved from this wholesale dispersal. What did he intend to do with it? Well, he said, in his lifetime it would remain hidden in his London flat, a source of comfort and solace to him (he was not a young man); after his death it could go to the National Gallery, he would make provision in his will. My aunt did not discuss the legality of this; that was not her province; she had, apparently, taken a fancy, as strong-minded women sometimes will, to the frail elderly man opposite her picking distastefully at his gingery curry. She accepted the commission, named her fee, a thumping one, which he paid on the spot, by Barclaycard, and the deal was agreed.

"When do you want it done?" she inquired.

The house, he told her, was in process of being cleared. Silver and china had gone already. A firm of art transporters would be calling in three weeks to remove the paintings; so there was no time to lose. The article that Mr Normanley wished to reserve for himself was a small painting by Goya; a portrait of an ancestress, Lady Maria Normanley, whose father had been British ambassador at the Escorial. "It is a very beautiful painting," he said wistfully. "And moreover it is exactly like my dear mother who died twenty years ago."

My aunt Gwen noted the particulars of the painting, and whereabouts in the house it was hung, and the client gave her a great deal more information about the Priory, in which he had grown up. Then the pair parted.

Aunt Gwen was somewhat exercised in her mind as to whether to undertake the crib herself or allow one of her journeymen-students to do so. Normally, since it was a rather superior piece of lifting, she would have done it; but lately she had been suffering from acute arthritis in the neck and shoulders (arthritis is an unfortunate occupational hazard of foisting, nipping, and all outdoor forms of knavery due to the long hours spent motionless, watching, in damp exposed spots); naturally my aunt would not let herself be deterred by such a small consideration as a little pain, but she was afraid that the affliction might impair her efficiency.

She therefore, after much thought, entrusted the job to her senior journeyman student, an extremely proficient Troll and Prigger, Tom Casewit, who had only six months remaining before he would have completed the full course and be a Master Cracksman. Tom was a silent, taciturn individual, dark, with a scarred cheek, result of a turn-up with the slops; his final graduation had been delayed by a four-year sentence in the pokey but he had not wasted his time while in jail as he had the good luck there to encounter a famous Australian safe-breaker who taught him some elegant variations of method.

"It's not a hard job, Tom," aunt Gwen told him. "There's no one living in the house at night now. You can do it on your own — you won't need a warp or a stand."

Warps and stands keep watch outside. And the gin who opens the window is called a tricker.

"You need not take your apprentice," Gwen told Tom. "The house is only protected by electric alarms; and any first-year can deal with *them*."

Tom nodded. He was never one for unnecessary words.

"It seems a bit odd that they should leave the big house empty," Miss Thornbush went on. "Even though it's liable to fall into the coal mine down below within the next six months, you'd think there'd be plenty of markers and curbers keen to get in and hook up the pickings. But apparently that's not so. The reason why is —"

At this point she dropped her voice, which was not loud at the best of times. A hidden listener, who was curled up under a loose floorboard in Miss Thornbush's study, strained his ears, but to his great annoyance was unable to hear what she said next. Some word like *glaar*? The *glaar* keeps them away? That was what it sounded like; but there is no such word in the language.

A moment later the door opened and closed; Tom Casewit had gone out. And not long afterwards Miss Thornbush followed him; and presently the listener uncurled himself and pushed up the floorboard and made his escape.

Who was this listener? Why, it was Tom's apprentice, Skin Masham; a thin, hollow-eyed boy, so bony and gangling in appearance that his skill in creeping through narrow places was continually amazing his fellow-students; he could slip through a crack that seemed hardly wide enough to pass a chisel or a picklock through. Where a ray of moonshine could go, Skin Masham could follow, they used to say. He had a tuneful voice, too, and could sing the college song very movingly:

> O when I am dead and go to my grave
> A flashy funeral let me have
> Let none but bold robbers carry my corpse
> And sing "There goes a wild 'un, a wild and wicked warp!"

But despite his voice and his agility, Skin Masham was not popular with the students; he had a spiteful, jealous nature, was always fancying himself overpassed and put-upon; he felt that nobody gave him his due, and he hated, he hated with the whole strength of his nature, anybody who had something that he wanted. An apprentice was supposed to serve his journeyman faithfully, stand below the window with the wresters, hold the curb, carry the garbage to the marker, watch at all times for the peelers, and, if necessary, interpose himself and hold them up while the senior prigger made his escape. So far, such a crisis had not arisen; but it seemed highly unlikely that Skin would act in so self-sacrificing a manner should it be required. Tom Casewit did not wholly trust him; but then Tom Casewit trusted nobody.

Gnawing his nails to the quick, Skin crept away down the passage. He was consumed with jealousy that Tom should be sent away to a crib without him. Normanley Priory was quite evidently a first-class crib, a really grand one; it would have counted at least thirty credits to him in his end-of-term marking. Why should Tom have all the credit — Tom who would be a Master soon in any case? It was unfair — hideously unfair! Skin decided to take action on his own. He would show the old bag who, in her ropey old college, was a really skilful cracksman. And if he could put a spoke in Tom's wheel at the same time, why, so much the better.

Students of the college were, of course, expected to study a crib intensively before attempting to crack it. Movements of inmates, arrivals of outside tradesmen, resident animals and their habits, surrounding vegetation, local weather conditions, even folklore if relevant — all had to be absorbed and taken into account.

Tom Casewit had immediately gone off on what was known as tolling-time; Skin went to Miss Thornbush and asked for leave of absence to attend the wedding of a sister in Newhaven, Connecticut.

"You must be exceedingly fond of your sister to want to go such a distance?" remarked Miss Thornbush looking at him sceptically over the tops of her steel glasses. Skin did not seem the kind for deep family attachments.

"Oh, it's just, ma'am — we haven't seen each other since we was kinchins." Skid tried to look properly wistful; actually he loathed his sister, who was married to a wealthy bookmaker, and would not have gone within fifty miles of her house.

"Very well; you may have two weeks. But you had better study your theory of termage and quitteries while you are away — if you expect to pass the Lent term examinations," his principal told him sternly.

Skin escaped, muttering spitefully, packed a small bag, and hitched a ride to Kinnockshire, in which county, he had discovered by study in the college library, Normanley Priory was to be found.

Kinnockshire is a wild, rugged county. The inhabitants speak a dialect hardly changed from the ninth century, when the valleys were overrun by Norsemen who stayed for a while, decided that the climate was too bleak to be endured, and returned home again. Towards the north angle of the county, which is one of the smallest in England, Kinnockdale lies between two gloomy crags; and, at the foot of Kinnockdale, Normanley Priory is uncomfortably perched on top of its coal mines.

Watching the house was not easy. In such a countryside, a stranger sticks out like a cactus in a cabbage bed; Skid had to steal a bicycle, and make do with cycling through daily, in different disguises: sometimes a punk, sometimes a boy scout, sometimes a messenger on special delivery. He found that, as Miss Thornbush had said, the house stood empty, except for the staff engaged on the daily work of dismantling and removal. It was a big, grey place, on its green slope of hill; very plain, Skin thought it.

He tried asking local people about it, but their accent wholly defeated him; and as for the *glaar*, if that indeed was the word that Miss Thornbush had used, at the end of ten days he had reached no further conclusion about what it could be. Probably some kind of weather: mist or fog or wind coming across the fells. It was a cold, gloomy countryside. One story Skid finally did manage to translate out of the local dialect, which only confirmed his feelings about the place: back there some time in history, two to three hundred years ago, the couple who lived in the place at the time, Lord and Lady Normanley of that date, had starved their daughter to death, one of their daughters; just took and shut her up in a room and starved her, because she refused to marry somebody they thought she ought; either that, or she wanted to marry some unsuitable young fellow of her own. So they let her die of hunger in her own bedroom. What do you think of that! Skin reckoned that such folk deserved to have their house fall into a coal mine and lose all their money; anything that he could prig from the house before the contents were all dispersed seemed like fair pickings.

Quite soon he spotted what must be Tom Casewit; it was a good disguise, he must acknowledge, an old dame rigged up as an archaeologist from Newcastle University with field-glasses and all kinds of measuring implements, limping about in the grounds of the priory peering at barrows and piles of stones. The ground was all cracked and heaved up, like molehills on a big scale; you could believe that, quite soon, the whole house would go crashing down into the black caves underneath. Jeez; what a spooky notion. Skin decided that he had reconnoitred quite long enough; he'd go in tonight, bag the painting of Lady Maria and any other little items he chanced across, then get the obloquium out of there.

At dusk he called the local slops. Putting on his sister's voice, which he could mimic very cleverly, he told them that the lady archaeologist was really a high-class cracksman, and that if they looked in her knapsack they'd find wall-climbing kit and a magnetic neutralizer for dowsing electronic burglar alarms. "Who is this?" the police-station operator naturally said, but Skin rang off at that point; however they had paid serious attention to what he told them and, later, hiding in a gully in the Priory grounds, he was delighted to observe them arrive and do a snatch on the old archaeologist dame. And — what a surprise! — when they took off her wig, it wasn't Tom Casewit at all, but old Miss Gwen, Miss Thornbush the principal; she must have decided to do the

prig herself after all. Skin did feel a trifle nervous at that; shopping Tom was one thing, that would have troubled him not a
whit; but to do in the Old Lady Troll herself, that was a bit
shattering and more than he had bargained for. How would he
deal with the simpler on his own? And who would take on the
Deanship and give him his degree in due course? Still, no use
crossing bridges before he came to them. The first thing was to do
this prig.

Skin entered the Priory as easily and as skilfully as a field-
mouse, nipping through the crack of a rotting door; he had of
course put his quietus on the burglar alarm first, and the slops
were no doubt by this time off at the slop-ken interrogating old
Troll Thornbush, and long might they keep her there!

Slipping up the carpetless stairway, silent as a cloud of dust,
Skin made his way to the picture gallery.

Along at the East end, the old simpler had told Miss Thornbush
and she had told Tom Casewit: a picture of a lady in a grey dress
and a pearl necklace.

Easy to spot. Couldn't mistake it.

The night was cloudy, not dark, and by the time he reached the
end of the gallery his eyes were accustomed. He could see the
outline of the picture well enough, and made out that it was a
bird, with hair done on top of her head and a strand or two of
cobbles round her neck; Jeez, what a size! Pity they weren't real
ones, they'd be a sight better worth prigging than an old bit of
painted canvas.

About to lift down the canvas, Skin had a bad fright; a voice
behind him whispered, "Here you are at last!"

He spun round, pretty fast, at that, you may be sure; and was
not pleased to see a dame standing as close to him as he was to the
picture.

"Who by the Troll are you?" says he, staring at this nan as well
he might; for in nearly all respects she was the image of the
picture: dressed all in grey, with her hair done up on top and the
rope of cobbles round her neck. The only difference was in her
face, which looked like all of hunger itself; the eyes, the gaping
mouth, the fallen-in cheeks, the ravenous despairing gaze she
fixed on him was enough to set the cold prickles coursing down
his back.

"Who am I?" says she. "Don't you know me, and I've waited

for you here for so long? I am the glaar," she says, and with that she steps forward and takes him by the hands, both hands, for he was so bedazed he couldn't fend her off; he lets out a little pitiful whimper, like a puppy as you wring its neck; and then a crack opens in the floor and down they go, both of them, and the walls as well, pictures, carpets, and the lot, with a rumble and tumble of falling masonry. And that was the end of Skin Masham, and the end of Normanley Priory as well; by the time the art transporters arrived there was nothing to be seen but a big hole in the ground, and if anyone has gone down into the mine to hunt for all those pictures and Sheraton chairs, they haven't found them yet.

If you ask me, Skin Masham was lucky; what he'd have got from his fellow students for shopping the principal would have lasted far longer and been a whole lot more painful than falling down a crack with a ghost.

What happened to Miss Gwen Thornbush? Serving a short sentence for being apprehended with burglars' tools.

Who's running the academy? Why, I am.

Toby Thornbush, transported to Botany Bay, was my great-uncle. Bug-eye Casewit, my grandfather, was a famous bush-ranger, Toby's brother-in-law; so when sentence was passed, aunt Gwen said to me: "Tom, you'll keep an eye on the kids till I'm out, won't you?"

Always one to keep things running and do her duty, aunt Gwen; that was why she'd decided she had better face the glaar, and not send a deputy to do it. Anyway, I reckon, as things turned out, it was all for the best; that Skin Masham was no loss.

GOOD INVESTMENTS

Celia Dale

EUNICE CHRISTINE HILDA Bradshaw grew up in the crisply stony seaside town of Seaham with her maternal Auntie Florence, her father having been killed on active service in 1944, her mother dying of heart trouble two years later. Eunice was in her late teens by this time, studying clerical skills at the local Polytechnic. She and Auntie Florence knew each other well, as the sisters had lived near to each other, and the transference from one terrace villa to another was painless. Auntie Florence was a dressmaker, a stout exclamatory woman who had never married, and she doted on Eunice — so clever, so competent, such a church-goer, a sweet girl. And it was all true.

Eunice graduated through several jobs, each better than the last; and for the past 27 years she had been head of the department dealing with Bereavement Claims in the Seaham branch of a national charitable organization.

She was a neat, refined woman now, neither fat nor thin, discreetly made-up (but nothing so vulgar as eye shadow, merely powder, pink lipstick, and on off days perhaps a brush of rouge), with hair parted at the side with a half fringe and which grew just a little browner with each fortnightly visit to the hairdresser. She ran her department impeccably, with a smile and a word of praise when merited. She ran Auntie Florence's house impeccably also, especially as Auntie grew older and fatter and weaker, leaving more and more of it to Eunice and never ceasing to exclaim what a treasure she was. And she was.

She liked everything to be dainty. Frilled curtains, cushions and aprons; flowered bed linen; potted plants in pretty containers standing on doilies; embroidered tray cloths and nightdress cases. She cooked delicious cakes, scones, puddings, even made fudge and fondants. She tried out whimsical recipes from magazines, such as Sponge Easter Bunnies, Chocolate Yule Logs, Guy

Fawkes Brandy Snaps. A spot of spillage in the kitchen was whisked away in a trice, the oven was almost as pure as the day it was installed, the teacloths rinsed and drying after each use, and herself and Auntie sitting in front of the television eating dainty snacks off trays daintily laid with embroidered cloths and matching flowered crockery.

"What a girl you are!" Auntie would wheeze, tucking in. "What a treasure!"

"Silly Auntie!" Eunice would murmur indulgently, "It's my pleasure."

And it was.

So when Auntie died Eunice felt it keenly. People were very kind; she had, of course, the support of the church among whose congregation she had many friends. Auntie had left the house to her and a few — a very few — thousand pounds in the bank. Eunice was due to retire the following year, when she would be sixty. The pension would not be much but she had some savings in the Building Society; she would be able to manage.

But she missed Auntie. She missed her wheezing presence, her cries of love and appreciation. She missed having an audience for her excellence; making rock cakes and peppermint creams for the Church Bazaar was not the same, glad though she was to do it, as making them for instant, face-to-face applause. She missed having someone to demonstrate her virtues to.

She had caused a rose-bush to be planted for Auntie in the crematorium's Garden of Remembrance, and she was pruning it one gusty November Sunday (she visited the Garden every fortnight and preferred to look after the rose-bush herself as Auntie would have liked) when she fell into conversation with a gentleman performing the same task a bush or two away. His bush was newer than hers by several months; his wife had passed away only recently, he still wore a black band on his sleeve, and had hardly any idea of how to wield his secateurs.

Eunice showed him; she had a ruthless way of pruning which would, she knew, result in a mass of dainty blooms in summer. Mr Stafford — Stanley Stafford, retired Water Board official — was full of admiration. The wind was cold, his nose dripped slightly, he suggested a cup of tea.

Eunice had never considered marriage. She knew nothing of men save socially (married or semi-celibate around the Church Hall) or in business (often overbearing or unreasonable, with cigarette ash everywhere and not too careful about how they emerged from the toilet). As a television viewer and a subscriber to the Public Library she had perforce had aspects of male behaviour presented to her; but television sets could be switched off, and although it was becoming more and more difficult to be sure no unpleasant antics or language appeared in novels, the librarians were fairly good by now at recommending those that might not offend, and there was always travel and biography — although even there one could no longer be sure nowadays, what with fertility rites and hitherto unpublished diaries.

No, men had never attracted her. They seemed, on the whole, selfish and dirty. But she did miss Auntie. And poor Mr Stafford was so pitiful, with his sad eyes and reddish nose, trying to look after himself in the rented flat he had shared with his late wife, the lease of which was nearly up. And there was she, lonely in Auntie's two-bedroomed house.

As a lodger? That would hardly be nice, people would talk . . .

They were married quietly in the spring. Eunice wore navy blue with touches of white and Mr Stafford wore a rose from his late wife's remembrance bush in his buttonhole. Eunice had made it quite clear from the beginning that there was to be none of "that", and Mr Stafford had thankfully concurred. He was seventy-four and had never had much of a taste for it. He moved into Auntie's bedroom and Eunice remained in hers, and they never saw each other unless they were fully dressed. But he revelled in her competence, excellence and daintiness (his late wife had not been much of a housekeeper), in her cheerful small talk, her tasteful presence alongside him in church or when viewing telly, and in the daintily delicious meals she set before him.

He was not used to them, and when they had been married less than a year he had a coronary thrombosis and died in Intensive Care.

Eunice was shocked. The arrangement had worked so well. Stanley had been no trouble, grateful for all she did, taking his own dirty clothes to the launderette so that she never had to handle them, giving up smoking so that there was no mess or fusty smell. He had praised her, comparing her favourably (but with good taste) with his late wife. He had been nearly as good as Auntie.

But better than Auntie in one way; he left Eunice £9,000 and his life insurance policy. He had, surprisingly, turned out to be rather a good investment.

She missed him. Perhaps not exactly him but the appreciation he, like Auntie, had given her. Besides, now she was retired (she had resigned at marriage but in consideration of her 27 years' service the organization had not diminished her pension) she had very little to do. She would be willing — on the same terms, of course — to take on another man. And there seemed to be money in it . . .

The Garden of Remembrance was a lovesome thing, God wot, and Eunice continued to visit it as regularly as before, for she now had three rose-bushes to care for — Auntie, Stanley and Stanley's late wife (as she considered only nice). She observed the other visitors discreetly, and if a funeral were taking place would find out who was the deceased. If it was a gentleman she took no further action. But if it was a lady she would slip into a pew at the back of the chapel and take tactful part. Afterwards she joined the mourners to view the floral tributes and, some months after Stanley's death, stood in line to press the widower's hand and murmur, "I was a friend of your wife's."

"Oh yes — thank you," he said, dazed, a small, bald man in a well-cut suit, his relatives prosperous-looking.

"Perhaps, when your grief has eased, I might call on you? So many happy memories . . ."

"Thank you. So kind."

She pressed his hand and moved on. She knew who he was from the cards, his address would be in the telephone book.

This time it took longer, about eighteen months; and this time she sold Auntie's house and moved into Kenneth Gratton's handsome semi-detached on the Cliff Road. The arrangement was as before: separate rooms and no intimacies. But Kenneth was not otherwise at all the same as poor Stanley had been. He had been head of a building firm and used to ordering men about and getting his own way. Although he was small and bronchitic he had a will of concrete, drank whisky in the evening, refused to give up his pipes, which made the whole house smell disgusting as well as leaving dottles of burned tobacco in every dainty ashtray and even on the floor. He expected her to watch Match of the Day and, horror of horrors, wrestling. He disliked made-up dishes, dainties of every kind; liked fried onions, pickles and stout.

It was no hardship at all for Eunice to slip a sleeping-pill or two into his bedtime whisky and, when he was snoring loudly, place a pillow over his face.

Kenneth did not leave her his house (he left that to his son who lived in Newcastle and took no interest in his father's affairs) but he left her a reasonable sum — not as much as she had expected but she realized that Kenneth had been an error of judgment in many ways, something of a disappointment altogether. But there was always tomorrow, and pressing yet another widower's hand the following autumn she felt her instincts could be relied on this time.

Gilbert Phelps was pale, frail and asthmatic, almost unbecomingly eager for someone to continue taking care of him. He ate little and worried about his health and was, in fact, a very poor companion, although he possessed some sound investments and a house in the best part of Seaham which she sold at a good profit as soon as Probate was granted; it had been a happy release for them both.

Now, on the whole, she thought it would be wise to move from Seaham and start afresh elsewhere. She moved further along the coast, into a genteel private hotel, found the local Garden of Remembrance and a neglected rose-tree, and in not too long a time became Mrs Reginald Crocker, with a nice first-floor flat overlooking the promenade and a husband who was eighty-four years old.

No one was surprised when *he* apparently died in his sleep.

As Mrs Christine Crocker, Eunice married the following year a retired solicitor called Wilfred Jessop, who left her some more useful stocks and shares and property in Cornwall. This she sold, and with the proceeds bought herself a luxury bungalow (but big enough for two) in Redcliff-on-Sea where, as Christine Jessop, she became the wife of Bernard Barnes, company director and diabetic, whom she nursed daintily till his peaceful passing during the night not very long afterwards.

Redcliff-on-Sea had a large population of senior citizens, and before long, as Hilda Barnes, she married an ex-Army man, Major Desmond Heath. She found him crying under the pergola of the Garden of Remembrance, shame-faced into a large handkerchief, and, as with the first, harmless Stanley, gave him comfort and accepted a cup of tea.

The Major was small and stringy; he had served under Monty at Alamein and liked to tell stories of how sometimes, at first glance, he had been taken for that great warrior, standing sharp and keen in his jeep, battle-browned soldiers cheering his passing.

"Great days, marvellous days!" he would say, take out his handkerchief and blow his nose.

He and his late wife had been living in one of Redcliff's more expensive hotels. "Never seemed to put down roots anywhere," he said. "Army life, rolling stones. Eleanor —" he gulped a little, as he always did in those early days at the mention of his late wife's name, "Eleanor was content to be an Army wife — camp follower, I used to tease her. Longed for a home though sometimes, both of us. Home is the soldier, home from the lea. And the hunter home from the hill. We were looking around, but then — left it too late."

He absolutely agreed with Eunice's provisos. "Companionship, that's what you and I are about, isn't it, Hilda? Grow old along o' me. And to tell you the truth, that wound I got at Mersah Matruh . . ." He coughed, embarrassed, and Eunice changed the subject.

The Major moved in and they settled down in a way now very familiar to Eunice. As a military man, used to being on the move, he was sparse and neat in his belongings, orderly in his habits. He did not smoke, drank only one gin and tonic before supper, enjoyed gardening and the same television programmes that she did. His late wife had left him comfortably off and, what with one thing and another, Eunice had accumulated an extremely tidy sum over the recent years. The Major had a sweet tooth and appreciated her cakes and dainties. He paid her little compliments, which none of the others since Stanley had done; but chivalrous compliments, gallant and with no nasty suggestive undertone.

She really was getting to like the Major very much. He was a perfect gentleman. If this was marriage, she could begin to see why so many people recommended it: companionship, appreciation, nothing messy or disagreeable, privacy and respect, nothing that wasn't nice. She really felt she might settle for this one; marriage with the Major, growing old along o' him, no more speculative attendances at unknown funeral services, no more business prospects to consider, for surely the two of them had quite enough between them to live comfortably to the end of their days?

She was very surprised, therefore, to be wakened in the middle of a night some months after their marriage by her bedroom door being opened and footsteps padding across the floor.

"Desmond? Is that you? What on earth . . . ?"

But he made no reply. And even if he had she wouldn't have heard it, for the pillow he pressed down on her face blanked out for ever all senses save terror and panic and an outraged incredulity.

GIVE HIM AN INCH...

Herbert Harris

"WE'RE LOSING HEIGHT fast," said the pilot of the small light aircraft, a tall rangy man with a lean brown face.

His name was Jim Tulley, and he spoke casually, as if discussing the weather, in a voice faintly tinged with Australian.

Van Leeman, the Netherlands businessman, was much less relaxed. His paunchy body moved forward jerkily, stiffening tensely, his creased, sallow face becoming visibly paler.

The girl named Valda asked, "What's the trouble?" But the man at the controls of the private plane merely shrugged.

Valda's voice was brittle, matching the slim body with its firm athletic lines, the spiky gold petals of her hair, the arrogance of her high-cheekboned face.

She had worked with Jim Tulley for over a year. Most people imagined they were married, since they were man and wife in all but name. Perhaps, one day, when he had freed himself from his real wife, he would marry her. Perhaps.

"Could be trouble with the fuel supply," Tulley ventured after a while. "We'll have to find somewhere to put her down."

"What — *here*?" Van Leeman demanded hoarsely. "Are you a lunatic or something?"

Valda smiled. "Give him an inch and he'll turn it into an airstrip," she said.

"Anyway, we're all lunatics, all three of us," Tulley remarked calmly. He stared downwards. "There's a bit of a clearing down there."

"Where the hell are we, for God's sake?" the Dutch businessman asked hysterically.

"Are you joking, mate? You don't use a bloody map here. Malaysia has a lot of jungle and most of it's right under our arses." Tulley's rugged tanned face was cemented into a grim dourness.

"Thick trees matted with vines and wild orchids," he added. "Blokes have taken two days to hack their way through one flaming mile." He heard Van Leeman draw in his breath sharply. "Then there's the Malay tiger — a wicked bastard, that one — and the snakes and the wild pigs . . ."

"For God's sake shut up!" the Dutchman cut in shakily.

"That's a good patch down there, pretty clear of trees," Tulley went on. "Just about big enough to land this perishing kite. Can you see it?"

"I have no wish to look," Van Leeman answered sharply.

"Ah, yes, I should have remembered. You can't look down from heights — you said so. I'm surprised you fly."

"I avoid it whenever I can."

"Anyway," Tulley continued calmly, "let's try and put the old bitch down, shall we?"

"You're sure you can make it?" Valda asked with a hint of apprehension.

"Keep your fingers crossed," Tulley answered laconically. "It's this or nothing, anyway."

"Hundreds of miles of jungle in any direction — that's just great." Valda sighed. "Still, I suppose you know best, Jim."

"But *does* he?" Van Leeman shouted in a choking voice. "Good God, this is sheer madness!"

"Look, chum, what do you want me to do?" Tulley argued. "Keep losing height till we hit something? — or land in this bit of clearing and sort out what's wrong with the old cow?"

"And suppose we can't take off again?" the Dutchman demanded angrily.

"Don't ask damfool questions," Tulley rapped back. "The chances are we should die here. The whole thing's a gamble, mate."

"After all," Valda put in, scowling at the Dutchman, "Jim didn't force you to come. You begged him to take you, so you'll just have to make the best of it."

Van Leeman clamped his jaws together tightly. There was stark terror in his eyes as he stared first at the girl and then at his tightly clenched hands.

He had flown over this jungle once before, but in a comfortable and comparatively safe airliner. And the jungle had seemed endless, they had said, a dense and impenetrable green hell, a

nightmare maze full of unimaginable horrors. He had never
dared to look himself.

He remembered thinking, and sweating as the idea came to
him: suppose we had to make a forced landing in the midst of that
green horror? And now there was no need to wonder what that
would be like. Very soon now he would find out.

Van Leeman wiped the sweat from his face with a handkerchief. It was worse than a Turkish bath in this God-forsaken
hole, he thought bitterly.

Of course, he should never have trusted a man like Jim Tulley.
What sort of madness had driven him into this? He might have
known Tulley was an adventurer, a soldier of fortune out to make
a fast buck even if it meant risking the necks of all of them.

All this would never have happened if it hadn't been for that
damned attack by terrorists on the airport of Kota Kohjang.
They had shut it down and there were no planes in or out until the
affair had settled down.

Then, late one night, in a bar near the airport, Van Leeman had
met Jim Tulley and this girl Valda.

"It's absolutely vital that I get to Kuala Batu," the Dutch
businessman had said. "There's a big deal waiting to be done
there, worth half a million to me. But time's short. If I wait for a
regular plane, I'll lose out to somebody else."

"I've got a plane," Tulley had told him casually. "No more
than a tiddler, and not so young, but she's in fair nick."

Tulley's candour had appealed to Van Leeman. A hopeful
gleam appeared in the Dutchman's small, mean eyes. "You mean
you've got it here?"

"A few miles up the road — in a field at Chingi-Langi."

A moment's hesitation on the Dutchman's part. Then his greed
for money had taken over. "You . . . you'd trust yourself in this
aircraft?"

"Sure. I've flown 'em in worse nick."

Van Leeman had turned to the girl Valda, who looked a
capable, sensible sort of girl, a bit like his secretary back in
Amsterdam. "And you?"

"I'd take it up all right. I love that old kite. Jim taught me to fly
in it."

"You have a licence too, then?"

"Sure. Jim and I take turns to pilot it."

The Dutch businessman had laid a hand on Tulley's arm. "Look, I'm not above taking a gamble, Mr Tulley. I've gambled in business all my life. That's how I've made my money. Will you fly me to Kuala Batu?"

It was Tulley's turn now to hesitate. "It's a fair hop. The fuel's on the short side, and it's hard to come by fresh supplies since the terrorists blew up the local oil tanks."

"I'd like you to do what you can, Mr Tulley."

Jim Tulley had pursed his lips. Then: "Okay, Mr Van Leeman. We'll shove off as soon as it's light. Remember it's a gamble, though." He crossed his fingers, smiled for the first time, a sardonic curl of a smile. "It'll cost you a thousand, Mr Van Leeman."

"A stiff price."

"A stiff assignment."

The Dutchman never guessed what sort of price he would pay eventually.

The diminutive aircraft made a number of circuits above the clearing, spluttering. Then slowly it floated down on to the treeless patch, landing a little bumpily but without mishap.

Tulley taxied to the limit of the clearing, then swung the small plane around to face the other way.

"Ready to take off again when the time comes — *if* the time comes," Tulley explained, seeming to take a malicious delight in seeing the fat little Dutchman squirm with discomfort.

"At least we can stretch our legs for a bit," Valda said in a calm and dispassionate voice. "I daresay Jim will take a little time to find out what's wrong. I've a pack of cards. You'd like a game?"

"Cards!" Van Leeman almost shouted. He stared in disbelief at the slim, wiry girl with the unevenly cut blonde hair. Hell, she was cool, this one, he thought. He shook his head. "No. I've some papers in my case I need to study. That will help me keep my mind off this awful nightmare."

As Tulley worked quietly on, his shirt drenched with sweat, the look of fear never left the Dutchman's eyes. Valda sat still and silent, her face expressionless as she watched Tulley making his routine checks.

Finally, Tulley strolled away from the plane, wiping his hands on a greasy rag. Van Leeman swallowed painfully as he studied the grim look on the pilot's face.

"I've got news for you," Tulley announced. "She'll only *just* do the remainder of the trip if we drop some ballast."

The Dutchman blinked. "Ballast?" he repeated.

"Human ballast," Tulley told him brutally. "I mean that one of us stays here."

"Are you crazy?" Van Leeman demanded, his chin trembling.

"No, mate, just practical," Tulley answered evenly. "And I want to make it clear from the start that I wouldn't consider leaving Valda here."

Van Leeman, his face paper-white, just stared at him, saying nothing.

"You do realize, I suppose," Tulley went on, "that Valda and I could very well fly off and leave you here?"

"But you'd get no money!" Van Leeman shouted.

"But we'd have our lives, Mr Van Leeman. Naturally, we would make every effort to find you again, but that could take a hell of a long time, and in the meantime . . ."

A lengthy shudder rippled over the Dutchman's squat body. "My God, you wouldn't do such a thing!"

"No, I should hate to," Tulley told him. "Which means that Valda flies you to Kuala Batu, and I have to remain here."

A look of unbridled relief flashed across the Dutchman's face. "Of course, Mr Tulley, I will pay you handsomely."

"Like hell you will," Tulley told him bluntly. "But I wonder if I shall ever enjoy the money? You realize, don't you, that when Valda comes back for me, she might never find this particular clearing. And I haven't a cat in hell's chance of getting out of here on foot. So I'm the one who's taking the gamble, Mr Van Leeman, bigger than any gamble *you* ever took."

Van Leeman swallowed. "You've got courage, Mr Tulley, I'll give you that. And I'm ready to reward courage."

"Good. You spoke of making half a million out of that big deal at Kuala Batu. Okay. You pay us ten per cent — fifty thousand."

The Dutchman stared at him for a long moment, then shrugged. "Very well."

"The moment you land at Kuala Batu, we'll have kept our part of the bargain. So you will then hand Valda a cheque for fifty grand. It will at least ensure that she lives in some degree of comfort when she hasn't got *me* to look after her."

Valda broke in: "Don't talk like that, Jim. I'll never rest till I find you, you know that. I'll be back."

Tulley's craggy face broke into one of its rare bleak smiles, and again he held up two crossed fingers. "And now," he said, "get to hell out of here before that old crate gets barnacles on her."

Van Leeman and the girl got back into the plane, and Tulley looked on with a critical eye as Valda took off.

She was a good girl, Valda was, damned good. A pretty girl, and passionate in her wilder moods. Yet level-headed and reliable at the same time. He could safely leave her to do all the rest.

In a matter of a day or two that cheque for £50,000 would be cleared, and they would be sitting pretty, because Valda would find him all right . . . oh, yes, she'd find him, he knew that. . . .

They could celebrate with a bottle or two of the best champagne in Harry's Bar.

That's where Valda would find him. She had only to walk into Harry's Bar in Selangri and he would be sitting waiting for her, her favourite brand of dry champagne all ready. . . .

"See you in Selangri, darling," she had whispered, winking, as Van Leeman climbed into the plane.

Tully struck off through the trees with his loping strides. A few hundred yards to go along a familiar track and he would strike the well-used road to Selangri.

The town was half a mile up the road — not too far, thank God, in this sticky heat.

And the quiet stroll was so uneventful that Tulley paused once to throw back his head in an unaccustomed way and bay with laughter at the hot blue sky.

A BOX OF BOOKS

Palma Harcourt

JENNIFER TRING, HER long apricot-coloured hair streaming behind her, came running down the stairs of the apartment building where she lived with her husband, George. Blinded by tears, she didn't notice the loose rod that the concierge had failed to replace. She caught her toe in a ruck in the carpet and fell, landing in a tangled heap almost at the feet of her neighbour, Pierre Bouleau, who was waiting for the lift.

"Ma chère Jennifer!" He ran to her aid. "Are you all right?"

"I — I —" Choking with sobs, the girl clung to him. "Oh, Pierre!"

"You have hurt yourself?" he asked, solicitously, and in English; even after three years in Paris Jennifer Tring knew next to no French. With a caressing gesture he wiped the tears from her cheeks. She was very young and very beautiful, but he felt no desire for her. She was, in his opinion, a stupid little bitch.

"Tell me," he said.

"It's George. He promised me a dress for my birthday, a real dress — *haute couture* — and he was to take me to Maxim's to celebrate." She swallowed a sob. "Now he says he didn't mean it. Not at this sort of price. He says my dress isn't worth the money. And anyway we can't afford it because he's being posted back to London. What do you think, Pierre?" She stood away from him and pirouetted slowly so that he could admire the exquisite line of the jade green dress she was wearing.

The Frenchman pretended to consider, his thoughts on what she had said about her husband's posting. Tring was a British diplomat, and if he was returning to England . . . "Dear Jennifer, if you weren't already perfect that dress would make you so." He blew her a kiss.

Jennifer laughed. She liked Pierre Bouleau. He talked a lot of rubbish, but he was fun. He didn't despise her because she wasn't an intellectual, as many of George's colleagues did — at the same time as they stripped her with their eyes. She could relax with him, enjoy herself. She took the handkerchief he was offering her, dried her tears, blew her nose.

"Thanks. Now I feel better."

"I'm glad, though you have made me feel worse. It's so sad that you're leaving Paris." He pulled a long face. "I shall miss you, both of you. When do you go?"

"I don't know. Soon, I think." Jennifer shrugged. The question had reminded her of George and his meanness to her. Her anger returned. "Pierre, can you lend me some money? If I'm not to be taken out to dinner tonight, I'm damned if I'm going to cook. I'll go down to Madame LeBrun's and spend a fortune. Stuffed vine leaves. Fresh salmon. Lots of cheeses. What's more, I'll make George open a bottle of champagne."

"Splendid!" Pierre grinned, showing very white, even teeth. "But, alas, dear Jennifer, I can't lend you any money. I have none. I meant to go to the bank today and forgot."

It was a lie. But once before he had loaned her a couple of hundred francs, which she had conveniently forgotten. He had been forced to ask George. George had repaid him at once. Nevertheless, it had been embarrassing. So, no more loans to Jennifer. As a Frenchman his sympathy was with the husband.

"Oh well, I dare say LeBrun's will trust me. They should. I spend enough there." With a wave of her hand, Jennifer departed.

Pierre watched her go, his handsome face a blank. Then slowly, ignoring the lift that had at last arrived, he mounted the stairs. His apartment was on the second floor. The Trings lived opposite him. He rang their bell.

The door was flung open and George Tring stood there, hair rumpled, tie awry, a glass of whisky in one hand. He stared at Pierre through round spectacles.

"Oh, it's you," he said ungraciously.

"I'm sorry. You were expecting Jennifer, of course." Pierre smiled sympathetically. "She'll be back soon. She's gone to LeBrun's to spend a fortune, she said."

George grunted. "She told you, then. We had a row. My fault really, but it's been a bad day, and to find she'd paid so much for a plain little dress — I lost my temper. It doesn't happen very often." He led the way into the living-room. "What will you have? Gin and tonic?"

"Please, yes." Tactfully Pierre changed the subject. "You are to be posted, Jennifer tells me, and soon."

George nodded. "Yes. We're going back to London in about eight weeks. It's rather a blow. I'd been counting on another foreign posting."

"Does it make much difference to you?" Pierre sipped his drink and looked around the room. The apartment was rented furnished, he knew, but the Trings had brought their own china, silver, linen, and all George's books. "Your government will move you?"

"Move us? Yes. The problem is where to. Places in and around London are prohibitive. Unlike some of my colleagues I've no private money. I can't afford to buy. And a First Secretary's salary, minus allowances, doesn't go far." George sighed.

"I've an idea." Pierre grinned. "Buy up all the liquor you can at diplomatic prices, have it shipped back to England for free, and make a nice profit when you get home."

He spoke jokingly. He didn't need the quick, involuntary shake of George's head to tell him the suggestion was unacceptable. He had discovered months ago, when he first became George Tring's neighbour and had tried to buy an odd bottle from him, that George was stuffed with scruples.

"Maybe we'll be lucky," George said. "Who knows? I've got to go over to London for a few days next week. Jennifer's coming with me, and we'll see what the situation is then."

After a few minutes' chat George offered Pierre another drink, but the Frenchman refused. He had learned everything he wanted to know. He returned to his own apartment and went immediately to the telephone. He dialled a Marseilles number. He spoke fast and in an *argot* that George Tring, excellent French speaker though he was, wouldn't have understood. It was a satisfactory conversation. Pierre was grinning broadly as he put down the receiver.

The next morning Pierre waited by his window until he saw Jennifer, a shopping basket on her arm, leave the apartment building. He hurried after her and, with little difficulty, persuaded her to come and have a coffee with him.

"I have a belated birthday present for you," he said as they sat down at a café table.

It was a silk scarf in her favourite shade of green, an expensive trifle that delighted her as he had known it would. She kissed him on both cheeks, then at once tied the scarf around the neck of her white dress.

"Oh, Pierre, how I shall miss you in London! You must come and stay with us as soon as we're settled."

"That would be wonderful," he lied. "Incidentally, my sweet Jennifer, I'm hoping you'll do me a favour when you go to England next week. Will you take a small packet for me?"

"Yes, of course."

"Ah, you are good and kind, and trusting." Pierre laughed. "But you must let me explain first. After that, if you wish, you must say no, because what I'm asking is not strictly legal."

Jennifer's beautiful amber-coloured eyes widened. She didn't believe him. She thought he was teasing her. "How, not legal?"

Pierre explained. An aunt of his had recently died. He was her executor. Among the bequests was a diamond brooch, which she had left to an old and dear friend, now married to an Englishman. He had considered sending it through the post but the risk was great; the brooch was quite valuable.

"And you would like me to take it for you?" Jennifer interrupted. "Why not? What's illegal about that?"

"Technically, I should get an export licence and pay a percentage of the assessed value."

"But that's absurd!"

It was what he had expected her to say and Pierre was more than satisfied, but he was careful to hide his feelings. "It's the law, Jennifer."

She made a contemptuous gesture. "You sound just like George." She hadn't forgiven her husband yet for spoiling her birthday. "Of course I'll take it for you, Pierre. But you mustn't tell George. I'm sure he wouldn't approve. He can be very — stuffy sometimes."

"Poor Jennifer! Never mind. It'll be our little secret." Pierre gave her his most charming smile. "I'll drop the brooch in before you go. And thank you, ma chère Jennifer. I'm very grateful to you."

But not nearly as grateful as I hope to be, he thought, as he watched her go swinging down the sunlit street and disappear into the butcher's shop. He grinned to himself. It had been even easier than he expected. She had asked no awkward questions about the supposed need for an export licence; she hadn't asked why he didn't take the brooch to England himself; and she had actually told him not to mention the matter to George. When he telephoned Marseilles later in the day he would be able to report that everything was going exactly according to plan.

The following Wednesday, Pierre delivered to Jennifer a small rectangular package, neatly wrapped in brown paper. She put it in her bag and thought no more of it until she and George arrived at London airport. They had only one suitcase, which George was carrying, and automatically they made for the "Green" nothing-to-declare exit.

"One moment, please, sir." A customs man stopped George.

Immediately Jennifer thought of the diamond brooch in her bag. And, for the first time, it occurred to her that Pierre Bouleau could have been lying. If it was a brooch, why was it so carefully packaged? Why not let her take it through customs as a piece of her own jewellery? Maybe it was something else, something she didn't like to think of. But head high, heart pounding, she walked straight on, pretending she wasn't with George.

A minute later George came hurrying after her. "You might have waited for me."

"What did he want, the customs man?"

"He had a message for someone, and he thought it might have been me. That's all."

Jennifer swallowed her relief. She told herself she'd been stupid. What could be in the package but a brooch? Nevertheless, she couldn't completely subdue the niggling doubt that had somehow sown itself in her mind.

As soon as she got a moment — they were staying with friends of George, called Colley, in a dreary flat in Paddington — she locked herself in the bathroom and carefully slit the tape on the package that Pierre had given her. From the brown paper she extracted a cardboard box which, with a quick intake of breath, she opened. Inside, on a bed of cotton wool, lay a brooch, just as Pierre had said. Jennifer nearly laughed aloud.

She examined the brooch with an admiration that was tinged

with envy. She wished she could possess a piece of jewellery as beautiful and expensive. And the diamonds — she couldn't possibly have known they were paste — catching the light, seemed to wink at her.

Someone tried the door. Quickly Jennifer did up the packet, flushed the toilet and left the bathroom. She found George very pleased with himself. He had been talking to the porter who had told him that before long there might be a flat vacant in the building. It would, George said, suit them perfectly. And he wondered why his young wife should suddenly seem on the verge of tears.

The next morning, having telephoned the number Pierre had given her and been invited to lunch, Jennifer took a taxi to an elegant block of flats in Knightsbridge — just the sort of place, Jennifer thought, where she and George should live. Suppressing her excitement, she rang the bell.

"Jennifer Tring? Come in, my dear. I'm Monique Pender-Browne."

Pierre had told Jennifer very little about Mrs Pender-Browne. Certainly he hadn't described her and, in spite of the warmth of her welcome, Jennifer found her disconcerting. For one thing, she was very tall for a Frenchwoman; Jennifer, who was five feet seven, was forced to look up to her. Then she was distinctly plain, with a big nose set in a nondescript face, which seemed to contradict her beautifully done hair. And she was younger than Jennifer had expected, a middle-aged matron — the sort who would run committees and chair meetings and organize good works — not the frail old lady Jennifer had pictured.

"Sit down, my dear, and let me get you a drink. Sherry?" Mrs Pender-Browne led the way into the drawing-room. "Or would you like something stronger? A gin and tonic?"

"Sherry, please," Jennifer said quickly; she never drank hard liquor. She glanced around her. If Mrs Pender-Browne was something of a disappointment, the flat, redolent of money and an eclectic taste, was a dream come true. She was filled with admiration. "What a super place this is! You've made it look absolutely fantastic," she said.

"Why, thank you, Jennifer. It's kind of you to say so." Mrs Pender-Browne didn't hide her amusement; the flat, leased for three months at a colossal rent, was serving its purpose. "Of course, it's very small, but it's just a *pied-à-terre*. When you're here again you must come and see our country house. It's extremely old and extremely interesting. I'm sure you'd like it."

"I'm sure I will." Jennifer sipped her sherry. "It's very good of you to invite us."

"Not at all. We're always pleased to have young people to stay, especially anyone as enchantingly beautiful as you." Mrs Pender-Browne let her glance linger over Jennifer, making her feel uncomfortable. "And now, my dear, the brooch? I'm longing to see it. I was so touched when I heard from Pierre that my darling Annette had bequeathed it to me. We were very close, you know, more like sisters than distant cousins."

Jennifer gave a quick smile that was meant to express sympathy and reached for her bag. Suddenly she was ill at ease, her mouth dry. She had tried to do up the package neatly again, but what would she say if Mrs Pender-Browne accused her of being curious, or worse?

"Here — here it is." To her annoyance her voice shook a little. She held out the packet. "It was no trouble."

"Thank you. Thank you indeed." Noting the creased brown paper and the uneven tape, Mrs Pender-Browne smiled with pleasure. There was no question. The girl hadn't been able to resist temptation. She had undone the packet, just as Pierre had said she would. "I can't tell you how grateful I am." She examined the brooch lovingly.

"There's no need." Jennifer was enormously relieved; Mrs Pender-Browne had noticed nothing. "I was glad to bring it. It's silly the French should expect you to pay tax on a gift like that."

"Yes. Absurd! Not that it's really the money. It's the principle. And the unkindness." Mrs Pender-Browne sighed. "But at least I have Annette's brooch — thanks to you, my dear."

"At least?"

"Oh, yes, didn't Pierre tell you?"

Jennifer shook her head, and Mrs Pender-Browne explained. It seemed that Pierre's aunt had left her not only the diamond brooch, but also an antique clock. The clock had been in their mutual family for more than two hundred years. It was of considerable value — far greater than the brooch — so that the duty on it would be huge. And, what was infinitely worse, Pierre, having made tactful enquiries, had discovered that it was most unlikely that an export licence would be granted for such an *objet d'art*.

"So it looks as if Annette's last wishes are to be disregarded, and I'm never to enjoy a wonderful thing that actually belongs to me." Mrs Pender-Browne gave a sad smile. "*Tant pis*. One has to accept, I suppose. Another sherry, my dear? No? Then let's go and lunch."

During lunch — a pleasant meal that Jennifer enjoyed — the clock wasn't mentioned. Instead they talked about Paris, and what it was like at seventeen to marry a diplomat almost twice one's age and go abroad for the first time. Jennifer did most of the talking, while Mrs Pender-Browne drank a great deal of white wine and curbed her impatience, knowing that a false move could ruin everything.

It was over coffee that the subject of the antique clock came up again. To Jennifer's surprise Mrs Pender-Browne suddenly went to a charming little escritoire and took an envelope from it.

"Jennifer, this is for you." She dropped the envelope in Jennifer's lap. "You won't be offended, will you, my dear? You're a sensible girl. But I did want to give you a little present for your kindness in bringing me Annette's brooch, and I couldn't think what. So I decided to be practical and let you choose for yourself. I do hope you don't mind."

"No. No, of course not." Jennifer picked up the envelope, not sure if she was meant to look inside at once. "Thank you very much. It's awfully good of you, though not a bit necessary. I was happy to bring the brooch. I only wish I could bring your clock."

"So do I, my dear." Mrs Pender-Browne's sweet smile didn't reach her eyes. "Ah well, I'll have to wait for an ambassador's wife for that."

"An ambassador's wife?" The question trailed away. Jennifer, tucking the open envelope into her bag, had been able to take a peek inside — Mrs Pender-Browne had tactfully turned her back to pour more coffee — and the banknote in the envelope wasn't for five or ten, but for fifty pounds. With fifty pounds she could buy a pair of shoes to match her jade dress! "An ambassador's wife?" she repeated.

"Yes. At ambassadorial level you travel with all sorts of possessions, I believe, silver, china, paintings — and, of course, there's no question of customs inspection. Everything's just packed and shipped for you — even your wines. Am I not right?''

"Yes. I think so." Jennifer hesitated, but the thought of a pair of jade green shoes decided her. Mrs Pender-Browne had been very generous about the brooch. "Look, I can't promise anything," she said, speaking rapidly, "I'll have to talk to Pierre. But it's possible — only possible mind you — that I might be able to bring your clock to England for you."

"My dear, that would be wonderful! But how? Your husband isn't an ambassador yet — unfortunately."

"No, but the government ships quite a lot for us, too." Jennifer was thinking quickly, her mind concentrated on the problem. "There are George's books, for one thing. They'll be packed in cardboard cartons, at least a dozen or more. No one would notice an extra box."

"I suppose not. It's certainly a clever idea and, as you know, I'd be more than grateful. But you mustn't take any risks for my sake, Jennifer. I absolutely forbid it."

Suddenly mindful of the agonizing moment when the customs man at Heathrow had stopped George, Jennifer had second thoughts. She shrugged. "Perhaps you're right. I couldn't tell George. He wouldn't approve. And it might be stupid."

Mrs Pender-Browne's smile was thin. She cursed herself for suggesting there might be a risk. Now she had to undo the damage. Deliberately she looked at her watch.

"I don't want to hurry you, my dear, but I do have to go out this afternoon."

"Yes, of course." Jennifer put down her coffee cup and got to her feet. The abrupt change of subject had bewildered her. "I — I'm sorry. I mustn't keep you. Thank you for the lunch, and for the present."

"Thank you too, my dear." This time the smile was warm. "I shall always be grateful to you. As for the clock —" Mrs Pender-Browne gave a heavy sigh. "It was such a part of the childhood that Annette and I shared. Maybe one day . . ."

"I'll try," Jennifer heard herself say. "I'll talk to Pierre. And if he thinks it would be safe to bring the clock, I'll do it."

"Oh, my dear!"

Suddenly Jennifer found herself clasped in Mrs Pender-Browne's arms and kissed on both cheeks. She didn't enjoy the embrace. There was something odd about it. It was too lingering. Too sexy? She said her goodbyes quickly and, thinking of the jade shoes she intended to buy, hurried from the building.

Mrs Pender-Browne watched from a window till Jennifer had disappeared from sight. Then she went into the bedroom. She took off her wig, removed the plumpers from her cheeks, slipped the coloured contact lenses from her eyes, washed off her make-up and changed her clothes. Mrs Pender-Browne had ceased to exist. Henri Chapelle, native of Marseilles, who liked the good things of life but didn't believe in working for them, had resumed his true identity.

Chapelle returned to the drawing-room. He poured himself a large whisky, lit a cigar and, sprawling on the sofa, thought about the beautiful English girl. After a while, he lifted his glass. "To you, Jennifer, my little darling," he said in Mrs Pender-Browne's voice. "How I wish you were lying here beside me — better still, under me." And he gave a loud, raucous laugh. It would have appalled Jennifer who, having just bought a lovely pair of shoes that exactly matched her dress, was that moment thinking very kindly of Mrs Pender-Browne.

Two months later the Trings moved to London. Their friend, Pierre Bouleau, had insisted on taking them out to dinner on their last night in Paris and, when it came to saying goodbye to him, Jennifer wept. Somehow Pierre seemed to personify all that she had enjoyed during the last three years, and she hated to think it was over. She was not looking forward to London.

In spite of her protests, George had signed a two-year lease on a flat in the Colleys' block in Paddington. It included carpets, curtains and some furniture. But when they arrived and Jennifer saw the broken-springed sofa and the marks on the wall where pictures had been removed, she wept again.

"It'll be better when our own things arrive from Paris," George said, trying to console her. "We've some nice prints, and the books will make a difference."

"The books, yes." Suddenly more cheerful, Jennifer agreed. The books — rather, one particular box of books — would make a lot of difference, or so she hoped. "When do you think they'll get here?"

"By the end of next week, with luck." George, relieved that

she was looking happier, beamed on her. "Darling, I know this flat isn't what you'd like, but for the moment, if we're to save for a house, it's the best we can do."

Jennifer shrugged irritably. She couldn't understand why, if a house was the object — and she'd much prefer a nice flat, something like Mrs Pender-Browne's — George didn't buy one at once. After all, he was almost thirty-six. Surely by now he must have enough money for a down payment, even if he had supported his invalid mother for years before she died.

"And meanwhile we live in this squalor," she said bitterly. "Can't we afford to have the place painted, at least?"

"Not all of it." George sighed. "It would cost hundreds, unless we did it ourselves, and I'm not much good at that sort of thing. Maybe we could get one room done."

Hundreds, Jennifer thought. Fifty pounds for bringing in a diamond brooch in one's bag. How much for shipping an antique clock worth thousands? She had told Pierre about the gift when he admired the jade shoes — George hadn't noticed them — and Pierre had said, laughing happily, that Jennifer could count on Mrs Pender-Browne being much more generous when she received the clock.

And it had been no bother. Pierre had arranged everything. She had given him one of the cardboard cartons that the moving firm had delivered — George insisted on packing his own books in order to keep them in the right order — and Pierre had returned the box with the clock, so he assured her, safely swaddled in plastic foam. She had nothing to worry about.

Any difficulty there might be would arise in London, when the box was delivered to the flat. George mustn't be allowed to unpack it. But that problem had also been foreseen. Pierre had put the letter "H" on one corner, so that she would be able to identify his box, and hide it away until she could deliver it to Mrs Pender-Browne.

ˋNevertheless, the following Thursday, the day the Paris shipment was due to arrive, Jennifer's nerves were jumping. And, as the hour approached when George could be expected home from the office and there was still no sign of the moving van, she became more and more fraught. Finally, however, it appeared, just five minutes ahead of George.

As Jennifer heard her husband's voice outside the open front door of the flat the first of the boxes of books was being brought in, and immediately her eye caught the letter "H". Without explanation she seized the box from the man and staggered into the bedroom with it. It was safely stowed at the back of her clothes cupboard when George came in.

"Hello, darling. Stuff's arrived, I see." He kissed her. "I told the men to put my books in the spare room. I've heard of a chap who might be prepared to paint the living-room for a reasonable sum, and there's no point in arranging the books if that's to be done."

"Oh, George, how wonderful! When?"

If Jennifer's enthusiasm was somewhat tepid, George didn't notice. He was tired. It had been a hard day, and his mind was preoccupied with problems connected with his new job at the Foreign Office. Jennifer too was *distraite*, and thankful to go to bed early. They didn't make love. Neither of them knew that it was the last night they were ever to spend together.

The next morning Jennifer could scarcely wait for George to leave and, as soon as the front door had closed behind him, she was on the phone to Mrs Pender-Browne. She expected to be asked to lunch again, but was disappointed.

"My dear, I'm terribly sorry, but I'm going down to the country today," Mrs Pender-Browne said, "so I'm afraid we can't repeat the delightful meal we had together — anyway, not until my return. But I should love to have my clock to take with me. Would you be very kind and bring it over, Jennifer? About twelve? Then perhaps we could have a drink before I leave."

Jennifer agreed at once. She could hardly do otherwise. And on the stroke of twelve she rang Mrs Pender-Browne's bell.

"My dear, how very kind of you. How very, very kind."

The box was taken from her and carried firmly into the bedroom. Mrs Pender-Browne didn't appear to notice its weight. She returned without delay.

"And now for a glass of sherry before I set off."

"Aren't you going to make sure the clock has travelled safely?" Jennifer was surprised.

"No. Pierre assured me that it would be packed with the utmost care and, after all, it hasn't finished its travels yet, has it?" Mrs Pender-Browne seemed amused. "Were you hoping to see it?"

"Yes, I suppose I was rather."

"You shall see it when you and your husband visit us in the country."

Once again Mrs Pender-Browne expressed her gratitude, but it was obvious she was in a hurry. She didn't offer Jennifer a second glass of sherry.

"My dear, I'm so sorry this has to be such a brief meeting." She drew Jennifer to her and kissed her, arms tightening round the girl, then abruptly released her. "And a little present." As on the previous occasion she gave Jennifer an envelope. "Just to say thank you."

"Thank you, Mrs Pender-Browne. Thank you very much."

Jennifer was now as eager to go as Henri Chapelle was to be rid of her. How much was in the envelope? Enough to have the whole flat painted? And for new curtains? This time the envelope was sealed. Jennifer tore it open in the lift, and her eagerness evaporated at once. For the priceless antique clock, as for the brooch, Mrs Pender-Browne had given her fifty pounds.

For the rest of the day Jennifer sulked, her temper unimproved by the absence of anyone to see her sulking. Nor could she explain her mood to George when he returned home, earlier than usual and carrying a large bottle of Spanish wine.

"What's that for?" she demanded.

"The Colleys are coming to supper this evening. Surely you hadn't forgotten."

"Yes, I had. Anyway, it's Friday. We always go out to dinner on Fridays."

"Jennifer, we used to, in Paris. This is London. We can't afford to go to restaurants now, except as a special treat."

"Then it had better be a special treat tonight. Because there's no food in the house, nothing for your Colleys to eat."

George was exasperated. "In which case you'd damn well better go and buy some. They'll be here soon."

Surprised by his tone, Jennifer found herself suddenly acquiescent. "Okay," she said. But she relieved her feelings by slamming out of the flat.

Fifteen minutes later the doorbell rang. George, thinking that Jennifer had forgotten her key, flung open the door to disclose — not his wife, but a much older woman, who thrust past him into the hall.

"Where's Jennifer?"

"Out. Shopping. Who are you? What do you want?"

"Your wife. Either she's a fool who's made a stupid mistake or the little bitch is trying to trick me."

"What do you mean?"

"She arranged to bring over a box of books for me in your shipment from Paris, guaranteed not to be opened by the customs. She delivered it this morning and it was just that — a box of books."

"What — what did you expect it to be?"

George passed his tongue over his lips. His mouth was dry. He didn't doubt the woman's story and he was afraid, not for himself, but for Jennifer. Any minute she would be returning with the shopping, and this extraordinary character . . .

"What did I expect it to be?"

The voice was a woman's, but the scornful laugh that followed was wholly male. George stared, his mouth gaping. And at that precise moment Jennifer fitted her key in the lock and came into the hall, kicking the door shut behind her.

"Why — Mrs Pender-Browne, what are you — ?"

Henri Chapelle, aware that he had betrayed his masculine identity to George, paused. Then, snapping open the crocodile handbag he was carrying, he pulled out a small automatic and levelled it at Jennifer.

"No!" George launched himself at the Frenchman. He didn't care a damn what Jennifer had done. No one was going to hurt her, not if he could prevent it.

Chapelle, caught off balance by the sudden attack, stumbled backwards, and involuntarily his finger tightened on the trigger. The bullet made a small, round hole in George's forehead. And George Tring, carried by his own momentum, fell dead at Chapelle's feet as if in supplication for Jennifer.

Chapelle, unworried by any such romantic thoughts, kicked him aside. He hadn't intended to kill George. It had been an accident. But it was done, and the girl was opening her mouth, about to scream. He reached her as the first sound emerged and knocked her back against the door with enough force to daze her. Then he picked her up, carried her into the living-room and threw her on the floor.

"Where's my box, the one Pierre gave you in Paris?"

Jennifer was incapable of speech. She was terrified. She didn't understand what had happened, but she knew that George, her dear, kind, clever, stuffy George, was dead. He'd been shot by Mrs Pender-Browne, who wasn't Mrs Pender-Browne at all, but a strange man with a crooked wig and women's clothes.

"Where's my box?" Henri Chapelle repeated.

"I — I brought it to you, this morning," Jennifer managed to say at last.

"That was the wrong box. It was full of books." He bent down and slapped her hard across the face. "Where's the one Pierre gave you?"

"That was it." Jennifer's voice was choked with sobs. "It must have been. Pierre put an 'H' on it so there could be no mistake. 'H' for clock — you know, *horloge* in French." Words tumbled over each other as she tried to explain, tried to stop the man from hitting her, tried to save herself. "He said it was a joke."

Chapelle gave a short, sharp laugh. "H" for *horloge* and "H" for — He appreciated the joke, but this was no time for it. He was getting desperate. He hauled Jennifer to her feet.

"You're lying! Where's the — the clock?"

"I don't know."

Against his will he believed her and, furious with her, with himself, with whatever had gone wrong, he seized the neck of her dress and ripped it to the hem. Beneath it she was almost naked. His expression changed.

"No!" Jennifer said. "No!"

"Why not?" Chapelle said softly. It would only take a few minutes, and he was going to have to kill the girl anyway.

She struggled hard, biting and scratching, no longer afraid. Somehow rape by a man whom she still thought of as Mrs Pender-Browne was doubly awful. But her struggles only excited him further, and it wasn't until it was all over and he held the cushion hard on her face that she knew she was about to die.

The bell rang as Henri Chapelle was searching the flat. He hesitated, his hand on the doorknob of the spare room in which George's boxes of books were stacked. It rang again. The Colleys had been asked to supper, so they were sure that George and Jennifer were at home. When there was still no answer, Bill

Colley peered through the letter-box. He saw George's body lying on the floor, the scattered groceries and what he took to be a middle-aged woman crossing the hall. He sent his wife to dial 999.

By the time the police arrived Henri Chapelle had fled down the fire escape. Subsequently he was caught, tried and convicted. During his trial he never mentioned the box marked "H". Some months later this, together with the rest of the boxes the meticulous George had carefully marked "A" to "N", came into the possession of the Reverend Arthur Tring. George's elderly uncle wanted no more scandal. He kept all the books, and the contents of the box marked "H" — worth at street value about three million pounds — he poured down the disused well in his garden.

THE SHADOW BEHIND THE FACE

Peter Godfrey

HE DIDN'T KNOW which was the face and which was the mask: the smooth softness of her cheeks and lips, the straight nose, delicate eyebrows, and widely spaced eyes, or the greedy lustful thing that lay beneath?

Each time he pondered the problem, he remembered their days of courtship, the sweetness of stolen kisses, the great longing in their arms and bones, the haunting agony when she went away, then the overcoming of obstacles, their marriage, the passionate impulse each to the other gradually merging and becoming a part of the great new spirit of camaraderie that was their life together.

And when he remembered these things he became certain that her face was her true face and the mask was a malignance, like a luminous shadow under her flesh. Then he would think, But how did it get there? — and other doubts would arise and his mind would go endlessly on through the old vicious circle.

It wasn't as though it had always been there. Or had it? He hadn't seen it when they were courting. It was only after two years of marriage that he began noticing the signs. Little things at first, slight accentuations of normal moods and emotions, pique that became irritability, sadness that developed into depression, mirth that laughed too loud.

Soon it all became more and more pronounced — or did he notice them more because he was watching for them?

He wasn't even sure that what he saw wasn't some morbid by-product of his imagination.

At least, not until that night in October.

He had lately given up smoking, and when the craving was on him he had developed the habit of washing it away with hot, sweet chocolate. They had been in the cinema, and from the commencement of the feature film he felt uncomfortable. The peppermint he sucked did nothing to alleviate the hollowness in the back of his throat, the intense need for tobacco. He thought of going out for some chocolate, but they were seated in the middle of a row and he throttled his impatience.

He began to be vividly conscious of how often the characters on the screen lit up cigarettes. The movement of their lips and hands tortured him. From somewhere behind him, the air-conditioning brought him a whiff of aromatic tobacco. Once, when the heroine stubbed out a cigarette she had barely lit, he felt his fingers tense to reach out and take it.

He was irritable in the car, but she never said a word. After his first few grumbles he too relapsed into silence, but over and above the purr of the engine it was as though the tension between them was crackling with invective.

At home she moved, not towards the kitchen, but down the passage to their bedroom.

"What about my chocolate?" he asked loudly, and when she did not answer he strode after her and gripped her arm. She pulled against his fingers momentarily and then turned and looked directly at him.

With a sense of shock he saw the face behind her face contorted with an anger and a brittleness that dwarfed his.

But when she spoke, it was her own lips that moved. "I won't be a minute. Go and heat up the milk. Please."

He still held her, and in a flash her lips narrowed cruelly and he saw the evil gleam of the white teeth of the other. "Let go, you swine!" she spat and tore herself loose.

At any other time he would have left her alone, but that night his anger spurred him. He followed her.

She had just emptied the powder from the blue paper on to her tongue when she saw him. There was a great fear in her eyes, but a force stronger than that fear made her hand lift the glass and drain the powder down.

He asked stupidly, "Did you have a headache?" But he knew it wasn't a headache powder she had taken, and she knew he knew. The next second she was in his arms, sobbing as though her heart would break.

The story came out between sobs. How she had first been persuaded to try the drug because she always felt so tired and listless, because she feared she was losing the flush of his love.

The marvellous feeling of exhilaration the powder gave her, and then the letdown and the need for more. Then larger and larger doses, and the terrible realization one day that her soul was irretrievably chained to a few white crystals in a slip of blue paper.

His anger left him. While she spoke, he cupped her face in his hands and looked deep into her eyes. He saw only the face of the girl he had married.

Her words bred in him a feeling of deep sadness, but underlying that was a curious sensation of elation and triumph. Perhaps it was because things that had been dark to him before were now crystal-clear.

While she lay quiescent in his arms, he thought about the mask and the shadow it had cast over their life together. "Now that we know what it is," he said, "we can fight it."

She shivered. "You don't understand. It's — too late for fighting. *Much* too late. I've tried."

"You tried by yourself before, but it's different now. Believe me, I know how to beat this thing."

She flinched away from him in sudden panic. "Not a doctor," she said. "I won't be put in a home. I won't."

He stroked her with his voice. "No, no doctor. Just you and I. And nobody will know."

Her words were calm, but there was desperation in the undertones. "It won't work. I've tried, I tell you. It won't work."

"Nonsense," he said. "You may have tried, but you didn't know the right method. The main thing is that you want to give it up."

He paused and then added, "Do you?"

She turned away from him abruptly.

"I'm not sure," she said, and went on fiercely, "No, don't interrupt me. I want to tell you about the last time I tried to stop. It was just ten days ago. I knew what I was doing was wrong — I was tortured by my conscience and I made up my mind to stop it there and then.

"That was at three in the afternoon. By five the craving was so strong my nerves seemed to keep up a perpetual jangling. At seven I said I had a headache and went to bed. I must have slept for a while, although I don't know how, but it couldn't have been for long because you hadn't come to bed yet.

"When I woke, the craving was gone and I felt a great peace in my mind. I remember thinking, I've won! That's all there was to it, a short sharp fight, and now I'm free!

"Then I saw there was no water in the glass on the bedside table and next to the table, on the floor, was a crumpled slip of blue paper.

"It took me a few seconds to realize the significance, and when I did I was unwilling to believe it. I sprang out of bed and rushed to count the powders. There was one less than there had been an hour before.

"Through my confusion I fell asleep, but the next morning I worked it out calmly and rationally. I thought, So I can't control my actions in my sleep? Right. Then I mustn't sleep. You see, I had become obsessed with the idea that if only I could keep away from the drug for twenty-four hours, the major battle would be over. That was why I didn't throw the powders away — I felt they would have to be there to make my victory complete.

"I rested as much as I could during the day, bracing myself against the craving that would come early in the evening. And when it came, it didn't seem so bad at first, but my initial satisfaction didn't last long. By nine o'clock my nerves were screaming.

"I went to bed only because it was torture to walk about and be spoken to, but I had no intention of sleeping. Over and above my mental agony came a drowsiness, but I fought against it because I knew what that would mean. Then a terrible thing happened."

She caught her breath in a pause.

"I was lying on the bed, willing myself to be still, vividly conscious in my defiance of the dreadful attraction of the drug. I want you to remember that — I was quite conscious and I was willing my body to lie still. But it moved all the same. It got out of bed and walked to the drawer. My hand reached forward. I tried to stop it, tried so hard that my consciousness seemed to stretch and tear, but the hand kept moving. The fingers twitched open a packet and poured the powder on to my tongue.

"I fought — how can I describe it? — my mind was in an agony of effort and frustration, but my muscles seemed to belong to someone else. I was filled with an anger and a resentment a million times more fierce than I could normally imagine, let alone experience. But I kept on fighting, right through the movement of bringing the water to my lips to the last second when my throat swallowed and it was over.''

She paused again, and this time he prompted her. "But why aren't you sure whether you want to give it up?''

"Don't you see? I don't know whether anything can make up for the suffering involved in fighting the urge, particularly now I'm sure it can't be beaten.''

"Come with me,'' he said, and put his arm about her shoulders.

Together they walked down the passage to his study. There she sat down while he selected a book from the shelves.

He began to read to her, drily and unemotionally, a tale of horror which was all the more horrible because it too was dry and unemotional, couched in precise scientific terms.

It told in objective phrases exactly what happens to a drug addict from the preliminary stages of exhilaration and exhaustion to where the difference between maddening pleasure and excruciating agony became the finest of hairlines, and on to the inevitable mental, moral, and physical disintegration. He put the book down. "Do you see now why you must stop?'' he asked. But behind the horror and fear in her eyes he saw also a bitter resignation.

He repeated, "Do you see now?''

"It's no good!'' she sobbed. "Oh, can't you understand? Even if what is going to happen is ten times worse than the book says, the fear isn't enough to kill the terrible need of *now*.''

Suddenly he realized he must throw everything he had into the struggle. "Listen,'' he said, and felt his fingers press through her soft flesh to the shoulder bone, "listen. Before we were married, when it seemed impossible we would come together, I fought for you and you helped me and we won. Now the choice is yours. Either you fight this thing with my help and win again or you give in and give me up too.''

She said, "What do you mean?''

His voice was like a whiplash. "I married a girl I loved and respected. I didn't marry a drug-crazed coward reconciled to an early lunatic grave. And I will not under any circumstances remain married to one.''

The lash had struck her a dreadful blow. She flinched, and at her next doubtful words he felt he had as good as won. "But — how can I fight this thing?''

"Will power.''

"I've tried that and failed."

"You've tried it, yes, but not intelligently. All you did was impose a prohibition on yourself. What you must do is force yourself into a substitute activity."

She looked at him queerly. "I'm not sure I understand."

"Let me put it this way. You know I've given up smoking — it's a week since I had my last cigarette. You're a nonsmoker, so you don't know what the craving for tobacco is like but, believe me, when you're used to sixty cigarettes a day, it's strong."

He sensed her unspoken suggestion and hurried on. "Your craving may be stronger, it probably is, but the general principle of the cure is exactly the same. When the urge to smoke becomes intolerable I force myself to drink the chocolate. Almost from the beginning I've found it relieves the craving, and daily it's becoming easier. The chocolate has become a sort of mental crutch. That's what I mean by substitute activity."

She said, hopelessly, "It's no good — "

Again his voice became brutal. "It's that or you must do without me."

For a moment her eyes were like those of a hunted animal, and then suddenly she softened in a mist of tears. "I can't do without you, darling," she said, and he gathered her into his arms.

With her wet cheek on his chest he talked on, in elation. "Now we must find you some substitute activity. What shall it be? I know — the chocolate. We're fighting it together, let's do the same thing. Will you join me with the chocolate?"

She nodded her head vigorously against him and he held her away gently. "That reminds me why I was so irritable," he said. "I could do with a cup right now."

"Go and put the milk on then," she said, "while I see what I can do to look human again."

While they sipped the beverage together, and until he finally fell asleep, he felt happily confident. It was mainly because he now knew all about the mask. One can fight what one understands.

He came back early from the office the next afternoon and after he had kissed her he searched her with his eyes. She read his expression and answered by direct action. From behind the mantel clock she took nine blue powder wrappers.

"I've been waiting to give them to you," she said and he kissed her again. But he thought it better not to let her see him wash the white crystals down the kitchen sink.

At six o'clock a nervous gesture of hers attracted his attention and he saw, quite clearly, the other face pushing through her flesh. "I think I'll have some chocolate," she said and moved towards the kitchen.

He called after her, "Don't forget mine," and swallowed two or three times in anticipation — he could do with a cigarette.

She brought in the cups and he tried not to let her see him watching her. He talked inconsequentialities and felt a great relief when she began to answer in the same vein. When they had finished she came and sat next to him on the settee and he put his arms about her. She snuggled her head on his shoulder.

She was quiet, and when he looked down at her she was fast asleep. And the face he saw was her own face, with no trace of the other showing.

When she woke she seemed a little nervous, but he held her close until it was time for dinner. After the meal they again curled up together on the settee. He turned down the lights and made love to her as he had done in the first flush of their honeymoon.

In the weeks that followed, the act of drinking the beverage together came to mean more than just a compensation for a craving. It began to symbolize a new life and happiness for both of them. He watched her, of course, or rather he watched the shadow behind her face. He saw when it came and how the chocolate drove it away and how gradually, when it did come, it seemed each time to be less and less distinct. Until even he could hardly see it.

It was only then he was able to explain to her about the mask, gently and with a quiet flush of triumph at their joint victory. She said nothing, but looked at him with a sort of wonder, kissed him, and lay for a long time with her head on his chest.

He was detained at the office one afternoon and came home late and irritable. For the first time since his newfound gentleness with her, he spoke sharply. "Sit down," she said, "and I'll bring you some chocolate."

She went out, but he didn't sit — and it seemed to him she was taking an unduly long time. He walked into the kitchen.

The two cups of chocolate stood on a tray on the table. She was drinking a glass of water. As she saw him she gave an involuntary gesture of avoidance.

A piece of blue paper fluttered to the floor.

His muscles seemed to react to the situation before his brain did. He stopped in his tracks as the implications of her action struck him. "My God!" he said bitterly. "Again? But why — why? What's happened to your will power? I thought when you stopped — "

"I never stopped." She was facing him with a sort of brittle calm that checked the rush of his words.

"But the powders, I threw them away — "

"Table salt. Ordinary table salt wrapped in blue paper."

Again anger bubbled past his tongue. "Why did you lie to me? God, it's contemptible! Why all the elaborate deceit?"

"I had to," she said and there was a fierce exultation in her tone. "Do you remember the alternative you offered me? It didn't do any good frightening me, reading from that book of yours. I knew I could never give up the drug, no matter what the consequences were — I knew it, not with my mind, but with every living tissue in my body.

"Then you told me the other thing, remember? You told me you'd leave me, and I heard in your voice you meant it. In that moment I realized that even though I couldn't do without the drug, I couldn't do without you either."

"So you resorted to lying and trickery! But it won't help you, do you hear? By God, I meant what I said: I won't spend the rest of my life with — a mask!"

"Yes, the mask." Her voice had a vibrancy even more compelling than his anger. "Strange how you misinterpreted that. You thought what you called the mask was something alien to me, an evil perversion injected into my normal personality by the drug. But what you see is the real me, the *hungry* me peering through the mould and expressions formed by years of social taboo and repression. We've all got that deprived, restricted inner self. Just weaken the social pressure by any means and the real face begins to come through. Why don't you look in the mirror?"

His eyes turned to the glass on the wall. He saw his features reflected back to him, perfectly normal, perhaps slightly flushed from anger. But behind his flesh a shadow moved, a gruesome travesty of his own face, and a lustful horror leered through his eyes.

"What have you done?" he cried out.

Her voice was still calm. "There was only one way to keep us together. I went back to the bedroom — remember? — to fix my face. That was when I fetched the powder to drop into your chocolate. And every time you've had chocolate since another powder has gone into your cup."

Emotion made him hoarse. "I'll beat it. Will power. I'll beat it."

She shook her head. "It's too late. I know. I've watched your eyes. I've watched you building up an attitude to the drinking chocolate, a sort of religious fanaticism as though it had a special and holy significance for both of us. You weren't wrong, you know. It was bringing us together again."

He repeated. "I'll fight it."

"It won't do you any good. You'll see for yourself in a minute. That's your cup nearest you."

He looked at the shaped china, and the bubbles on the surface of the liquid winked at him with translucent purple eyes.

His face must have shown what he felt, because she leant forward and touched him and her eyes were suddenly wet. "Oh my poor darling," she said, "don't hurt yourself like this. Drink your chocolate."

"No," he said. "No!"

But even as he spoke his finger crooked around the handle of the cup.

SUPERGRASS

Clare Dawson

DOWNSTAIRS, THE TELEPHONE rang in the hall. Bernard emerged from the bathroom, towel over his shoulder, chin covered in shaving soap and descended the stairs, without haste.

"Christie here," he said in that deceivingly gruff north-country tone which could be off-putting to those unaccustomed to it.

"Mike Grimley, sir."

" 'Morning, Mike. You're bright and early. That can only mean trouble."

"There's been a serious development, inspector. The Super wants everybody in before ten o'clock for a conference."

"Keen as mustard, our Superintendent Preston," said Bernard, good-humouredly. "What's up, anyway?"

"A prison escape, sir. Ivan Thornburn, no less."

"Good God!" exploded Bernard. "After all our efforts to put that slippery villain inside, they can't even manage to keep him locked up. How the hell did he get out of Parkhurst?"

"It was Brixton, inspector. Report says he was granted special permission to visit his mother in hospital, Paddington area. They brought him down yesterday under heavy guard. He was due to be taken back today after an overnight kip in Brixton. He absconded sometime during the night. It's not clear yet how he did it but he had help, of course."

"I bet he did. Half the bloody underworld. Okay, sergeant. I'll be there as soon as I can."

Back in the bathroom, he finished shaving, guiding his razor along a lean jaw and square chin, up to the edge of thick lips and then above them, his clear blue eyes following the exercise carefully.

Less than fifteen minutes later, having settled for a coffee-only breakfast, he was in his car heading for the Yard. His thoughts were on Thornburn and his earlier good humour was gone. Putting Ivan Thornburn away had been his greatest triumph and it had happened barely two years ago.

The fifty-five-year-old gangland boss who had skilfully evaded arrest for numerous serious crimes over a period of ten years had been rounded up, together with 26 other villains, in a series of dramatic and carefully planned early-morning raids on houses in London and the Home Counties. Twelve unsolved crimes, ranging from attempted murder to armed robbery, had been cleared up and Bernard had moved up from inspector to chief inspector as a result.

And it was all thanks to one man, he reflected. Beppo Marachini. Bernard's very own supergrass.

After Bertie Smalls, he was one of the best supergrasses the Yard had ever had. Beppo's testimony had rid society of some of the very worst elements of the criminal fraternity in London and Bernard, for one, would never cease to be grateful to him.

After twenty years in the force, he had learned to take nasty shocks in his stride but Detective Sergeant Grimley's news left him shattered. Thornburn of all people — escaping from jail. It was at times like this that he felt a fleeting disenchantment with police work although, deep down, he knew he loved the job. Despite its unsavoury nature, the long and unsociable hours, frequent frustration and tedium, the fight against crime was something he firmly believed in. Winning the battles was what it was all about, even if the cynics complained, as they did, that the war was never won.

His thoughts drifted back to Beppo Marachini. A revenge killing was plainly on the cards for him if Thornburn ever caught up with him. And it was well known that a swift merciful bullet was not Thornburn's way. In the past, he had arranged slower and more painful departures from this world for his enemies and would, doubtless, ensure that Beppo's wife and three daughters were made use of before they were killed.

And then, of course, there was young Claudio. He would be about four years old now. Thornburn was callous enough to dispose of the child too, probably taking pleasure in forcing Beppo and his wife to witness the child's execution.

It was seldom Bernard allowed himself to become emotionally involved where villains were concerned, but this one aroused more anger and revulsion in him that he had believed possible.

Ivan Thornburn was the "brains" behind every sort of vice, a man who had reigned in terror for over ten years and whose evil methods for dealing with his enemies were notorious.

How much, if anything, did Thornburn know about Beppo's whereabouts, he wondered. Had his underworld pals been beavering away while he was in jail? Had they discovered the supergrass's hideaway and was this why Thornburn had been sprung from jail? He consoled himself it was highly unlikely. Beppo was no fool.

A small group of senior officers were gathered in the operations room when he arrived at the Yard and he was greeted with nods and some apprehensive stares.

Everyone knew the extent of his involvement in Operation Beppo, as it had been known at the time, and few had any doubts about the chief inspector's feelings about the escape.

"We all know what this means," Superintendent Preston began without meander. "Thornburn's got to be caught and put safely back inside as quickly as possible and that means a nation-wide net. Then there's the question of Marachini. Chances are Thornburn will be after him, so we've got to be one jump ahead. What's the man's last known address?"

An officer came forward with a bulky file but Bernard answered the question promptly.

"After the trial, he took off for Canada, superintendent. He was back in this country within the year because he and his family couldn't settle."

"Damned stupid thing to do," snapped Preston but Bernard went on as if he hadn't heard him. "According to my sources, he spent some time in the Pennines, then moved up into Scotland. Last report was that he'd bought a house in a small town near Dundee and got himself a job in a factory nearby."

The discussion went on for another hour and when Bernard returned to his office, he groaned at the sight of all the paperwork which had accumulated during his three-day leave from work.

Sergeant Grimley tapped on the door and came in with a cup of coffee, putting it down on his superior's desk before saying quietly: "Think Thornburn's mates on the outside *have* managed to trace Beppo, sir?"

Bernard shook his head.

"The man's been moving around a lot since the trial. He only settled down properly six months ago."

"He'll be feeling pretty sick when he hears the news. I can't help feeling a bit sorry for him, even though he was a villain. It took some guts, after all, to grass on somebody as big as Thornburn."

"Beppo had plenty of good reasons, sergeant. Firstly, he had spent a lot of time inside and was sick of prison. He was knocking forty-five and, with his form, he knew he could get as much as twenty years for that armed bank robbery in Shepherd's Bush. He'd have been close to sixty by the time he got out. He wanted to see his kids grow up. One girl was eighteen but the other two were still at school. Then there was the son. He and his missus had waited a long time for a boy and he was only two years old when we nabbed Beppo for that bank job.

"Secondly, he believed someone had tipped us off about the Shepherd's Bush job and suspected Thornburn. But what really put the cap on it was the business over his eldest daughter. He'd got to hear, while he was on remand, that that stupid brother of his, Angelo, had taken the girl to a party organized by Thornburn. She was a good-looker and Thornburn had fancied her for some time. It seems the girl was slipped a mickey-finn during the evening and ended up in bed with Thornburn. Beppo was almost murderous when he heard about it. After that, he began singing like a bloody canary — I'm glad to say."

"The Marachini brothers are twins, aren't they?"

"Yes," said Bernard, unable to keep the contempt out of his voice. "Incredibly alike, physically and facially, but when it comes to character, they are poles apart. Beppo never wanted to get involved with the gangs. He preferred planning and carrying out his own jobs, with brother Angelo to help him, of course. Unfortunately, Angelo had other ideas. He wanted to get in on the bigger, dirtier rackets. Prostitution, drugs, hard porn — you name it — so he sucked up to Thornburn and Beppo despised him for it. Angelo took the girl to Thornburn's party, knowing full well what the slimy Ivan had lined up for her. His own niece! Right bastard he was and probably still is."

"How come he didn't do time for his part in the Shepherd's Bush job, guv?" asked Sergeant Grimley.

"He got away before we could grab him. His girlfriend gave

him a solid alibi and, although Beppo spilled the beans on him too, we didn't have enough evidence against him. His case was dismissed and he took off somewhere abroad. Word is he's back in London again and hanging around Thornburn's old bunch. He's one bloke I'd really like to see get his come-uppance!''

When Superintendent Preston called Bernard into his office later, he asked bluntly: "Any ideas, Bernard?"

"One or two, sir. But I need a while to think them out. Our best bet of catching Thornburn, of course, is to use Beppo as bait."

"Beppo's not likely to agree to that."

"He might — as long as we promise him protection. After all, as long as Thornburn's on the run, he and his family remain permanently at risk. If Thornburn doesn't know where he is *now*, he'll find him."

"You're suggesting we have a word with Beppo?"

"It's worth a try."

"If he says yes, then what?"

"That's what I need to think about." Bernard glanced out of the office window at the sun-bathed London streets. "Feel I could do with some air. Okay if I disappear for a while?"

Five minutes later, Bernard was out in the sunshine and strolling along the Victoria Embankment, mulling over a variety of ideas. When he got back to his office, he called Sergeant Grimley in.

"Have they made contact with Beppo yet?" he asked.

"No, sir. Dundee C.I.D. have promised to come back to us."

"When they do, I want to speak to Beppo myself on the phone. He may need some persuading and I'm the best one for that. Now, I want the whisper to go around that Beppo has been hiding out in London for over a year."

"Hiding out here?" repeated Mike incredulously. "Who's going to believe that?"

"The criminal fraternity, that's who. It's just the sort of thing Beppo might do — the old Beppo that is. Villains all over the country scouting for him and he, right here, under their noses all the time. Would appeal to his sense of humour. Also I want you to contact that snout Pete Guzzi. He proved very useful that last time we needed him. You know where he hangs out. Look him up and get it over to him that Beppo is in real danger and that Angelo should be told."

Mike ran his hand through his blond hair and frowned.

"Beppo testified against Angelo, inspector. He's not going to care if Thornburn catches up with his brother — "

"Don't I know it — BUT, your snout *won't*. I spent a lot of time in Italy after the war, sergeant, and I got to know the Italians pretty well. Family is very important to them. No matter what you may have done, when it comes to anything as serious as your life being threatened, the family close ranks and old grievances die fast. Your snout is straight. He's going to judge Angelo by his own standards. Hatred is one thing but letting somebody kill your own kin without trying to do something to stop it, is quite another matter. Take my word for it. Your snout will contact Angelo and tell him Beppo's in London. We'll supply an address he can give to Angelo."

Sergeant Grimley stared at his superior. As much as he admired the older man for his distinguished work in the force, at that moment he thought he had gone right off his rocker.

"What if he decides to settle a score with Beppo himself?" Bernard grinned.

"Angelo Marachini is a yellow-livered creep. He gets other people to do his dirty work. Besides, he's always been a bit scared of his brother. Then there's Thornburn. He wouldn't do anything which might amount to treading on the villain's toes. He knows better than anyone that Ivan the Terrible wants Beppo for himself."

"Ah, I see. The snout gives Angelo the address and Angelo makes it his business to inform Thornburn, via his mates?"

"I'm banking on it. Judging by past form, Angelo is as predictable as night following day."

"Then what?"

"We'll set a trap for Thornburn. I'm going to have a word with the superintendent. Keep yourself available. He might want to talk to you before you go."

Later that morning, Bernard got a call from Dundee C.I.D. and learned that Marachini would be home from work in the lunch-hour and would wait near the phone for his call.

Bernard rang the ex-directory number and spoke to the super-grass for almost half an hour. Persuading him to go along with his plan wasn't easy. Twice Beppo rang off and twice Bernard dialled again. He almost gave up when the phone rang solidly for several minutes and he feared Beppo really wouldn't pick up the receiver again.

"You're the obvious bait, Beppo," he argued.

"Thornburn will have worked that one out for himself — "

"Of course he will! But we all know how much he wants to get you. We'll be that bit smarter, I promise. Will you co-operate?"

By the time he replaced the receiver, Bernard was sweating and it had nothing to do with the summertime heat permeating his small stuffy office.

He consulted Superintendent Preston again and another conference was called. This time it lasted for several hours and when it ended, every man involved looked tired and ready for a pint at the pub down the road.

The Italian restaurant was closed, but in a back room the proprietor and Angelo Marachini were sitting, drinking red wine and waiting impatiently.

"Another five minutes and I'm going," said Angelo, breaking the uncomfortable silence between himself and his companion.

"He *will* be here, Signor Marachini. I saw him only last night at my place. He was very anxious to talk to you — about Beppo."

Angelo, small and dark and almost painfully thin in his well-cut suit, spat at the mention of his brother's name. The proprietor was shocked but made no comment and nervously refilled his visitor's glass.

There was a tap on the door. A waiter popped his head into the room and announced Pete Guzzi's arrival. When the short, fat Italian joined them, the proprietor made himself scarce. Guzzi sat down.

"What do you want to talk to me about?" demanded Angelo, eyeing the newcomer suspiciously. "It had better be important. I don't like people wasting my time."

"I've got some news about Beppo."

"What about him?"

"He's here. In London."

Angelo's thin hand shot out with lightning speed and hit Guzzi so hard across the face, the man toppled from his chair. Pale and shaken, he stayed on the floor looking up at the younger man, plainly scared.

"It's the truth. I swear it. I've even got an address."

"Where did you get the information?"

Guzzi told him he had got it from a bent copper and after a moment's thought, Angelo seemed satisfied.

"Okay, so he's in London. That'll make it easier for Thornburn, won't it?"

"Dio mio!" gasped Guzzi, back on his feet now, his fear momentarily forgotten. "He's your *brother*, Angelo."

"So? He grassed on me too, remember."

"But it's his life we're talking about, Angelo. You know what Thornburn will do if he catches up with him. You can't just sit back! At least warn him and give him a chance to — "

"Shut up. I want to think."

The thin Italian lapsed into a lengthy silence. Presently, he said: "Okay, what's this address you've got?"

Guzzi told him and, getting up, Angelo tossed two tenners on to the table with characteristic arrogance. "Split it with Luigi or keep the lot for yourself. Makes no difference to me. And remember — no blabbing about this."

"You *will* warn Beppo, won't you?" asked Guzzi in anxious tones.

Angelo grinned over his shoulder as he reached the door.

"Course I'll warn him. He's my brother, *vero*?"

In the car, Angelo drove around for a while in case he was being followed. He didn't trust Guzzi — in fact, he didn't trust anybody. When satisfied that he wasn't being trailed, he drove off towards Battersea.

A plan was already forming in his mind and it sent the blood racing through his veins. This was the opportunity he had been waiting for. A chance at last to become part of Ivan Thornburn's gang — still active despite its leader's imprisonment which no one in the underworld believed would be lengthy. If he could deliver Beppo on a plate, Thornburn would be more than casually grateful.

He felt pleased with himself as he stopped outside a neat row of semi-detached houses. He knew in which of them he would find Thornburn's men. This time, he was confident, they would welcome a visit from Angelo Marachini.

Beppo had changed a lot since Bernard last saw him. He looked much thinner but reasonably fit and in good health. His bushy hair was shorter and slicked down against his head but he still looked tough and met Detective Chief Inspector Christie's gaze directly.

"This plan of yours had better be safe, inspector. My wife nearly did her nut when I told her where I was going."

"We've put a lot of thought into it, Beppo. Nothing will go wrong. I've put the word around that you're lying low in London, as I told you on the phone."

The London-born Italian nodded wryly.

"Straight into Angelo's ears, I suppose?"

"Who else?"

"You know he'll shop me to Thornburn?"

"I'm banking on it."

Beppo sighed. "Thornburn's too smart for an old trick like that, inspector. He'll know you're setting me up as bait."

"He won't KNOW. He'll suspect. Just remember how badly he wants to get even with you. His kind of hatred overrides caution. My bet is he'll send Angelo to sniff out the address, check you are on your own and make sure there's no sign of us in the vicinity. When Angelo gives him the green light, he'll make his move, assuming of course you won't be expecting him."

"So where do you come in?"

Bernard grinned and offered his visitor a cup of coffee, promising to explain later.

The unusually hot spell of summer weather had given way to sporadic thunderstorms and when Angelo set off to keep his rendezvous with his brother, the rain was falling fast and furious.

He drove with care, going over in his mind what Thornburn had told him to do. Nothing must go wrong. This was his big test and if he passed it with flying colours, he knew he was in.

Forty-eight hours earlier he'd been driven to Thornburn's hideout — a secluded farmhouse in Hertfordshire. The gang leader had looked pale and ill but none of his old aggression had left him and he seemed even more dangerous than before he had gone inside.

Angelo had kept his nerve while the older man questioned him about his sources. The questions were asked over and over again, rephrased sometimes to try and catch him out in a lie. In the end, Thornburn was finally convinced that Angelo's information was genuine and the two men spent half the night discussing his, Angelo's, plan.

When the Italian left, his instructions were clear. It would involve him in no danger at all. All he had to do was go to the address Guzzi had given him and speak to Beppo.

With or without his brother's agreement to Angelo's escape plan — cooked up by Thornburn just to make Angelo's visit appear genuine — he would leave the premises and pass a signal to the gangland boss and his men hidden nearby.

The rest would be up to Thornburn. Angelo would be well away before his supergrass brother got what was coming to him.

The downpour had lessened but a steady drizzle kept his wipers busy. On the outskirts of Finchley, be consulted the route plan to find Beppo's address, although by now he knew it almost by heart. He'd been to the place, after dark, several nights running to study the area and report back to Thornburn.

He glanced at his watch. Almost ten o'clock in the morning. The house was in a cul-de-sac just off the busy main road and he parked a few yards away from it.

The street was deserted. Two cars were parked half-on and half-off the narrow pavement and it went through his mind that Thornburn's fear of a police ambush was without foundation. There was no room to conceal vehicles in such a narrow road.

Leaving the car, he walked boldly up to number 22 — a small, end-terraced house — and pressed the doorbell button. A curtain moved in a downstairs window. No one came to the door. Angelo pressed again, pulling up the collar of his brand new mackintosh against the drizzle. Still no one came to the door.

He began to feel nervous. Pete Guzzi had phoned him the previous evening and sworn that he'd persuaded Beppo to see Angelo that morning. Had he lied? Or had Beppo changed his mind about trusting him? He cursed under his breath and pumped at the bell button impatiently as the rain increased.

Water dripped from the peak of his fashionable tweed cap, bounced off his thin shoulders and raced down his light-grey mackintosh. Angelo began to worry. He knew Thornburn was watching him from the house opposite.

Part of the plan was that Thornburn and his men would forcibly enter the house in the early hours, tie up the occupants and use the place to lie in wait for Angelo's all-clear signal. He knew they were safely installed because the gang leader had phoned him early that morning.

He began to feel sick. If Beppo didn't admit him, he was sunk. Fear suddenly began to take a grip on him. In desperation, he hammered on the door and relief flowed over him as he heard a sound behind it and then slowly it began to open.

He stepped into the darkened hallway and, at once, felt the muzzle of a gun pressed into his back. He spoke quickly, nervously.

"It's okay, Beppo. I'm alone and I'm not carrying a shooter."

"Into the front room. And make it snappy," came a voice near his ear and when Angelo spun around, he let out a cry but it was swiftly stifled by a hand clamped over his mouth as he was dragged, protesting, into the front room.

"He's been in there for almost half an hour," grumbled Thornburn, pacing the carpet. "Why is it taking so long?"

"He said he might have trouble convincing Beppo he was on the level, boss," said one of his five henchmen. "Beppo's probably got a shooter. He won't let Angelo go if he thinks he's likely to betray him."

"That creep Angelo said he *could* convince him. He'd better be right."

"Something's happening, boss. I think Angelo's coming out."

Thornburn moved back to the curtained window, binoculars raised, watching as the front door of the house opposite opened. "As soon as we get the signal, we move in — fast. If he puts up a fight, start shooting but remember I don't want him killed. He's mine."

A small thin man emerged but it wasn't Angelo. This man was wearing a dark-brown overcoat and green trilby and he halted at the garden gate to stare directly at Thornburn's window.

"Christ!" exclaimed Thornburn, lowering his binoculars. "That stupid Angelo has fluffed it. That's Beppo and he's making a run for it. Come on. Let's get him!"

As they emerged, the man in the overcoat and trilby began waving his arms at them but as the gang raced towards him, he turned and started to run.

"Aim for his legs. Shoot, you fools. Shoot!" yelled Thornburn as several bullets whistled through the air. The running man stumbled and fell on to his face in the rain-sodden street. When they reached him, he was dead.

Behind them, all down the narrow cul-de-sac, doors were beginning to open. Uniformed and plainclothes officers poured into the street. Thornburn and his men turned in panic and set off in different directions. They didn't get very far but when Bernard snapped the handcuffs on Thornburn a few minutes later, the villain looked elated rather than crestfallen.

"Bit slow off the mark this time, Christie," he jeered. "I might be going back inside but Beppo Marachini ain't going nowhere. He's paid the price for grassing on me!"

"Sorry to disappoint you, Thornburn," said Bernard. "But the man you just filled with lead wasn't Beppo. It was Judas, his brother. Take a look for yourself."

Beppo came to the door of the house, Superintendent Preston at his side, and when Thornburn recognized him, he exploded with rage, screaming abuse as several policemen dragged him, struggling, to the waiting police car.

"That's what I call a good morning's work, sergeant," said Detective Chief Inspector Christie as he slipped quietly into the back of the police car, some time later. "We've got them all this time — *including* Angelo Marachini."

GERMINATION PERIOD

Jean McConnell

I WENT ROUND the garden being very selective. Only the best for John. The little gift would not come amiss. After all he had been so poorly. His heart again, I had heard. There were friends who made a point of keeping me up to date with news of him.

It was early evening, and the dew was already clinging in droplets to the asparagus fern — as it will in autumn. Mist hung under the yew. But the dahlias still blazed in the last of the blood-red sun. This year they had done better than ever. Even though John had not been there to tend them.

It was the early evening of our lives when he'd left. Without conscious thought, I had supposed we would advance into old age in our set pattern of habits. That John would eventually have more time to work with me in the garden. More leisure to concentrate on our speciality. Except in September, of course. It was an understood thing that John did not work in the garden in September. Because of his — what was it he called it? — allergy.

But then the whole prospect had changed.

Unlike most women, I never expected him to come back. He was too good a catch for that. Whatever else I thought her, I knew she was no fool. And no man is any sort of match for a really determined woman. He'd never come back of his own accord.

I knew this, but it hadn't stopped me thinking about him. Thinking about them both, for the whole year they had been together now. And far from time healing, as everyone always says — though on very little evidence it seems to me — on the contrary time had simply provided a pause in which to assess what had happened and to consider the appropriate steps to take.

I had made no contact with John at all during the period. No weeping phone calls. No letters begging him to return. No messages sent through those mutual friends. Such pointless exercises are not my style. Why give her more prizes?

The one advantage I had was in knowing John better than she did. Knowing him from 25 years of marriage. In such a length of time a host of attitudes and quirks and fancies are revealed. John had an outward show of strength and confidence — even hardness. A very convincing one, that served him well in his business. But I knew, as only a wife of many years can, that he was not without vulnerability.

I knew he'd never tell her of his little problem. I'd not known myself for years. Until a certain incident in the bedroom, in fact. On holiday in a hot climate. That time he'd been reduced to a shivering, weeping wreck of a man. I had been able to deal with the situation then, and ever afterwards when the need occurred. Would she cope, I wondered? Some women might not be able to face it. For me, strangely, this single proof that the man had his sensitive side had been endearing. There had been little other evidence.

In a year, the first fine flush of passion must have waned. Now, surely, she would be starting to watch him for signs. The long stares out of the window, or into the fire — the backward thoughts. The journeys inside the head — without her.

Now my time had come into bloom. As hers had done, those twelve months before. And I would use the moment with pleasure. As she had done.

He was chairman that year of the Autumn Show. She was secretary. The Expert had come down to select the winning entries. We had entered our dahlias as usual. Scarlet, as usual. To enhance the heads, John had widened the opening of the florets, pressing a cotton bud into each orifice, delicately caressing and probing, until it responded and stayed fully flared.

As always, I observed this process with interest. His skill in this field always struck me as ironic. She had been watching too, I recall.

The judging completed, the awards were to be made. John, the Committee and the Expert gathered behind a table, where silver cups flowered out of the green baize. The crowd assembled in front. I hovered nearby, waiting for John's usual signal to join him. It didn't come. Instead, she took the place by his side, smiling and nodding to everyone in the blanket coverage of royalty.

No bell rang at that moment, as it might have. After all, she was secretary, I reasoned. And the Expert this year was indeed a very great one, which could account for John's distraction.

I infiltrated back into the crowd, clapping the prize-giving with a fine enthusiasm. At last the green baize was bare — except for ours, which John had accepted. The winners, smug with triumph, ran a gauntlet of jagged congratulations as they hurried off with their silverware. The remainder dwindled away in the usual rancorous discussion.

"There's a little supper laid on," I heard her announce. She was gesturing towards a long table at the end of the room, where, with lightning speed, a meal was being laid. The Committee guided the Expert in that direction. I stood and watched as she placed a hand on John's arm and drew him to follow.

He looked towards me. "Why don't you go on home, dear," he said, reasonably, politely. "I won't be long. Take the cup with you." They moved off together to the supper table. And she glanced back at me with a little smile.

I think I might have accepted everything that came after quite differently, if it hadn't been for that little smile. Might have viewed the turn of events with some equanimity — but for that little smile.

Still I stayed. Standing quite alone now. Holding the cup cradled in my arms. The serving girls, knowing who I was, lowered their eyes. Their absence of any delight in the situation warmed me into life.

When everyone was settled at the long table, I walked up the length of the room. John was seated next to the Expert. With her beside him.

I offered words of appreciation to the Expert. Remarks sincerely meant, for his comments had been witty, encouraging and knowledgeable. He murmured his thanks, and smiled up at me vaguely. "My wife," said John, without moving. The Expert's eyes slewed fractionally in her direction, then back to me, as he half rose and shook my hand.

At this point, she began offering a basket of bread rolls round the table. On her face she was wearing that same expression as the gardeners who had carried off the cups.

It was then I had gone home.

He'd had one heart attack soon after they'd set up together. No doubt the going had been energetic, commented our mutual friends. Heart attacks are a hazard for men to whom the seven year itch comes twenty years late. And now, I was told, he had suffered yet another tremor. Not at all well, it seemed. But in good spirits. She was very anxious about his health, they said. I could well imagine. When you've reeled in a record fish, the last thing you need is a hole in the net.

I came in from the garden as the light faded, and began to pack up my present with the greatest care. I had boxed some up the week before as an experiment — to see how long they would stay at their best. You can't rely on the post these days — even first-class. Four days seemed to be the limit before they started dying off. I would have to hope for the best. I put as many as I could into the box. So as to be effective without overcrowding it.

I knew as soon as he saw them he would know who they were from. And in that moment he'd appreciate everything I still felt for him.

I travelled up with it to London — a thirty-minute journey. I didn't want the postmark to give any hint to her of who the gift was from. Then she might intercept it — as any jealous woman would — and that would spoil everything. I wanted him to open it. To get the full benefit. To react as I knew he must. And when she saw the effect it had on him, why, that was when she would suffer.

That was how I intended that things should go. The fact that I was still able to make an impression on him. That my knowledge of him from our past life together still gave me a power over him. This was what would be my pleasure. And her pain. Wasn't that a fair reversal of the coin?

I heard a week later that they had found him dead. Slumped across his desk. A massive heart attack, reported our mutual friends. Beside him was found an empty, perforated, cardboard box — apparently just unwrapped from its brown paper and string. What it had contained had been a matter of some specula-tion. She had been in the bath when he had opened it and had come down to find him lying there. She was distraught, they said. Distraught.

Today, I walked round the garden again and plucked a bunch of our celebrated dahlias. In memory of John. For a table arrangement. Perhaps some grey foliage would blend. Soften the colour, which I had always felt a little harsh for the house. Good for showing, of course. To hold its own against the rest, with their fierce onslaught of hues. Grey. Or even better some russet leaves. That would make quite a heart-warming display.

John always let me cut the flowers in autumn, because of his phobia. Yes, in truth, one could call it a phobia.

The day was drawing in and the dew had already formed. In the dark yew tree it had risen in a magnificent web. A sparkling lace mat hung between the branches. Quite beautiful, I thought. In the centre poised its owner, a symmetrical pattern of beige and brown etched on her fat, oval body. Quite the largest specimen I had seen this season. How had I missed it? What a waste. However, the others had been sufficient. Clearly they had travelled extremely well, and made a lively escape on arrival. Full marks to the G.P.O.

Will it ever be suspected what happened? I don't think so. I never betrayed John by telling anyone about the screaming, hysterical man on that tropical paradise holiday. Nor the shuddering, stricken jelly he could still become on certain occasions. And I certainly won't now.

AUTUMN CROCUS

Ella Griffiths

"OUCH!" INGRID BERGERSEN gave a start as someone or something suddenly prodded her elevated posterior. Annoyed, she extricated her head and shoulders from beneath the steering-wheel and swung round to confront the prodder. Only by a considerable effort of will did she restrain herself from lashing out as she struggled clear.

Her "attacker" proved to be a diminutive old lady who at first glance appeared to be as broad as she was tall. A fringe of tight white curls peeped out from beneath a broad-brimmed straw hat and she was wearing a chequered coat which was clearly too small for her.

"I'm sorry if I made you jump," the old lady said apologetically. "Only — well, my sister's feeling a bit faint and . . . I wondered if you'd drive her home. Us, that is."

"Drive you home?" Ingrid Bergersen gazed around her. There wasn't a soul in sight. "I've got a right one here," she thought to herself. "Cracked, obviously." Aloud she said: "I'm sorry. I'm afraid I can't. I'm only going just down the road here. To Ikea — the furniture depot, you know."

"My sister's just over there in the wood," said the old lady, as though Ingrid had never spoken. "She had to, er . . . relieve herself." She gestured towards a clump of bushes some way off the road. "Then she came over funny. My name's Emma Baardsen. My sister's name's Astrid."

"Pleased to meet you," Ingrid Bergersen said for want of anything better. "Only I still can't drive you home. I only stopped here because I was fiddling with my beads and the string broke. That's what I was looking for."

"I'm glad you did stop," Emma Baardsen said. "I do wish I could persuade you. My sister's not at all well . . ."

"First my beads, now this," Ingrid Bergersen thought

despairingly, gazing around in search of the other sister. "Well," she said at last, relenting a little, "I suppose I could run you to the nearest telephone box, so's you can phone for a taxi. But I can't drive you home. Ikea'll be closing soon, and then I'll have wasted my whole journey."

"We don't live far away," the old lady pressed. "Nordraak vei. Number 16."

"That name rings a bell," Ingrid thought. She knew it as a better-class area, all detached houses with large, well-cared-for gardens. "Genteel" was the word that came into her mind. Before she had time to answer, however, another old lady suddenly emerged from the bushes and made her way towards them.

"Here she is!" the woman who had introduced herself as Emma Baardsen exclaimed. "How are you feeling, Astrid? This lady's kindly offered to drive us home."

"That's very nice of you," the new arrival said, beaming at Ingrid. She was as scrawny as her sister was chubby. "Very nice indeed. Nordraak vei 16. Just up the road and turn right."

Then, without waiting for a reply, she clambered into the back seat of the car.

Faced with such a *fait accompli*, Ingrid Bergersen capitulated with as good grace as she could muster and indicated to the other old lady that she should slip into the front seat. "It'll be quicker than standing here half the day arguing the toss," she consoled herself. "Might as well talk to a brick wall."

All the way to their home the two old ladies kept up an incessant chatter — mostly about health foods and herbal beverages. "Damn those beads!" Ingrid thought to herself. "If it hadn't been for them I wouldn't have had to sit here listening to all this drivel." She was tired and hungry, and it was clear now that she wasn't going to make Ikea whatever she did. "When am I going to learn to say no?" she wondered.

When they reached their house the two sisters insisted on her coming in with them to have something to drink. Ingrid looked at the house. It stood well back from the road and fairly oozed respectability and a quiet opulence. Mentally she replaced "genteel" with "well-to-do". She protested that she hadn't time, but in vain, and in the end she again gave in and accompanied the two old ladies into the house.

"Do sit down," urged the tall thin one. "I'll go and get you some of our home-made cordial. It's very refreshing. Just the thing on a hot day like this.'' It occurred to her that the woman had made a remarkable recovery.

"Thank you," Ingrid murmured resignedly, settling herself into a deep armchair.

As she sank back into the plush she was startled to hear Emma Baardsen call to her sister: "Take the ice from the tray on the right. The colour's not real."

"Shouldn't I bring in some biscuits?" the other sister replied from the kitchen.

"No, just the cordial," said Tubby, as Ingrid had mentally dubbed her.

"Stingy devil," she thought to herself. And what was all that about colour? "They really are round the bend," she decided. But when the cordial finally appeared she had to admit that it was very pleasant indeed. Refreshing, as Astrid Baardsen had said it would be.

As soon as she decently could, she made her excuses and took her leave. For some reason she was unable to fathom she felt relieved to be out in the fresh air again. There was something strange about the two old ladies. It wasn't just their crankiness. Without knowing why, she felt oddly depressed.

Next day Ingrid told some of her friends at the office about her encounter with the Misses Baardsen, the two old biddies as she called them. She didn't exactly dramatize the incident, but her version of it certainly lost nothing in the telling. Three weeks later one of the secretaries, Vera Dahl, came across to tell her that her parents had just bought a house in Nordraak vei. "And do you know," she finished up, "it's right next door to those two old biddies you told us about."

A month after that Vera came with the news that she had met "the thin one". "Mother says they're very well liked," she went on. "Gad about all over the place. She's got to know some of the other neighbours, and they say they often come home in cars. Nearly always a young lady driving. Not the same one, mind you. The neighbours think they must be nieces — hoping to inherit a packet, you know. Seems they're absolutely stinking."

"More likely mugs like me they've shanghaied into driving them home," Ingrid Bergersen snorted. "They're probably running a regular racket. Never mind," she added with a laugh, "at least the trees get watered!"

And with that she dismissed the two sisters from her mind.

A couple of weeks later Ingrid attended a reunion with the sixth-form girls of the old school. It was the first time they'd had such a get-together for ten years, and practically everyone turned up. Drink in hand, she made the rounds, stopping for a word here and there. It was mostly lighthearted cocktail-party chit-chat — until she came to Marianne Melbye. After an opening exchange of pleasantries and the inevitable "Remember whens?" Marianne suddenly said: "Awful about poor Kari, wasn't it?"

Ingrid knit her brows. "Kari? Kari Randen?"

"No," said her friend, "Kari Nissen. *You* remember her — mass of lovely auburn curls."

"Of course I remember her," Ingrid Bergersen replied. "But what's so awful about her?"

Marianne looked at her, hesitated a moment, then blurted out: "She's dead. Suicide. The shock nearly killed her parents."

"Kari? Suicide? Why on earth would she . . . What was it, a man?"

"That's just it. Nobody seems to know," Marianne answered. "She was always so chirpy, wasn't she? Life and soul of the party. That made the shock of it even worse."

"She must have had some problem no one knew anything about, then," a third member of the group put in. "Got on top of her, probably, so that in the end she felt she couldn't go on living. They lose their sense of proportion, they say."

"But she was so outgoing," Marianne Melbye protested. "Up and down, granted, laughing one minute, sobbing her heart out the next, but aren't we all? And the day she — the day she did it, she was on top of the world, apparently. Told her mother she'd driven two old ladies home. Done her good deed for the day, so to speak. Reckoned it had earned her a good holiday."

"Yes, I heard about that," another woman chimed in. "Drove up to her parents' cabin, didn't she? Some forester found her a few days later."

"That's right," Marianne replied. "She was still in the car. Run head-on into a tree. Never believe it, would you? Brand new car, too. Toyota Corolla. Lovely, it was — I saw it. Green. She was stuck tight, down between the steering-column and the seat, they say. How'd she get down there, do you think?"

"I don't know," said Ingrid. "But was it the crash that killed her? You said it was suicide."

"So it was. At least, they *said* it was. Overdose of sleeping tablets."

"*Said* it was? Don't they know? There must have been an inquest, surely."

"Of course there was. And a post mortem. But the pathologists don't always find the answer. Not the whole answer, anyway. How can they? They don't say much, either. I haven't plucked up courage yet to talk to her mother and father . . ."

"Neither have I," said a girl on the edge of the group. "And I don't live far away from them, either. I can't go on avoiding them, though. They're probably beginning to wonder already."

After that the party appeared to lose its momentum. It seemed that everyone was thinking of Kari.

Some time later Vera Dahl invited Ingrid to a party at her parents' new home in Nordraak vei. "They've more room than I have," she explained. "My flat's so tiny, you know."

Ingrid determined to get there early in the hope of meeting the two old ladies next door once again. It was a lovely autumn day. As she pulled up outside the house she couldn't help wondering what it was that impelled her to want to see them again. The last time she'd been in the house, she'd been glad to get out of it. She came to the conclusion that there was something decidedly odd about the two, something that set them apart and made her feel sorry for them despite their obvious affluence.

It was Astrid Baardsen, the thin one, who opened the door when she rang. Ingrid hastened to apologize for arriving unannounced: "I'm going to a party at the house next door," she explained, "and I thought I'd look in and see how you were getting on."

"How nice!" the old lady exclaimed. "We don't get many visitors. Come on in."

"No, we don't," agreed Emma Baardsen, suddenly materializing behind her sister.

"That's not what I've heard," Ingrid thought to herself, but said nothing. Instead, she seated herself in the chair indicated by the tubby one. A prolonged silence ensued. To break it, Ingrid enquired where they bought their health foods and asked if they could recommend something that would really do her good and which also tasted reasonably pleasant.

This prompted the sisters to produce a number of recipes they thought she might like. One was for homemade jam.

"We have some she could try," said Emma Baardsen.

"Thank you, but I've inconvenienced you enough as it is, I'm sure," Ingrid protested feebly.

"Nonsense. You try it. You'll love it," declared the other sister, disappearing into the kitchen.

A moment later, confronted with a biscuit piled with gooseberry jam, she decided to put as good a face on things as possible and eat it. She quickly popped the biscuit into her mouth, chomped it, and swallowed it, washing it down with cordial from a glass Astrid Baardsen had placed beside her chair.

"Yes, it *was* nice," she agreed. "Thank you. I shall have to have a go at making some myself."

"Let her take a jar home with her, Astrid," said Emma Baardsen. "She'll be able to enjoy it with her breakfast."

"No, really, I couldn't . . ." mumbled Ingrid miserably.

"Of course you can, my dear," declared Astrid, emerging from the kitchen with a jar in her hand. "Here you are. Take it!"

Shortly afterwards Ingrid made her farewells and left, the two sisters standing on the doorstep to wave goodbye and urge her to come again soon.

The party was a decided success, but before it could get properly under way Ingrid began to feel unwell. She was preparing to leave when Vera stopped her. "You stay here," she insisted. "You can go upstairs and lie down. Living alone like you do, what if you get worse and need a doctor?"

"Oh, it'll pass, I'm sure," Ingrid protested. "Can't for the life of me think what it can be. I was as right as rain when I came. I don't want to spoil the party."

"You won't," her friend assured her. "Go on up and have a lie down. You'll probably be okay in an hour or so. D'you know what?" she asked abruptly, going off at a tangent. "Mother's been talking to an old lady who used to know the son of one of your 'friends' next door. The tubby one, as you call her. Real tragedy, apparently. Committed suicide because of a woman. Quite a beauty too, by all accounts — auburn hair, green eyes, the lot. Had a green car, too, to match her eyes. It's some years ago now, but they've never got over it. Well, who would? Still, come on, let's get you on to that bed. That's more to the point.''

"I thought they'd never been married."

"They haven't," said Vera. "Neither of them. They named the boy Viktor Joachim. Quite a mouthful. There was a lot of talk at the time — it was thirty years ago, remember. People wondered if the names were supposed to mean something. Indicate who the father was sort of thing. Nobody knew, you see. Never found out, either, apparently. There must have been a helluva scandal. Anyway, come on, have a nap and see how you feel later."

As she lay on the bed Ingrid began to think about her class reunion and the story she'd heard about two old ladies that Kari Nissen had driven home the day she died. She hadn't thought much about it at the time, probably because she was so shocked at the news of Kari's suicide. Kari had been a redhead and driven a green car.

Her mind was racing. There *had* to be a connection. She started to get up, intent on telling Vera of her suspicions. Instead, she fainted.

When she came round it was to find herself in a hospital bed. "The jam!" she thought to herself as soon as her head cleared. "That's what it was — the jam." She rang the bell and asked the nurse who answered it if she could speak to a doctor.

Dr Olsen was young and too good looking to be true. "You've got to do something," she implored him, and told him of the jar of jam she'd left at Vera's parents' in Nordraak vei. "It's poisoned!" she finished desperately.

The doctor acted quickly, and next day the results of the lab test were on his desk. There was nothing wrong with the jam Ingrid had been given by the two sisters.

"We could see from the contents of your stomach that you'd been eating gooseberries," he explained. "We had to pump you, of course. But that's not all you've had. We're still analysing the rest."

"Nothing wrong with it?" exclaimed Ingrid unbelievingly. "I can't understand that. I took it for granted that it was the same as the jam I ate on that biscuit I told you about. That's what poisoned me, I'm sure. Though it could have been the cordial, of course.'' There'd been no ice the second time. "They only use that in the summer to cool people off,'' she thought to herself, forcing a grin at the gallows humour.

They kept her in hospital for almost a week, so she had plenty of time to think things through. One day a policewoman came to see her. Detective Constable Anne Bakke.

"Seems to me there just has to be some connection between my school friend Kari Nissen and her green car — that must have had local licence plates, too, same as mine — and me and my car. That's green too, you see.'' Ingrid sighed. "She was a real beauty, Kari. Mass of auburn curls. D'you think the two old ladies she drove home that day could have been those two sisters *I* drove home? Sounds a bit far-fetched, I know, only . . . .'' she said, frowning, "only there *is* something odd about them. Can't put my finger on what it is, but there's something funny somewhere.''

"I could tell you lots of things you'd never believe,'' said the policewoman. "They're true, even so. So I wouldn't write off anything as being too far-fetched if I were you. Though for the life of me I can't understand what the connection could be,'' she added.

Ingrid suddenly remembered the peculiar exchange between the sisters that day she drove them home. What was it Emma had said? "Take the ice from the tray on the right. The colour's not real.''

Of course! It was neither the ice nor the tray they'd been talking about. It was her hair. It was naturally red, just like Kari's had been. Only that day it had probably looked dyed, because the evening before she'd given it a colour rinse to liven it up and bring out the highlights. That was what had saved her the first time!

"Shouldn't I bring in some biscuits?'' Astrid had asked. "No, just the cordial,'' her sister had replied.

The next time she visited them they'd realized that she really was red-haired, hence the biscuit with the jam. That was what had poisoned her.

She told Anne Bakke what was in her mind. "I don't what they'd put in the jam,'' she went on earnestly, "but it must have been something. I'm sure of it. Can't have had much taste to it, either, otherwise I'd have noticed, wouldn't I? Doctor Olsen says they're all still analysing what was in my stomach. How long'll it take do you think?"

"I really couldn't say," the policewoman answered. "They always have a lot on at the lab, you know."

Shortly afterwards she left, with a promise to come back soon.

"Think if you'd insisted on going home that evening," said Marianne Melbye when she came to visit Ingrid next day. "You'd probably have had it. Nobody would have found you before it was too late."

"Cut it out, Marianne, please," Ingrid implored her friend. "I thought you came to cheer me up. I can't seem to think about anything else but those two damned women as it is!"

Detective Constable Anne Bakke was as good as her word and returned the day before Ingrid was due to leave the hospital. "I've had your two old ladies in for questioning," she said. "Gave them as good a going-over as I could under the circumstances, but no go. We even got a warrant and searched the house. Not a thing."

"What do *they* say about it all?" Ingrid wanted to know.

"Say? They say they're being persecuted. Threatened to take legal action if we didn't leave them alone. Clear consciences, both of them, never done anything wrong in their lives. Just paid a fortune in rates and taxes and the only thanks they get . . . you know the sort of thing."

Ingrid could imagine. She remembered how far she'd got with her protests that time she'd been asked to run them home.

Towards the end of September Ingrid Bergersen drove slowly past the sisters' house. She was convinced that they weren't anywhere near as innocent as they pretended to be. But would they ever be caught out? And if so, for doing what? And what could their motive be? She stared thoughtfully at the house as she cruised past. Her eyes fell on a flower-bed in under the wall. It was full of what looked to her like crocuses. But crocuses in Norway in September?

She parked the car a little further up the road and made her way back on foot to Number 16 to have a closer look. She could see now that they weren't crocuses, but they were very similar. White, lavender and white, and purple flowers and bare stems.

She hadn't the faintest idea what they could be.

When she got home she phoned her Uncle Sigmund, her mother's younger brother. He was a botanist. "*Colchicum autumnale*," he said without hesitation. "Sounds like it to me, anyway. Of course, I'd have to see them to be sure. *Filius ante patrem*'s another name for them. 'Son before Father.' That's because the flower comes before the leaves — the opposite of most plants, in other words. Their common name's Autumn Crocus. Meadow Saffron's another. They're very poisonous, by the way. Hang on a sec and I'll let you know exactly how poisonous they are. I seem to remember reading that about four grammes of the seeds is fatal for an adult — " He put the phone down and Ingrid could hear him leafing through the pages of a book. A moment later he returned: "Yes, that's right. Four grammes. One and a half will do for a child. Colchicine is very much a toxin," he went on. "It's a lot like arsenic. That's why it's known as 'vegetable arsenic'. Without medical attention people usually die after two or three days. Affects the respiratory system — they just collapse. They usually remain conscious right up to the end, it seems. I didn't know all that, by the way — I just looked it up."

Ingrid thanked him and rang off. Then she phoned Detective Constable Anne Bakke. The policewoman was out, but a friendly male voice assured her that Detective Constable Bakke would call her back as soon as she came in.

Two days later Ingrid was asked to go to police headquarters and have a word with Anne Bakke at her office.

"Sit down," the policewoman said. "I'll make it as short as I can. One of our lads had discovered those flowers before you phoned. But thank you anyway. After all, it was you who put us on to the case in the first place. We have them now, of course. We kept the house under observation and went in not long after we'd seen them picking those damned flowers. They denied it all to start with, naturally, but in the end they admitted it. Seems they extracted the poison from the seeds and corms — bulbs, you know. That's all they lived for, apparently, to avenge Emma Baardsen's son, Viktor Joachim. It's quite true, by the way: he *did* commit suicide some years ago because of a red-haired girl with a green car. They'd got it into their heads that if they kept at it long enough they'd be bound to get the right woman in the end. Crazy, obviously. Quite apart from anything else, with winters like ours, who keeps a car for ten years? They'd never thought of that, of course! Seems that they'd expected such a lot of the lad. Both of them. He was quite young, only twenty-five, so it really was a tragedy. The worst of it is, they don't seem to have any idea how many women they've given poison to. Or what happened to them. I'm inclined to believe them on that point. They're quite detached about it all. No remorse or anything like that.''

"It's awful," Ingrid exclaimed, her voice trembling. "Just think, I could have been dead by now, and all for nothing. Funny you didn't get on to them before, though, isn't it?"

"It's easy to say that now," Anne Bakke replied, "but you've got to remember that they'd never done anything to call attention to themselves. To all intents and purposes they were just two harmless old ladies, comfortably off and perfectly respectable. Why should we have suspected them of *anything*, never mind something as horrible as this? Besides, there was nothing to link Kari Nissen's death with others in the district. We shall get on to that part of it now, of course, but that's with the advantage of hindsight."

It transpired that Astrid, the thin one, had come across the "recipe" in the gardening column of a women's magazine and that her sister had reasoned that gooseberry jam was best suited to camouflage the taste. Cordial, too. She'd been right about that, Ingrid thought wrily.

It was not until Christmas, when the whole family was gathered at her parents', that Ingrid Bergersen had a chance to talk to her Uncle Sigmund again. He was curious to know why she'd been so interested in autumn crocuses.

Briefly Ingrid told him her story. "Not much of what I've just told you got into the papers," she concluded, "but that's the way it was."

"Viktor Joachim?" her uncle mused when she'd finished. "There was a chap by that name in my year at university. Died suddenly. Could it have been the same one, d'you think?"

"Well, neither name's very common these days," said Ingrid, "and together . . . It *must* have been the same man."

"If it was, he was quite a card," her uncle said. He wrinkled his brows thinking back. "Strange type. Full of hare-brained schemes and always telling stories. Trouble was, you never knew whether they were true or not. Used to go on for hours about the girls he'd bedded. We used to egg him on, go along with him, you know. It was some years ago, and people weren't as frank about things then as they are now. But girls? Never in this world! He was as 'gay' as they come!"

HEAT WAVE

Cyril Donson

I WAS ENJOYING a rare day off when Jim McBride rang.

Most of the country had been sweltering for days in temperatures in the nineties. The papers claimed it was the hottest July we'd had for years. The city shimmered, air dancing off the pavements. Strange smells, resurrected and cooked by the uncommon heat, added to the discomfort of sweat. Contrary to popular belief, the heat was not making people more affable.

In the street it was like being trapped in a great oven turned on full, with no air, no relief. That was why I was clad in cotton shorts, open-necked shirt and open sandals.

Jim McBride, in my confessedly biased opinion, is the best copper in the city. A Detective Sergeant, I rated him higher. He was tough, resilient, human, with the teeth of a bulldog once he got them into a case.

I found him in his office sitting in his own private pool . . . of sweat. He was cursing the heat and the regulations which insisted that he must wear a minimum of clothing on duty that in this weather was sheer purgatory.

"Christ," he greeted me. "You look positively indecent, Russ Kidd. Jesus, you've got funny legs haven't you?" He laughed. I scowled.

"I bet yours wouldn't win any prizes, mate," I retorted.

Still chuckling, he said: "At last I've found your Achilles heel. You're touchy about your legs."

"The hell I am," I said. "What did you ask me to call in for?"

Serious again he shoved a tatty piece of paper across the table.

"Take a look at that. It was sent to Sir Peter Hartford."

I read the crudely contrived note. It was a warning. Letters cut from magazines had been used to form the words:

"Hartford your latest mistress is going to be killed".

I passed it back. Soberly, he told me: "Hartford came in to see somebody this morning. The buck was passed to me. What do you think?''

''The note is amateurish. The language is no way that of the average criminal. Could be just a hoax, maybe somebody who wants to scare Hartford and this new bird of his. He's quite a guy. I reckon he must change his birds once a month. Last I knew he was in tow with a chick called Anita Baines.''

''Yeah. With the kind of money he's got he could change 'em every day. He told me the new girl moved into his apartment, the one he rents for his current mistress, only three days ago.''

''And Anita Baines was made redundant? Maybe she got mad and sent the note — ''

''Maybe. I'd like to believe it is as simple as that. I can't see the Baines girl murdering anybody.''

I left him to brood over the note, feeling that he'd wasted part of my day off with a trivial matter. The next day, at six pm, I had drastically changed my mind.

Jim telephoned me at my editorial office. The new mistress of Sir Peter Hartford, Dora Prince, had just been found dead on the pavement, ten floors down from the apartment she was keeping warm for Hartford.

I met Jim at the scene. The forensic boys were moving the corpse.

''Suicide?'' I asked. Jim grunted.

''Evidence points that way, so far. She was badly sunburned and had a nasty rash breaking out, all over her face, neck, breasts and thighs. She was wearing only the tiny bottom half of a bikini.''

I went with him up to the apartment. There was a uniformed copper outside the door. The key was in the door.

''We got the key from the caretaker,'' said Jim. ''I'm expecting Hartford along any minute.''

We looked around. Nothing had been touched since the girl had been found. Nothing appeared to be out of place. It was luxurious. I went to the double doors which led out on to a balcony.

There was a key in the right-hand door. And the doors were locked.

''Hey, how about this?'' I said. ''When that girl went off the balcony this door was locked. There was no way she could have locked herself out there.''

Jim came across. He went to speak to the man on duty outside. He came back into the room, looking grim.

"Nobody has been inside. Nothing's been touched," he said. "Which looks as if it wasn't suicide."

He unlocked the doors and walked out on to the balcony. I followed and the heat hit me like a physical blow.

It was the biggest balcony I had ever seen, with plenty of space for sunbathing. There was a Lilo out there, a bikini top, and nothing else. We spotted something else simultaneously. There were scratches, which could have been made by someone desperate with finger nails.

We went back into the main room. Jim looked at me and said: "Russ, for the time being, I want it kept between ourselves that we found the balcony doors locked."

I nodded. "Sure. I'm a clam. It looks like you're going to have to take that warning note seriously now."

"Yeah," he said ponderously. "But there's something odd about all this . . . something that doesn't quite add up. Don't you feel it?"

I had already felt it. I told him so. Hartford arrived. He looked truly overwrought, like a man stricken with shock and grief.

Jim kept him only for as long as was necessary. Hartford answered questions without demur, like a man in a trance.

"Yes, sergeant, the dead girl is . . . was . . . Dora Prince. She . . . she moved in here only three days ago. God . . . why? Why did she have to kill herself?"

Jim let that pass. "What makes you say that, sir?"

Dully, he said: "Dora was . . . very beautiful. She was also very highly strung, you know, temperamental. She could fly into hysterical fits one minute and the next be . . . well, all tender and loving. I warned her not to go out on to the balcony and take too much sun at once. She was allergic, and tended to break out in a hideous rash. And she was so fussy about her looks, almost fanatically so."

Jim clicked his teeth sympathetically. "So you think she went out to sunbathe, probably fell asleep and stayed out there too long . . . and when she woke up and saw herself temporarily . . . er . . . disfigured by the rash, she lost her head, and in a hysterical fit, climbed on to the balcony rail and threw herself off?"

Hartford nodded, his face grey with grief. "It must have happened that way."

Jim let him go, informing him that for the time being the apartment was not to be entered by him or anyone else until police investigations had been concluded.

"Do you know if the girl had any friends who might call?" asked Jim.

Just for one instant I thought Hartford hesitated before he said:

"No . . . no, I don't know of anyone."

"How soon can I use this, Jim?" I asked. "I'd like to be the first with the news that the girl's death was murder and not suicide."

"As soon as you want to," he said. "It has to come out now. I purposely didn't say anything to Hartford because I want to see his reaction when the news does come out. The point is, where the hell do I start?"

"Let's go and talk to the caretaker," I suggested.

"Yeah," he said. "Come on. Let's do that. I suppose you did notice that Hartford immediately thought it was suicide — he never even mentioned the warning note . . ."

"I noticed," I said. "And I don't think hysteria caused by a sun rash enough to drive a girl to suicide either."

We found the caretaker in his cubby hole of a room on the ground floor, reading his paper. He told us his name was Ted Franks and there were times when he wished he'd never taken the frigging job.

He struck me as being a man who would be half asleep most of his time, but he claimed differently when Jim talked to him. According to him, nobody went in or out of that apartment block without him knowing about it.

I had a job not to burst out laughing when I saw him. He was in grubby shorts, unshaven, and like a big, greasy bladder of lard on fat legs. He had bulbous eyes and a habit of sniffing permanently. At first he proved to be uncommunicative until Jim flashed his warrant card at him and invoked a bit of discipline and respect.

"Did you know the girl who occupied the apartment rented by Sir Peter Hartford?" asked Jim.

"Knew her by sight," he sniffed. "She moved in three days

back. The girl who used to be in there moved out."

"From your tone you don't seem to have much time for either of those young women?"

Scowling, which made him look even more comical, he said: "It ain't none o' my frigging business what folks get up to in these apartments, but, if you ask me, none of 'em are any better than they ought to be. I sometimes think I might as well be running a high-class bleedin' brothel. Some of these apartments where the well-off gents keeps their bits on the side . . . I reckon the only difference between them girls and street whores is the girls here sell theirs at a higher price. I'm a God-fearing man and one as goes to church regular, and it ain't fitting."

I wanted to laugh again. He looked about as God-fearing as Old Nick.

"Did the girl in that apartment, Hartford's, have any visitors today?"

"Yes, she did. I never miss a thing goes on here. My job, see? Now let me just think a bit . . . first there was that high and mighty Sir Peter Hartford. He come about ten this morning. He left again half an hour after."

"Anybody else call?"

"Yes, yes . . . I'm telling you, ain't I? God damn it, can't any of you lot be patient? Soon after Hartford left, that young feller called. I can't tell you his name 'cos I didn't know him. He left again about half an hour after. Then that girl came, the one who used to be in the apartment. I talked a bit to her. She told me she'd left some of her things and had come to fetch 'em. No . . . wait a bit, there was the other woman come before the young one. I didn't know her. She looked about forty. But very smart she was, and not all hoity-toity like most of your bleedin' rich folks. That's right. She come first. I didn't see her leave because I was in the toilet, but she must have. The young woman come after."

There was nothing further to get out of the caretaker and, soon after, Jim and I left the Midas Apartment block. Before I left him to go to my car, he said:

"I think I can take our man off the apartment. I'll see to it. The place must stay locked. The key can remain with the caretaker for the time being. I ought to do some work tomorrow, but if I do I'm in dead trouble. I have a heavy date with the missus and the kids to take 'em to the seaside for the day — "

I made a suggestion. "You go have your day out, Jim. I'll follow up on what you've so far got and fill you in on Monday morning, okay?"

He gave me a suspicious look. "You just pull anything funny, Russ, and I'll have your guts for garters. Anything you come up with, I'll want to know first." His scowl slipped a bit and then he said: "Thanks, mate. I'd rather face half a dozen villains than my missus when she gets her dander up."

Sunday was even hotter. The heat wave did have its definite advantages. I didn't have to turn to any page three to see half-naked birds. They were strolling around, all over the place.

I knew I was going to have to start with Hartford. I had no notion at all where I could find either Hartford's ex-mistress or the young man the caretaker said had called at the apartment. I hoped I might also get a chance to talk to Hartford's wife and that one of them would be able to supply me with the address of the ex-mistress, perhaps of the young man too, and also identify this latter character for me.

I arrived at the impressive home of the city big wheel, Hartford, at a little later than ten am. He was out playing golf, but my luck was in. Lady Ruth Hartford introduced herself and asked me in. I was thus easily presented with my chance to talk to her.

We went through to a big airy room she called "the parlour". I accepted her offer of a drink. She said:

"Are you with the police? I was expecting someone to call. I don't mind answering your questions. I assure you I have nothing to hide. That poor girl . . . and imagine it turning out to be murder."

I didn't comment on her question, and she didn't press it. She was a remarkably attractive woman, aged about forty and well-preserved. I found myself wondering what the hell Hartford was doing messing around with young girls when he had such a wife?

She was so frank and forthcoming that I decided not to pull my punches. I told her I knew she had visited Dora Prince at the apartment on Saturday. Would she care to tell me why?

"I suppose it will all have to come out now," she said. "So why not? My husband has had lots of mistresses. He . . . he is that type of man. Mostly I ignore his goings-on. He would never divorce me, because he loves me and he always comes back to me.

But Dora Prince was different."

A dark shadow seemed to flit across her face. "I knew there was something different, so I tackled Peter about it. I knew that he wanted this girl more than any of the others. But she had told him that she would not have sex with him until he married her. The reason I went to see her was to make her understand that she could never hope for Peter to divorce me and marry her. This may sound odd to you, but I did this to help Peter, because I love him more than anything in the world."

"How did Dora react?" I asked.

"As I had expected. She said Peter truly loved her and I must wait and see. I was about to leave, feeling I had failed in my mission, when Anita Baines called. She had come to collect some of her belongings she had left at the apartment. They both seemed to forget I was there, so I slipped into the bedroom. They had a terrible slanging match. I heard Anita call Dora a whore. Dora replied that she wasn't like *her*. . . Anita, because she would never go to bed with Peter until he married her."

She paused, hesitated, then went on: "I suppose I have to tell you the rest of it. When things went quiet, I came out of the bedroom meaning to let myself out and leave. I saw Anita locking the doors to the balcony. I went across. Dora was sunbathing with her eyes closed, plainly determined to ignore us until we had had enough and left. I asked Anita what she was doing. The girl was obviously scared at being caught. Plainly she, too, had forgotten my presence. She told me she only wanted to lock Dora out in the merciless sun, and prevent her getting back into the main room, so that she would suffer.

"I pressed her, thinking there was more to it, and she broke down and confessed. She hoped no one would come and Dora would be on that balcony for hours and probably die. Of course, you know I was once a doctor. I told Anita that it was most unlikely being in the sun for even longer would kill her. Anita begged me not to say anything to anyone. She said she was sorry, and I unlocked the balcony doors. We then both left."

It was at this stage that Sir Peter arrived back. When he saw me, he was angry, and when he knew I'd been questioning his wife, he was even more angry. His wife stared at me accusingly. "You told me you were from the police — "

About to leave, I said: "No, ma'am, *you* said I was. And I

wouldn't get too uptight about this, Sir Peter. Better talk to your wife. She may have placed herself in the position of being a possible suspect.''

Hartford suddenly changed his tune. He became very anxious.

"You can't believe that Ruth . . . my wife . . .''

"She had a motive," I said flatly. "But if it's any comfort — there could be others. Your ex-mistress, Anita Baines . . . and a certain young man, both of whom, like your wife, visited Dora Prince yesterday morning. I need the addresses of both.''

He became eager to help me, but he could only come up with the home address of Anita Baines, which he gave me.

"The young man's name is Harry Corby. He is Dora's exboyfriend. He has already paid me a visit and called me a few names. He also told me that if I didn't leave Dora alone he would kill me. Unfortunately I do not know where he lives.''

I thanked him and left. I drove straight on to the flat where Anita Baines lived, in sadly reduced circumstances.

She was suspicious at first, but after I had told her that I knew she had been at Dora's apartment on Saturday, the day she died, Anita Baines let me in.

She went to her kitchenette to make coffee. That was when, looking around, I found the clippings in her fancy waste-basket.

I let her finish her coffee, then I started in on her. "Why did you send that warning note to Hartford?" I demanded.

She looked shocked, then flustered. She started to deny it. I showed her the clippings in her tidy-basket and she broke down.

"I was so blazing mad at Dora taking Peter from me," she sobbed. "I just wanted to hurt . . . to frighten them both. I swear that was all I did it for — you don't think I would — ''

"Never mind that," I said brusquely. "You went to see Dora. You tried to lock her out on the sun-balcony, and if Lady Hartford hadn't been there you would have left her locked out, wouldn't you?''

Very distressed, and sobbing, she confessed that she would have done, but again she swore she only wanted Dora to suffer, she had never wanted to kill her.

I left with Harry Corby's address, and the information that Dora had worked as a model where Anita had once worked. Anita knew Dora and her boyfriend.

I got very little out of Corby. He was a big, muscular and very volatile young man and he told me where I could go. An after-thought sent me back to see Anita again.

It was just a hunch, but so far it was all I had going for me. I put the pressure on, and she admitted she had gone back to the apartment. The caretaker hadn't seen her slip in and make her way up the stairs. She went on:

"I had taken the door key out of Dora's handbag which was on the wall-cabinet. I let myself in. I had to duck into the bedroom when Harry arrived. He didn't stay long. He and Dora had a blazing row and I heard him threaten to kill her. He said if he couldn't have her, no man would."

"Then he left," I continued for her. "You waited until Dora went on to the balcony again and locked her out. You put the key back into her handbag and then you left?"

"Yes . . . yes . . ." she sobbed. "But I swear I didn't mean to kill her."

I saw Jim on Monday morning and wasted no time in telling him what I had found out.

"So we've got three suspects," he said. "All with the same motive . . . jealousy: Ruth Hartford, Anita Baines and Harry Corby."

"Include Hartford," I said. "Maybe he was regretting having a girl around his neck who insisted upon him marrying her? He could have had a motive."

"Yeah. But now we have to prove which one it is. Anita Baines looks to me the most likely. But Hartford had a key. He could have gone back. And maybe his wife could have too. Hell . . ."

I left him to stew over what we had, doing likewise myself. I didn't get a chance to see him again, even after I had another hunch. I rang him and told him what I had in mind.

"It's worth a try," he said. "Give it a go."

I had it printed on the front page of my paper in a nice little box nobody would miss seeing:

"Police investigating the murder of Dora Prince have a clue they hope will lead to the killer. Fingerprints were found on one article in Dora Prince's apartment which could identify the murderer."

It was in the evening's early editions. I was hoping Jim had acted and got himself settled in the bedroom at the apartment with another man.

I waited outside the Midas block in my car. I saw Anita Baines arrive. As I'd figured, it was only her word against mine and she was going to deny anything she had told me. But first she was going to cover up any evidence against her.

She went inside with so much caution that I left my car, locked it, and followed, but not too close. Again, as I'd suspected, the bragging caretaker missed more than he saw in that apartment block. Anita crept past him, and went up the stairs, so that the sound of the lift wouldn't give away her entrance. The caretaker was still snoring his head off, it seemed to me, when I also went past him and up the stairs.

A newsboy arrived and tossed the caretaker's evening paper into the cubby hole through the window. The lad either didn't see me or he took no notice.

With a sigh of relief I followed Anita. She took a key from her handbag and opened the apartment door, letting herself in. Before she could close the door again, I moved in. Jim appeared with his companion and nabbed her.

She started crying and denying that she had killed Dora Prince. She confirmed my earlier hunch that she still had her own key to the apartment, but on the Saturday she didn't have it with her so had to steal Dora's to do what she had in mind.

"That about wraps it up . . ." Jim broke off as we heard someone else at the door. We scuttled out of sight into the bedroom dragging the girl with us. We heard somebody come in and cross the room. Then we all pounced. It was Ted Franks.

He had not made for the handbag. He had made straight for the key in the balcony door.

Jim and I were stunned, but not enough to stop us tackling Franks. He turned on us. He was like a madman and fought with the strength of one, his big eyes bulging and crazy, thick lips slavering, breath coming in rasping gasps. I hit him with a short crisp left and he went down.

Jim and his man pinned him down and put the bracelets on him.

And suddenly he collapsed into a snivelling, blubbering heap. He was taken away, and the girl also.

Later Jim gave me the details, and what had been a confusing and puzzling end to the case became clear. Franks was a psychopath, much of his time quite normal and rational. But he had developed a crazy and fanatical hatred of the women who became mistresses, especially Dora Prince who had insulted him, calling him a filthy pig.

In one of his crazy fits he had killed her. He had gone up to the apartment on Saturday, just before six pm, found the balcony doors locked, and Dora still on the balcony in a terrible state. He threw her over the balcony rails, locked the balcony door again, and left. He'd been sly enough, even in his madness, to work it out that whoever had locked Dora out in the hot sun would be blamed for her death.

"We never suspected Franks," said Jim. "Yet he did have a key. He thought that story about us having prints meant he had left some on the balcony door key. Lucky for us. I guess we found the killer this time by not looking in the right place."

"Yes," I said. "It sort of flattens one's ego a bit, doesn't it?"

He laughed. "What the hell?" he said. "Come on, I'll buy you a pint."

Anita Baines didn't quite get off scot-free. They gave her a suspended sentence.

OPEN AND SHUT CASE

Tony Wilmot

HE FELT MARJORIE move beside him in the bed. "You awake, Tom?" He didn't answer right away but he knew from her tone of voice that it was no use pretending. He'd done nothing but toss and turn ever since he'd come to bed. Now it must be nearly morning.

"What's wrong?" Marjorie asked, switching on her bedside light.

"Nothing. I'm hot, that's all. Too many bedclothes."

"There's something bothering you, Tom. I know the signs."

"It's nothing, love. Try to get some sleep." In the morning, he told himself, he'd definitely go to the police . . .

"There *is* something, Tom. I'm going to make some tea. I couldn't sleep now, anyway."

He stared at the ceiling, listening to the sounds from the kitchen. Yes, he would tell the police.

Marjorie came in with the tea and sat on the bed. "Something happened on your walk yesterday, didn't it?"

She always seemed able to read his mind. He knew he'd have to tell her; there was no point trying to lie.

"Bunty found a briefcase in Badger's Wood." He still couldn't bring himself to admit the whole story, almost as though he felt he was guilty of some awful crime. But he hadn't done anything wrong, so why did he feel guilty?

"A briefcase?"

"Yes." He took a deep breath then slowly began to relate the events of his walk in the wood.

The briefcase, he told her, had been stuffed down inside the hollow bole of a gnarled old yew tree and covered with leaves and bracken. He would never have spotted it had it not been for Bunty, their basset, sniffing it out. He'd had no doubts that it had been hidden there — nobody could possibly have lost a briefcase in a place like that. It had been there some time, judging by the damp leather and dull metal clasps. It wasn't locked and what he saw inside had made him sick with excitement — banknotes. Wads and wads of them.

For a while he'd just stood there, paralysed with indecision — peering into the gloom, half fearing some other walker would come upon him. Then, feeling like a criminal, he'd shoved it under his overcoat and made his way back to the car.

"I was going to drop it in at the police station on the way home," he told Marjorie, "but something made me drive straight home. I know I should have reported it right away. But it's not too late — I'll go first thing in the morning."

"Where is it, Tom?" Marjorie cut in, a curious look on her face. "Where did you leave it?"

"It's locked up in the car boot, in the garage. Why?"

"You'd better bring it in, Tom. Suppose somebody broke in or stole our car in the night and got stopped by the police? We'd have a hard job explaining how all that money came to be locked in our boot."

Tom went down to the garage and got the briefcase. It was the middle of the night and no one was about, but he was relieved to get indoors again.

Marjorie stared at the case as though it were a prize specimen in a museum. "How much is in there?"

"No idea — thousands, I should think."

"Don't you think we should count it, Tom?"

"Better let the police do that tomorrow."

"Counting it can't do any harm. Besides, I'm curious. And so are you."

It took them nearly half an hour. The notes totalled £100,000. For a while they just stared, awestruck. Then Marjorie sniffed the air and said: "What's that funny smell?"

Tom picked up a wad of fivers and held it to his nose. "It's this. You wouldn't think money would smell like that.

"Perhaps that's what people mean when they talk about tainted money . . . that smell?"

He caught an odd look in Marjorie's eyes and felt his heart miss a beat. For suddenly he knew she was thinking the same thing he was — they had been married too long to have many secrets from each other.

"Tom . . . ?" she began.

"We'd better get some sleep," he said firmly, scooping the bundles back into the briefcase. I'll drop it into Inspector Keneley first thing after breakfast. He's an old pal from the golf club."

Over the breakfast table, Tom said: "Where do you think the money was nicked from?"

"Bank, I expect."

"I'm not so sure. I've been wondering all night. Those old notes are more likely to have come from a payroll."

"You'll have to take Bunty back to the woods before you hand it in. Otherwise they're going to wonder why you delayed and kept it overnight."

"I hadn't thought of that." He gave her a quick smile. "If I didn't know you better, Marjorie, I'd say you had a criminal mind."

"Tom . . ." she began again.

He felt his mouth go dry. He knew from her voice that she'd been thinking the same thing he had ever since he'd first told her about the briefcase. He waited.

"Tom — I suppose you *have* got to hand it in? I mean, supposing we just kept it? It wouldn't make much difference. After all, the money has already been given up as lost . . ."

"*Presumably* given up for lost," he corrected. "There may be a reward out for its return, for all we know."

Marjorie was staring wistfully into space. "We could pay off the mortgage . . . change the car . . . take that trip to Australia you've always talked about . . . my, wouldn't Jane be surprised to see us."

"Yes — and very surprised that her parents had used stolen money to pay for the trip! And afterwards we might take another trip — to Wormwood Scrubs."

"Don't be so negative. That's always been your trouble, Tom. You've always shied away from risks."

She looked at him calmly.

"You've been toying with the same thought, Tom. That's why you drove past the police station."

When Tom admitted she was right, and Marjorie began to analyse the situation, he found she was two steps ahead of him.

"Let's suppose you hand it in to your Inspector Keneley. If it's money that's genuinely been lost and it's not claimed within a reasonable time, it'll be returned to the finder — you.

"But it won't be returned to you if it's stolen money. Handing it in is the last you'll see of it.

"True, you might get a small reward — but is that going to change our lives? You could just as easily end up with nothing but a pat on the back for your public-spiritedness.

"No, Tom, we're not going to pass up an opportunity like this . . ."

"I couldn't stick it out, Marge," Tom protested. "My nerve would crack, tempted though I am. The police would get on to us sooner or later . . ."

"No, Tom," she cut in, smiling. "I've thought of a way. Now, finish your tea . . . while I tell you how we're going to do it."

Tom parked at his usual place at Badger's Wood. He took Bunty on her usual walk but made sure there were no other walkers in the vicinity of the yew tree where the briefcase had been hidden. Then he put the case back in the hollow bole and covered it with leaves.

As he walked back to the car, the thought struck him: suppose the robber chose today of all days to come back for his loot? For a second, he almost went back for it himself — then he shrugged. It was no good worrying about it. If it happened, it happened.

He got in the car, waited for Bunty to jump up into the back seat, then headed back to town. Twenty minutes later he was parking outside the police station. He took a deep breath, willing himself to act naturally, and went in. As long as he followed Marjorie's plan, he told himself, nothing could go wrong.

But things went wrong right away: the nice Inspector Keneley had been transferred to another division and the desk-sergeant kept looking at him suspiciously when he explained about the briefcase.

"I see, sir . . . if I can just have your name and address . . .

"Right, sir . . . briefcase full of money . . . found in hollow tree in wood . . . nothing to indicate ownership . . ."

Tom blurted out how Bunty had sniffed it out during their usual Sunday morning walk. He watched as the sergeant made notes in the log book.

"Will you want me to make a statement, sergeant?"

"Probably, sir. Detective-Sergeant Mills will take care of that."

"Oh?" Tom said, uneasily.

"It's a CID matter, sir."

"Oh yes — of course."

Detective-Sergeant Mills was nothing like the golfing Inspector Keneley. His features might have been carved from granite; he had eyes like laser beams. His voice had a steely edge.

"Left the case exactly where you found it, you say?"

Tom nodded. "I thought it best."

"Quite right. Didn't want to run the risk of getting mugged, eh?"

Tom smiled. But the detective's face remained like granite. Tom was beginning to feel distinctly queasy.

"Right, sir," the CID man said when Tom had gone over what happened for the second time. "We'd better get along to Badger's Wood before someone else does, eh?"

A fresh-faced constable was at the wheel of a patrol car outside. He gave Tom a wintry smile. Tom indicated Bunty in his own car. Could he bring her along?

"Why not?" Mills said. "She's the heroine of the day, after all."

They parked in the clearing at the beginning of the walking-track through Badger's Wood. Tom and Bunty led them to the yew tree. Tom stood back while Mills uncovered the briefcase. Trying to keep his twitching nerves under control, Tom watched the detective flick through the bundles of notes.

Back at the police station, Tom waited while the money was counted. He hoped he looked suitably impressed when Mills told him there was £50,000.

"We'll want you to make a statement, sir," Mills went on. "Saying how you found it. And we'll be running a stolen-money check through the Yard's computer.

"If there's a reward, you'll be hearing from us."

Tom cleared his throat. "But if it isn't stolen money . . . and is not claimed . . . it's usually returned to the finder, isn't it?"

"Usually, sir. But there's no doubt about this little haul, sir. Most definitely stolen. Stands to reason, doesn't it? People don't *lose* fifty grand in hollow trees!"

"I suppose not," Tom agreed trying to sound like the average dutiful citizen.

When he got home, Marjorie said: "I've found the perfect

hiding place for the money, Tom . . . that recess at the back of the preservatives cupboard.''

"You know," Tom said, "it's ironic. We're rich, yet we can't spend a penny of it until the police lose interest in the case.''

What he didn't say was that he had a gut feeling that Detective-Sergeant Mills was not one to lose interest quickly.

A few days later his fears were confirmed. Mills called at the house. Just routine, he explained to Tom. He thought Tom should know that the serial numbers on the money tallied with a payroll snatch six months earlier.

"So the case is closed then?" Tom said.

"Not quite, sir. You see . . . there was a hundred thousand quid in that payroll . . .''

Tom felt his blood run cold.

"Perhaps the thieves split it — fifty-fifty . . .''

"Possibly, sir. Anyway, we'll be in touch if anything else turns up.''

Tom heard nothing more until one night when he called into his local pub. As he was sipping his pint, he heard Mills's voice.

". . . if I could check the £5 and £10 notes in your till, landlord? We've reason to believe somebody might be passing . . .''

Tom was still shaking when he got home. Marjorie told him to bluff it out, stop worrying; if they didn't spend any of the money, there'd be no proof. Sooner or later the police would have to drop the investigation.

But the police didn't drop it.

If Tom bought cigarettes at a kiosk, Mills did too. If Tom went into a café, Mills would be right behind him. When Tom took a lunchtime stroll from his office, Mills would be hovering nearby.

Tom was sleeping badly. It was all very well Marjorie telling him not to worry; *she* wasn't being shadowed. One lunchtime, Tom sat on a park bench by the duck pond. Inevitably, a voice said: "Nice spot, isn't it . . . mind if I join you?"

Detective-Sergeant Mills chatted on, seemingly unaware of Tom's tenseness.

". . . I often sit here by the pond, in fact I used to play in this park as a kid. I used to imagine myself as a pirate or a high-wayman . . .

"It's a pity we have to lose our childhood dreams, isn't it?"

Tom wasn't fooled by Mills's blandness; it just made him more certain that Mills had rumbled him.

Suddenly he was sick of subterfuge; he just wanted to make a clean breast of it.

"Look, I know you think I kept half of that payroll money, so why don't you say so? You've been following me in the hope I'll start passing some of it. So why don't you charge me and get it over with?"

Mills said softly: "Well, sir, I must admit it had crossed my mind. Fifty thousand pounds is a lot of temptation."

"I'll go to prison, won't I," Tom said flatly. "Receiving stolen money, or whatever the charge is."

Mills looked thoughtful. "In the normal course of events, yes. But I'm a human being as well as a copper; and I can tell you're a decent enough fellow. And you *did* find the money in the first place. That in itself deserves some kind of reward."

He paused, then went on: "Now, sir . . . supposing a *second* briefcase full of money were to find its way under a tree in Badger's Wood . . .

"Constable Rodgers and I will be doing another search there next week and, well, we'd just sort of stumble across it, accidental-like.

"And the case would be closed, if you get my meaning."

Mr Richard Turpin, entrepreneur, stretched himself out on the golden sands of Bondi Beach. He was a very contented man.

Never in his wildest dreams had he expected to come into £50,000 so easily. Fancy just picking it up in a briefcase in a wood! It had been more than enough to make him quit his job and take an early retirement — and to start a new life in Australia. Of course, it meant assuming a new identity and kissing Britain goodbye forever.

But that was a small price to pay, ex-Detective-Sergeant Mills told himself.